SNEAK

OTHER BOOKS IN THE
SWIPE SERIES:

SWIPE

SNEAK

THE SWIPE SERIES

EVAN ANGLER

BOOK 2

THOMAS NELSON
Since 1798

NASHVILLE   DALLAS   MEXICO CITY   RIO DE JANEIRO

Published in Nashville, Tennessee, by Tommy Nelson. Tommy Nelson is a registered trademark of Thomas Nelson, Inc.

Tommy Nelson® titles may be purchased in bulk for educational, business, fund-raising, or sales promotional use. For information, please e-mail SpecialMarkets@ ThomasNelson.com.

Scripture quotations are from the Holy Bible, New International Version®, NIV®. Copyright © 1973, 1978, 1984, 2011 by Biblica, Inc™. Used by permission of Zondervan. All rights reserved worldwide. www.zondervan.com

Library of Congress Cataloging-in-Publication Data

Angler, Evan.
 Sneak / Evan Angler.
  p. cm.—(Swipe series ; bk. 2)
 Summary: In a future United States under the power of a charismatic leader, thirteen-year-old Logan and his friends, a group of dissenters called the Dust, receive some startling information from the Markless community, opening their eyes to the message of Christianity and warning that humanity is now entering the End of Days.
 ISBN 978-1-4003-1842-1 (pbk.)
 [1. Science fiction. 2. Government, Resistance to—Fiction. 3. Fugitives from justice—Fiction. 4. Christian life—Fiction.] I. Title.
PZ7.A5855Sn 2012
[Fic]—dc23

                                                              2012005919

Printed in the United States of America

13 14 15 16 QG 6 5 4 3

QG 08-10-15

For Logan, Lily, Tyler, and Shawn

CONTENTS

CONTENTS

A NOTE FROM
THE AUTHOR

DEAR READER,

By the time you read this, the book you are holding in your hands will most likely be banned. Inside you will find the second volume in the chronicles of Logan and Lily Langly, Erin Arbitor, Daniel Peck, and the Dust. Their story is dangerous; the knowledge within it is forbidden.

You must not be seen reading this. You must not be noticed holding it. Breathe not a whisper of it, even to your closest friends. For the walls have ears—and DOME is always listening.

But *if* you are committed to freedom . . . *if* you are determined to place yourself on the right side of history, no matter the cost, then here is what you must know:

For the last five years, Logan Paul Langly was watched. By a group of outlaws. By a secret society of Markless teenagers just waiting for the right moment to kidnap him. He spent every day terrified that it was his last. Five years ago, his sister, Lily, disappeared. Logan was sure that he would be next.

And then about a month ago, Logan found out that these teenagers—Peck and the Dust, the "Markless threat of Spokie"—were in fact the only thing protecting him from a far bigger danger: his own government.

You see, Logan was born into the worst years of our States War, terrible in its own right, and yet merely one small part of the Total War that threatened every nation on earth. All of us were determined to end the years of slaughter, the decades in which environmental devastation forced more and more people to fight over less and less land, water, food. . . . By the time Logan was born, our global civilization faced a choice: unify, or perish.

As you know, our world chose unity. The desperate few of us remaining banded together into two great countries, East and West, hoping that it might bring peace.

To this day, it has worked. None would question that our new European Union now thrives under the charismatic leadership of Chancellor Cylis, or that our American Union, where Logan lives, has done the same under our general in chief, Lamson.

It has been over a decade since General Lamson and Chancellor Cylis worked together to institute DOME's Mark Program, by which all who wish to gain the rights of citizenship may receive the Mark in exchange for their binding Pledge of allegiance to Lamson, Cylis, and country.

And it was around this same time that the chancellor and the general cooperated to bring about the worldwide Inclusion—the doctrine that systematically rid our world of all religions and conflicting worldviews, replacing them with a single, unified belief that the Mark is the only answer, the only security, the only peace anyone will ever need.

Every schoolchild knows that through these two initiatives—the Mark Program and the worldwide Inclusion—General Lamson and Chancellor Cylis are working toward a Global Union, promising a future of peace and prosperity for the entire world.

But what if I told you, dear reader, that Lamson and Cylis's intentions are not what they seem? What if I told you their Mark Program is just one part of a more sinister plan than we ever could have imagined?

A month ago, Peck and the Dust opened Logan's eyes to this truth—that when Logan's sister, Lily, disappeared five years ago on the day she was supposed to be Marked, it wasn't by accident. And it wasn't the Markless, or Peck, or anyone else who took her. It was DOME.

And just as all this was sinking in, just as his whole world was turning upside down before his very eyes, Logan's new best friend, Erin Arbitor, betrayed him, bringing DOME right to the doorstep of the Dust's hideout—Logan's last remaining sanctuary—and burning it to the ground. Now Logan is on his own, running from the law, determined to find his sister . . . whatever the price.

My name is Evan Angler. I was there for many of the events transcribed on the following pages. What I missed, I've learned through firsthand account.

I am part of Logan's world. I am Dust.

As are you, should you choose to turn this page . . .

Are you ready to learn the truth?

Evan Angler

PROLOGUE

07:16:32

THERE WAS A CLOCK IN THE CORNER THAT counted the seconds, an old-fashioned analog-type with long hands and a slender needle that tapped a maddening beat. The room was dark, and a team of men and women stood with their arms folded and their faces cast in canyon-deep shadows. A line of noses and the tips of chins, but no eyes, no lips, no ears. . . . They loomed over the man lying at their feet, but were they smiling? Frowning? It was impossible to say.

"I've done nothing wrong," the man pleaded. "What is all of this?"

"When did it begin?" someone said in the crowd.

"I don't . . . who . . . when did *what* begin?" The man shivered violently.

A young Advocate stepped forward to the pulse of the clock. The room's light shifted over the pieces of her face, and the blue tint of her eyes now shone even as the rest of her disappeared. She bent forward and touched the man's flushed cheek and said, "*This.* The fever. When did it start?"

The man lay bound at the Advocate's feet, soaked in a cold sweat and trying to make sense out of her question. "About . . .

1

I'd say . . . about a month ago," he said, looking up. "Maybe. Yes. About a month." He sneezed twice.

No response from the Advocate leaning over him.

"I don't understand. You come to my work, you pull me from my desk, you bring me here, poke me with needles . . . because of a *fever?*"

The Advocate sighed.

"What is it you *want* from me?"

"Nothing," she said. "Nothing anymore."

"Then . . . then you'll let me go, won't you?" Rapid breathing now from the floor, rasping and wet. The clock counted seconds on the wall.

It counted for a long time.

"No."

"I have a family!" the man cried. "A wife. And kids. Marked, everyone of age. Loyal citizens!"

The young Advocate knelt down now, into the light, beside the man. "We know," she said ominously.

He looked up in horror. This woman had no Mark on her wrist. This woman was Marked on her face.

"Who . . . who are you people?" the man asked.

The young Advocate tucked a wisp of her chin-length hair behind one ear and smiled, beautiful in the harsh, fractured light. "The International Moderators of Peace," she said. "I'm the Advocate here. Behind me are my Coordinators."

The man squinted at them through his watery eyes. "Then there must be some mistake. I've never heard of any of those things. My record is completely clean. I'm not a threat to peace anywhere!"

A Coordinator stepped forward, stone-faced, and knelt down

beside the Advocate. "Very sorry to say that you are, sir. Very sorry to say that you're wrong."

The Advocate put her hand on the bound man's shoulder. "No fault of your own," she apologized. "It's just . . . this fever . . . we're going to have to do something about this fever . . ."

In his delirium, the man looked past the young woman, past the team who'd captured him, up and over to that old, analog clock. Sixteen minutes after seven, it read. And the man tallied his last few seconds on earth.

07:16:28.

07:16:29.

07:16:30.

07:16:31 . . .

ONE

NEW CHICAGO,
NEW RULES

1

LOGAN PAUL LANGLY RAN UNTIL HIS LEGS gave out and his insides burst with pain. He ran until there were sparks in his eyes and splinters in his lungs. He ran until he collapsed.

The sun had long since dipped behind the skyline's abandoned rooftops, and Logan Paul Langly slumped now against the side of a building that gave no shelter, under lampposts that gave no light.

Ahead of him, outlined against the dying glow of a purple horizon, was an overpass, silent and slowly crumbling. This was the Ruined Sector, the outskirts of New Chicago, destroyed in the States War and never rebuilt. He was fifty miles out from Spokie. Another twenty from downtown.

Downtown was where he needed to be.

So Logan stood and stumbled on, blindly, paranoid, walking backward half the time, under the shadows of the dead neighborhood. A winter stillness held him at arm's length from any sense of hope these city streets might have given him, but even in his exhaustion, he knew that this was progress. For the moment, he wasn't being followed. For the moment, he wasn't lost.

"It's better than the woods," Logan told himself, emerging from the shadows and finding some small comfort in the thought. He had to wipe his face on his sleeves so the tears wouldn't freeze to his cheeks, but he laughed a little and said it again. "It's better than the woods, and the view here is nice tonight."

He looked out as he said it. Beside him, the water at the Ruins' edge stretched all the way to the horizon, peaceful and frozen and smooth. A soft wind slid over the ice, hitting Logan with waves of clear blue chill, and he could feel the Lake Michigan air lodging, jagged, in his throat.

Three months ago, Logan Paul Langly could not have imagined he'd wind up here. Three months ago, Logan Paul Langly was a normal kid with a normal life. He went to school, he mostly did his homework, and like all kids his age, he waited patiently for his thirteenth birthday—the day he would finally be Marked. By now, Logan should have been a full American Union citizen with full American Union benefits. But instead, he was here, a Markless fugitive stranded and alone—and that was the least of his worries.

Growing up, Logan had always thought of New Chicago as being familiar and close. He and his family had visited often to see his grandmother on birthdays or for the Inclusion Day parades. New Chicago always reminded him of cakes from his aunt and uncle's bakery downtown, of school trips to museums or family trips to sights and shops. He had felt like he belonged there. It had felt almost as much like home as Spokie did.

But New Chicago did not feel like home tonight.

And Logan did not belong anywhere now.

"Hands out, hotshot!"

Logan spun in the direction of the voice behind him.

"I said hands *out!*"

Under darkness, Logan could see the silhouette of a teenager in front of him, poking up from behind a trash can and holding its lid as some type of defense.

"I'm not . . . I don't . . . I'm no hotshot," Logan stuttered, barely even knowing what that meant, but the girl was already rushing at him, fumbling with Logan's coat, tearing at it. Finally she had Logan's wrist, and with the hand that held the lid, she pushed Logan's sleeve up tight past his forearm.

"Stop it! Stop it!" Logan yelled, wide-eyed and horrified, as the girl twisted his arm painfully to get a better look. "I'm no hotshot! I'm Markless, you beggar! I'm Markless! Like you!" And with these words, the girl paused finally, her arms slackening ever so slightly. She peered down at Logan's wrist, squinting severely in the dim light.

Logan was right, of course. His wrist was empty.

"Oh. Well, then it's nice to meet you," the girl said suddenly, smiling big and toothy. "Welcome to the Ruins!"

2

"It's how we get by." The girl shrugged, sitting cross-legged next to Logan by the lake. "I'm sure you understand."

But Logan rubbed his elbow tenderly, not understanding at all.

"Oh, get over it!" she scoffed. "As if you've never accidentally attacked a friendly stranger."

"I haven't," Logan said. "And where I come from, no one else does, either."

"Oh yeah? Where's that?" The girl rolled her eyes. "I'd love to visit."

Logan rose to his feet. "Slog Row," he said. "In Spokie." Then, more quietly, "You can't visit anymore."

The girl paused for a moment, cocking an eyebrow and taking in the sight of him. "You're a long ways from home," she said.

Logan laughed. "You have no idea."

The two of them walked along the water's edge for some time after that, Logan still nursing his elbow, the girl swinging her trash can lid playfully. "So you looking for anything in particular?" she asked. "It isn't an easy hike from the suburbs to the Ruins. Especially not this time of year."

"I wasn't headed for the Ruins," Logan said. "I'm headed downtown. I'd still be on my way if you hadn't stopped me."

"Well, then you're lucky I did! Markless like us don't stand a chance downtown anymore."

Logan looked at her, narrowing his eyes.

"Don't tell me you haven't heard."

He shrugged.

"DOME. They've gone bonkers!" She raised her eyebrows, pausing for effect. "Come on. You must know this by now. What they're doing—"

"I've been on the road a long time," Logan said, shaking his head. "Hiding in alleys, lost in the woods . . ." But the truth was that Logan did know. The truth was that Logan knew exactly what the Department of Marked Emergencies had been doing in the month since his Pledge. The Department of Marked Emergencies had been looking for *him*. He knew because they'd chased him in circles for weeks. He knew because they'd barricaded every last entrance to his hometown of Spokie. He knew because it took him three false starts to make it even this far toward New Chicago without getting caught in his first few steps.

Logan shrugged. "I haven't exactly been keeping up with current events. Been about a month since I've spoken to anyone at all."

The girl eyed Logan sideways for just a moment longer than he would have liked. "Well, that's when it started," she said. "'Bout a month ago. DOME has agents everywhere now, patrolling the streets. Someone with a dirty coat or unwashed hair or a skinny face comes along, DOME asks to see a Mark. Any poor tightwad can't show one . . . off they go."

"Where?"

"Hard to say." The girl shrugged. "They don't come back. Anyway, you can understand why I get a little jumpy around strangers these days." She took his hand playfully, twining her fingers in his and pointing his wrist upwards to examine it again.

"Still not Marked," Logan said.

"Yeah, well . . . can't be too sure." The girl rolled her eyes and let his hand drop. "So where's your huddle, then, Mr. Lone Wolf?"

"Huddle?"

"You don't have a huddle?"

Logan cleared his throat nervously.

"A huddle's, like . . . you know, your tribe or whatever. A circle. A family. Maybe not a real family, but—"

"I get it," Logan said. For a moment, Peck and Blake and the others flashed into his head. "I almost had one once, I guess. I didn't know you called them huddles."

"Well, what do *you* call them?"

"I dunno," Logan said. "A gang?"

The girl laughed. "*Gang* is a tycoon word. Markless stick to huddles."

"Tycoon?" Logan asked.

"Sure. Tycoons, bigwigs, hotshots, moguls—you know, the big spenders. The *haves*. The Marked."

Logan had heard the words before, but in Marked culture only the most foulmouthed people would dare use them in such a disparaging way.

"Oh, don't look so offended," the girl said. "The day the Marked stop calling me 'miser' and 'skinflint' and 'tightwad' and all the other awful slurs they've thought up over the years is the day I'll apologize for calling them moguls. Until then . . . well . . . they started it."

The two of them looked out at the lake for a long time.

"I need to get going," Logan said, shivering a little. "I've got a long way to walk tonight."

"What? Have your ears frozen shut? I told you, kid, downtown is off-limits. We stick to the Ruins now."

"No." Logan frowned. "I need help."

"Well, then let me. I have warm clothes, food—"

"I don't need to *survive*. I need to *move*." The girl looked at him, not understanding, and Logan sighed. "I need to get to the capital, to Beacon City. I have an aunt and uncle downtown, and as far as I can figure it, they're my only ticket there."

"They Marked?"

"Yeah."

"Then they're not family anymore."

"Look, whatever," Logan said, turning to leave, but the girl grabbed his shoulder before he could.

"You won't make it—"

"I've made it this far—"

"*They won't help you.*" The girl looked desperate now, her voice shaking suddenly. Logan wondered how many friends she'd lost in the last couple of weeks. "DOME's turning them on us. I'm telling you, it's like Mark-Unmark warfare or something. Your family won't take you to Beacon. They'll take you to the *Center* to Pledge and align yourself with Lamson and Cylis, like all the other moguls and hotshots. They'll take you to be *Marked.*" The girl ran her fingers through her hair, looking down and sighing deeply, trying to compose herself. "And that's if you're lucky. That's if they don't just send you straight to DOME on some trumped-up charge, like the good little tycoons they are." She looked out at the lake again, frozen and peaceful, and she took a few more deep breaths. "The one thing they will not do"—she spoke slowly now, her energy spent— "is get you to Beacon."

Logan sighed, feeling the cold creep in under his skin again. He wrapped his arms around himself. "They'll have to," he said, simply. "They're my only shot."

"Only shot at what?"

Logan frowned, and for a moment his mind traveled far away. To his sister, to Lily, a flunkee, swiped by DOME during her own Pledge five years ago, shipped halfway across the continent to Beacon City, to be punished in ways so secret that even most DOME employees didn't know the specifics. Logan thought of her, hidden away, alone and scared and confused. He had to save her.

"It doesn't matter what," Logan said finally.

"Well, it'd better. It had better matter a lot, actually. 'Cause you'd be risking everything for it."

"You'd be amazed," Logan said, "at how little I have to lose."

The girl stared at him, frowning, and he stared back. Then she knelt down, and she laid her trash can lid on the ground. She had a small bundle slung on her back, and she untied it and opened it, spreading out its contents on the ground. "Hungry?"

Logan didn't quite know how to answer that. He hadn't had a real meal since his birthday breakfast almost a month ago. Anything he'd eaten since, he'd found discarded among garbage or growing in the woods. In the moment, out of pride, he intended to shrug the girl's question away, to reinforce his status as the Lone Wolf Markless, able to fend for himself. But the thought of food sent a lurching wave through his system, and Logan must have grimaced.

"Here," she said, holding out a stack of crackers. "Take 'em. I have lots."

Logan could see that she didn't, that there was almost nothing there. "I can't take your food," he said. But Logan was smiling for the first time in so long that it made his face feel strange.

"Well, I don't want them back." The girl shrugged. And she pressed every last cracker she had into his hands.

Immediately, he was eating them, eating so fast that he choked a little and coughed out a cloud of pieces, the mouthful falling to the ground. At once he dropped down to scrape them up, crumbs and dirt and lint all mingling together, sticking to his fingers, and Logan licked all of it off, not caring what parts were crackers and what parts weren't. His eyes watered from the quick intake, and he coughed a few more times before he could speak. But when he did, it was with contentment and relief, a dry, grateful whisper. "Thank you," he said. "That's the most I've eaten in . . ." But he honestly didn't know, and he knew better than to remind himself.

"I'm Bridget," the girl said, putting out her Unmarked hand and letting it hang there for several moments.

Finally, Logan nodded. But he didn't take her hand. He didn't say a word.

"You may be Unmarked." She laughed. "But you aren't one of us."

"What makes you say that?" Logan asked.

"Because you still won't trust me."

"You just attacked me!"

"Well, sure, when I thought you were some bigwig," she said, as though it were nothing. "When I thought you were a mogul. Doesn't mean you have to hold it over me forever."

Logan frowned. The fact was, he didn't trust anyone anymore. But he couldn't go into all that now. "You just don't need to know my name, is all," he said, and he rubbed his elbow to drive the point home.

"Fine," Bridget said. A strange expression flashed again across her face, but it was gone before Logan could decipher it. "Even if you are set on going downtown, though, you're not gonna get there tonight. So the way I see it, you have two options. The first is that you stay with our huddle and get a good night's sleep. Andrew's down there by the trash cans, and he has an extra blanket you can use."

Logan frowned.

"What? Are you scared of *him*, too? Listen. You've got a friend now with me around, and I'm not going anywhere. I'll be here all night, and I'll be here when you wake up. If anyone gives you trouble . . ." Bridget swung her trash can lid like a shield and smiled.

"Thanks," Logan said. "I think." He nodded, unable to look at her through some combination of humility and paranoia. "But what's 'option two'?"

"Option two is that you run off and freeze to death, and I get to say I told you so."

"Excuse me?" Logan said.

But Bridget only winked, and she walked off toward the huddle in the distance, laughing to herself all the way.

∃

"The underpass is ours," Andrew said as Logan wrapped a blanket around himself. "It's decent shelter from the worst of the weather, and if you can manage to climb up to the highway, the road makes for a good lookout. *Hey, Ron, you up there?*" Andrew called abruptly.

"All clear!" a voice floated down.

"Why not keep to the buildings?" Logan asked. "Doesn't look like anyone's claimed them."

"Can't risk it," Andrew said. "Not since DOME started clamping down. They've already chased us out of New Chicago's main streets, and you'd better believe they're looking for an excuse to follow us out here and arrest us once and for all. Couple of squatting charges would give it to 'em—it's illegal to stay in a building that ain't yours, even if it's empty."

"But how would DOME know?"

Andrew laughed. "This huddle around you? We're the ones still out here, the ones who got away. Now, why do you think that is?"

Logan shrugged.

"It's 'cause we're the careful ones. DOME's thinking two steps ahead these days, so it's our job to think three. Now, the way I see it, we can't be sure those buildings aren't smoky with that electronic chalk dust DOME's always using to spy on us. Whaddaya call it? Surveillance powder. All it takes is one building filled with the stuff for DOME to hear us walkin' around inside, and then it's just a matter of time before they're banging down the doors and dragging us away. But the underpass"—Andrew swept his arms out around him and smiled at Logan—"the underpass is safe. It's open. It's ours." Andrew dropped his arms and shrugged. "For now, that is. Whether or not they're admitting it, DOME's rules have changed. Join Cylis and get Marked or die, am I right? One by one, if they have to—they're cleaning us out."

Logan's mouth went dry. "You, uh . . . you have any idea why that is?"

"Sure," Andrew said. "Simple. Little band of skinflints poked the sleeping giant."

"A little band of . . ."

Andrew laughed. "Look, Mr. Slog Row, do yourself a favor and try not to lie to me. There's no way you don't know this story."

Logan sat with his knees tucked up against his chest. He buried his chin into the edge of the blanket wrapped up around his shoulders and stared intently into its worn fabric. Thirty feet away, Bridget leaned against the next row of overpass pillars, arms crossed, one leg tucked up, totally still, just watching.

Andrew glanced at her and laughed. "I know Bridget says you're new at this, kid, but you can't honestly think I'd believe that you've never heard of the Dust."

Logan sat still.

"The Dust? You know, *Peck's* group? Come on; you *must* have heard of Peck."

"Rings a bell . . . ," Logan said, swallowing hard.

"He's been famous for years! The guy's, like, our biggest recruiter—our *only* recruiter, probably. Like a, uh—whaddaya call it?—a Robin Hood–type." Andrew laughed. "You know, stealing kids from the rich and giving them to the poor."

Bridget walked over to Andrew, joining in on the conversation by hitting him squarely on the back of his head. "Don't say it like that! Makes it sound like he's kidnapping 'em. That's exactly what DOME wants people to think."

"Yeah, yeah," Andrew said. "I just like the thought of it, you know? Sure, the kids wanna go. I know that. Sheesh." Andrew rolled his eyes.

"You ever met him?" Logan asked.

"Me? Nah. Guy's a ghost. Doesn't poke his head out for hardly anyone."

"So, uh . . ." Logan bit his lip. "Where do you think he is now?"

Andrew shrugged. "Probably dead."

"Dead? Why dead?" Logan asked a little too quickly.

"Boy, you really have been underground these last few weeks." Logan nodded.

"Well, listen, who knows what's really going on, right?"

Logan shrugged, leading him on.

"But from what I heard, Peck bit off a little more than he could chew. First he botched some kidnapping at a battle of the bands in September, which got DOME mad enough to justify all the street cleanings. Then—get this—the poor miser doubled down. Tried to recruit a kid *so* nuts-o that the flunkee actually went straight to some DOME agent's daughter, ratted Peck out, sabotaged his own Pledge, attacked his Marker's nurse, and then *escaped*."

All the cold of a mid-December night, and Logan began to sweat. "What, um . . ." He cleared his throat. "What makes you think all that?"

"You kidding? It's all any of us are talking about. Kid's, like, a legend." Andrew elbowed Logan's blanketed arm playfully. "He's a dead man walking! If DOME doesn't get him, the Dust will soon enough. But what are ya gonna do?" Andrew shrugged. "Rumors and hearsay, that's all it is. Just a little bit of laughs for the dark days."

Logan wiped a few beads of sweat from his hairline and smiled nervously at Bridget, who continued to stare at him silently.

Through Andrew's whole story, she hadn't looked away once.

That night, Logan slept lightly, waking what must have been every twenty minutes. On one side of him, buildings crumbled and waited for renovations that would never come. On the other, the lake lay still with a quiet dawn glow. And in between, all across the underpass, a couple hundred Markless boys and girls and men and women curled themselves up on the hard ground and shivered so hard that their teeth chattered, even in their sleep. How many were dreaming of food they couldn't eat or comforts they couldn't have, of rights they weren't given or futures they wouldn't get? How many dreamed of friends and family taken from them these last few weeks . . . of homes they had lost . . . of loved ones they would never see again?

And how many dreamed of Logan, the cause of all that? How many right now dreamed of the mystery kid fleeing DOME's grasp, carelessly sealing the fate of countless Unmarked, throwing all of them under the bus for his own selfish plans?

Half of them?

All of them?

Finally Logan gave up on any real rest and allowed himself to sit up. He rubbed his eyes and leaned back, propping himself up on his elbows. Andrew was there next to him, snoring just a little. And Bridget . . .

Bridget was . . .

"Where is she?" Logan whispered frantically, shaking Andrew awake.

"Whadder you talkinbout?" Andrew slurred, rolling halfway over and squinting at Logan with dry eyes.

"I watched Bridget fall asleep *right there*, Andrew. Now you tell me—where did she go?"

"Wheredas she evergo?" Andrew said, and he waved his hand dismissively before pulling a blanket over his face. "She'll be back inna morning." Another breath and he was snoring again.

Immediately Logan stood, heart pumping and mind racing.

It was probably nothing, right? Probably nothing at all. Certainly nothing to be suspicious of . . . right?

But the sky was blue at its horizon, and in the presunrise light Logan could see the whole huddle.

There was no question about it.

Bridget was gone.

TWO

WHERE ERIN
COMES IN

1

THE SUN WASN'T EVEN UP, AND ALREADY ERIN
was ready for school. She'd fed her iguana, she'd showered and
dressed, she'd made herself breakfast . . . by the time her alarm
went off, Erin had been sitting on the edge of her bed for thirty-five
minutes. She'd watched the minutes turn thirty-five times.

"Sleep well?" Mr. Arbitor asked when Erin emerged from her
room.

"Like a log," Erin said.

But this was a lie.

Erin hadn't slept well in a month.

Life at Spokie Middle was quiet these days, dull and colorless. It
didn't help that the school had been built underground to save space
among the too-cramped streets of the small, New Chicago suburb.
But at least in the past, the school's virtual "windows" had brought

a *little* humor to the space. These days, students at Spokie Middle were simply too downcast to care. Erin would walk through the Beach Wing, where not a single classmate stood soaking up the artificial sun. She would sit through lunch in her corner of the cafeteria, counting stains on the laminate table under weak fluorescent light, not even looking at the hushed "mountain landscapes" all around her.

In class, the teachers were somber, boring, apologetic, even, for continuing to teach under the circumstances. In every hallway, room, and stairwell, Erin could feel in her gut the low, trembling sadness given off by a student body still reeling from the one-two punch of losing Logan Langly so soon after losing Dane Harold.

And still no one at Spokie Middle was hit harder than Erin. By the time news struck that Logan had gone missing, everyone in school knew that she and Logan had become something of a pair. So after one too many questions about where Erin thought Logan might be and whether or not she thought Logan might ever come back, Erin decided once and for all that she was done being friendly to these people—the whole lot of them—and after that she just sort of retreated into her own private world of anger and suffering.

In economics class, Erin sat with her head on her desk, staring sideways at the empty seat where Logan would have been, just two rows from the front of the room. She sat that way the entire lesson, and no one said a word about it.

Things were no easier on Hailey Phoenix. For years, Hailey had been friends with the missing boys, and just this fall, she'd been the source of a major falling-out between them. Now it seemed there wasn't anything Hailey could do to avoid the gossip surrounding her, with some kids even wondering openly whether Hailey might have been responsible for Dane's and Logan's disappearance *herself*.

"After all," girls would whisper in the locker room behind her back, "the last anyone knows of Logan, he was on a date with *her*."

They were right, as it turned out. Hailey had, in fact, brought Dane and Logan to the Dust, one at a time, over the course of the fall. She'd betrayed them, even if it *was* for their own protection. But this was her secret. She hadn't been caught, and she hadn't confessed it to *anyone*. Certainly, in all their gossiping, none of the students at Spokie Middle actually *believed* the things they were saying . . . right? Even if they did happen to be true?

Hailey was a careful person. Had she known about what Logan told Erin the night before his Pledge—that Hailey had been working with Peck, and that she was a part of the Dust—she would surely have stayed away. She might even have left town with all the others.

But Hailey *didn't* know what Erin knew. And she *had* to risk it. She *had* to stick around—just a little while longer, at least. Because the only thing Hailey did know for certain was that Erin was working with DOME. And if Hailey ever wanted to see Logan again, if she ever wanted to find him and bring him back to Peck . . . well . . . then that made Erin Arbitor her single best lead.

"Rough day?" Hailey whispered as Erin made her way out of economics class and into the Arctic Wing.

"As bad as all the others," Erin said. "Today some jerk asked if I thought Logan might have been eaten by wolves."

"They roam around these parts." Hailey laughed.

"So he said." Erin rolled her eyes, and the two of them walked together down the hall, acting not entirely unlike friends.

"Hey, your dad works for DOME, though, doesn't he?" Hailey asked, seizing the opportunity to bring it up.

"Oh, uh . . . yeah. Government work," Erin said.

"That's right, that's right. Cool, cool." Hailey looked at the ground. "I heard, actually . . . uh . . . I heard, I think on the news or something, that when Logan ran away, it was during his Pledge . . . or something. Isn't that weird? I just . . . sometimes I wonder if that means DOME might be looking into it—"

"Oh, I wouldn't know anything about that," Erin said, too quickly. "Dad never tells me anything."

"No, I guess not," Hailey said. She laughed, a little nervously. "I guess . . . I guess I'm just hoping we'll see him again, is all."

Erin frowned. "You ever feel like maybe he and Dane are still around, sometimes? Like maybe they haven't actually gone too far?"

"No," Hailey said, narrowing her eyes. "What makes you think I would?"

"Oh. Just wishful thinking, I guess." Erin gave Hailey a sad smile and backed up onto the escalator. "You're right. Let's not kid ourselves. We'll never see either of them again."

2

When Erin made it home a half hour later, her father was sitting at the kitchen table with a DOME agent beside him.

"What do you want?" Erin said, still standing in the doorway. "I have homework."

"Johnson's here to see you," Mr. Arbitor said.

"Again? I'm flattered." Erin dropped her backpack onto the

floor with a *thud*. "You gonna take me seriously today, or are we all just here to insult me some more?"

"Erin. It's good to see you," Johnson said. "You remember where we left off?" He stood and reached out to take Erin's coat, but Erin made no motion to accept the gesture. Instead she took her time closing the apartment door behind her, letting the sound accentuate the room's awkward silence before answering.

"I do remember," she said. "We had just finished the part where you didn't actually listen to anything I had to say, and, if memory serves, we were about to begin . . ." She frowned and thought for a moment, tapping her chin. "Oh, that's right! Wasting my time."

Mr. Arbitor stood from the kitchen table and straightened his sweater. "Erin, we are not wasting your time, because this time is not yours to begin with. It is borrowed. From the government. It is time we are *allowing* you not to spend in Corrections for your suspected involvement in Logan Langly's escape."

"We're hoping this'll just take a minute," Johnson added, smiling uncomfortably.

"Don't bother, Johnson." Mr. Arbitor laid his hands on Erin's shoulders. The two of them stood there for a moment by the head of the kitchen table. Then Erin's father pushed her, hard, straight down into the chair where he had been sitting. "Let's not forget who got us into this mess."

"For the last time, Dad, I don't know what you're talking about." Erin looked at her father blankly, leaning back and letting the snow fall in chunks from the coat she was still wearing. All three of them listened to the wet sound of slush hitting the apartment floor.

"There is *no way* Logan Langly evaded those DOME agents on his own," Mr. Arbitor said. "There is *no way* he made it out of DOME's

Pledging Center by himself. So I am more than well enough aware that you do, in fact, know what I am talking about, *dear*."

Erin shrugged.

"But we are not here to talk about that," Erin's dad continued. "Not this time. Not anymore. We are putting those details behind us—"

"About time," Erin mumbled.

And Mr. Arbitor spoke through gritted teeth. "We are *here*, Erin—if you would be so gracious as to listen to me, your father, who has been nothing but patient and kind and forgiving ever since you decided to help that little miser—we are *here* to talk about next steps."

"Next steps," Erin repeated.

"Next steps," Johnson agreed.

Erin raised her eyebrows in a sarcastic display of excitement and surprise. "You mean, finally, that you're not just here to blame me for your mistakes? That you're not just here to yell at me and threaten me because you and the idiots you call agents were too slow to catch half a dozen *kids* hiding out in a warehouse, just waiting to be arrested, after I *told* you exactly where they were and how to get there? You mean you two are actually thinking of moving on from all of that? Of actually *investigating* something? You're really planning to play detective with your little friends over at DOME?" Erin laughed. "That's adorable!" She leaned forward, resting her elbows on the table and looking from her father to Johnson.

A vein in Mr. Arbitor's forehead throbbed visibly as he glared at his daughter.

Johnson cleared his throat and fiddled with his tie. When he spoke, he spoke calmly and slowly. "What we are doing here is spearheading a two-pronged strategy to find the Dust as well as your friend Logan Langly." Johnson smiled, ignoring everything about Erin's attitude. "We are hoping that with your help, we might maximize our chances of success."

Erin rolled her eyes. "I already told you—I don't know where Logan is. I don't know where the Dust is. They ran off and you lost them. What else do you want me to say? Follow Hailey Phoenix. She's in league with all of them, and we know she's their spy— Logan told me so before his Pledge."

"We are following Hailey." Mr. Arbitor shook his head. "No luck. Her movements are strange, no doubt, but they haven't led us anywhere. Peck must know she's a liability—he hasn't met with her at all."

"Have you powdered her house?"

Johnson nodded. "And a lot of good it did us. Hailey's extremely careful about what she says to her mom. They're both clearly aware of the risk she's put them under."

"Then bring her in and question her yourselves." Erin hated herself for saying it. She really did like Hailey. But she just couldn't stand this anymore. She desperately wanted Logan back. And failing that, she at least wanted this whole thing to be over so she could go back to Beacon. So she could be with her mom. So that she might have a real, functioning family again.

Mr. Arbitor paced around the table now, thinking. "She'll never rat Peck out, and you know it. If she's anything like the rest of the Dust, she'd sooner let us kill her."

"Besides," Johnson said. "That's an endgame for us. As soon as Hailey gets even a whiff of DOME—as soon as she has so much as the slightest sense that Logan might have told you anything, that you might have gone to us, that we might have proof to hold against her . . . she'll disappear. Much better, instead, for you to continue keeping tabs on her for us. See if she slips up and lets her guard down."

"How'd it go today?" Mr. Arbitor asked. "You talk to her?"

"Yes, Dad, I talked to her. Obviously. How many times do I have to tell you she's *way* too suspicious of me to say anything helpful?" Erin looked down at her hands. "And besides, I don't like doing it." She looked up again, at her father. "We need another angle."

Johnson smiled. "We're here today because we think we have one."

"Well, I can't wait to hear it. I'm sure it's a doozy. In fact, if it's anything like your last dozen plans—"

"We found Logan," Mr. Arbitor said. And he relished the look on his daughter's face. "Yeah. Thought that might get your attention."

"What do you mean you've found him? Where is he?" Erin turned to Johnson, speaking urgently now, her tough attitude forgotten.

"To clarify—we don't actually have the boy in custody. In fact, we're basing this off a rather unreliable source that has yet to be confirmed and . . . well . . . it could easily turn out to be a false alarm. But Erin"—Johnson leaned forward—"between you and me, I don't think it is."

Two more ice chunks fell from Erin's sleeves. They splashed on the table in front of her, and she leaned back slowly.

"Okay," she said, unzipping her jacket. "So what do you need me to do?"

3

There was a perfect stillness to the woods outside of Spokie. The trees were bare, and the sky behind them was a bright, clear blue. There were no birds or squirrels. Even Hailey's footsteps barely made a sound.

She arrived at the glade just as the sun slipped into the trees, casting long shadows across the grass. Hailey knelt down, scanning the ground and counting the rocks and the sticks scattered about. To anyone else, they were nothing. But to Hailey, they were a lifeline. Each rock a dot and each stick a dash, they spelled out exactly what she was looking for.

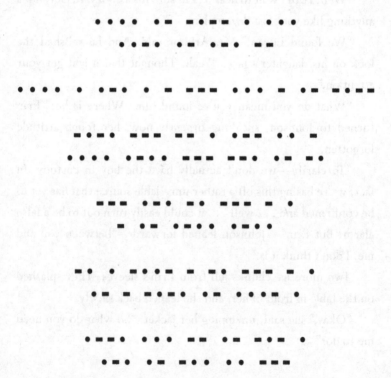

● ● ● ▬   ▬ ▬ ▬ ●   ▬ ▬ ▬ ▬   ▬ ▬ ▬ ▬

▬ ● ▬   ● ● ● ●   ▬ ▬ ● ●

It was Morse code. The oldest code in the book. But who would think to look among the rocks and the dirt?

It was a system Hailey and Peck had devised the night Logan ran off, when they realized that even notes burning away on paper would be too much of a liability from then on. The game had changed. Even a single visit between Hailey and Peck was now an impossible risk.

They set the first location together that night in November. Each would be in the woods, they decided, but each after the first would be in a different spot. Keeping it the same would invite DOME to look too closely, and perhaps notice the code. So the first location would be by the birch tree next to the wide stream, and the second location would be included in the message at the first. The third in the message at the second. And so on. In this way, Hailey's nighttime strolls seemed arbitrary to anyone not reading the code. Pointless, even.

But this visit to the glade was anything but pointless.

Hailey translated the message in her head and smiled.

Hayes farm.

Here to stay.

Come with Logan

or not at all.

Next note at cave.

PS Make radio

3900kHz

Erin had her jacket off, and it lay in a wet crumple on the floor. The room grew dim in the waning daylight, and she listened intently to each word Johnson said.

"They are fractured, and they are desperate. Throughout New Chicago, the Markless community is reeling. We've cracked down on squatters; we've cracked down on loitering; we've even redefined probable cause."

"These orders have come straight from the top," Mr. Arbitor assured her.

"The top?" Erin asked.

He smiled. "With the Global Treaty in place, the game is changing. Rapidly."

"What do you mean, 'in place'? I thought all that G.U. stuff wasn't happening until the spring, when Parliament could vote—"

"It wasn't. But Chancellor Cylis and General Lamson are pushing it through."

Erin knew as well as anyone that the general in chief of the American Union had always been a supporter of the European Union's chancellor. She knew that the two of them had been advocating for a true Global Union ever since Lamson adopted Cylis's Mark program in America, just after Erin was born. Erin's mother, a top economic software analyst on Barrier Street in Beacon, had even helped facilitate the merger of the A.U. and E.U. economies over the past decade. But Erin never could have imagined that the Global Treaty would pass through the American Parliament so quickly; it was a process she figured would take years.

"We are close, Erin, very close, now, to a single-nation world.

Never again will we worry about another Total War. Never again will we suffer from fractured cultures or incompatible views. *Unity*, Erin. Complete unity is upon us."

"This is classified, you understand, what we're telling you." Johnson looked nervously between Erin and her father.

"Okay," Erin said.

And Mr. Arbitor continued. "The American Union is merging, as we speak, with the European Union. They aren't waiting for the new year. It's happening now."

"So then . . ."

"As a sign of good faith, Lamson is redoubling efforts to reach a 100 percent Marked populace. To show our solidarity, you understand, across the A.U., in support of Chancellor Cylis."

"All right . . ."

"Well, Erin, your good friend Logan Langly has given us just the excuse DOME needed in the New Chicago area to . . . *revise* our stance against the Markless. No more turning a blind eye. They're criminals, Erin. And they're traitors. They've refused allegiance to Lamson and Cylis, and they are trying to convince others to turn against the government as well."

"I *know* that, Dad. We all know it."

Johnson nodded. "And yet, just six months ago, if we went around locking up Markless, what would we get? Unrest. We'd get whining about rights and free speech and respect for dissent and all of that, even among the Marked communities. You know—the idealists."

"The idealists," Mr. Arbitor growled.

"But the bigger the threat the Markless pose, the easier it is, from a public relations standpoint, to deal with them properly."

Mr. Arbitor leaned forward. "The Dust is that threat. And

now that we can tie them to Logan's premeditated assault on a Pledge Center nurse—which was nothing short of a direct and aggressive attack against DOME's New Chicago headquarters— we have all the proof we need that Unmarked communities are a hostile and dangerous public enemy. Logan's escape was an opportunity for Lamson—and he's taking it."

"That's ridiculous," Erin said. "You're manipulating Logan's intentions to prove your point."

"Oh, are we?" Mr. Arbitor sneered at his daughter now.

"We've been raiding Markless gangs for weeks," Johnson said. "Slog Row was just the beginning. We've swept all the surrounding neighborhoods. We've swept downtown New Chicago. We've clamped down on every bit of known activity."

"Good," Erin said sincerely. "It's about time, if you ask me."

"But there's more." Mr. Arbitor smiled. "Because in every raid since the escape, we have made one thing perfectly clear: DOME's priority is Logan. And any leads resulting in his capture will be rewarded accordingly."

"We know there are more Markless out there in the shadows and the alleys and the woods. But now all of them are the survivors of one raid or another. All of them have heard the terms of our deal."

Mr. Arbitor nodded. "And today, one of them has come forward."

"The tip sounds credible."

"Logan has surfaced."

"Our agents are standing by."

"You're not gonna hurt him," Erin said. "Once you have him. You're not gonna hurt him, are you?"

"No," Johnson said. "We would never hurt him."

"He's not one of them," Erin insisted. "He's not Dust. He's Unmarked at the moment, I know, but that's . . . temporary. He's isn't Markless, Dad. Peck *tricked* him. I told you that—Peck tricked him into thinking DOME has Logan's sister. It's ridiculous, I know. It was just a trap, and Logan fell for it. But you can't blame him for—"

"We're not, Erin. We're trying to help. That's all."

Erin sighed, and another chunk of slush fell to the floor. "Okay. And what about finding the Dust?"

"Can't pit Markless against the Dust," Johnson said. "Not in the same way. All anyone knows about Logan is that he's the miser who caused the raids. But the Dust . . . Dust is revered in this city. Peck's a symbol to those Unmarked beggars. They'd never turn him in."

"And anyway, he's too smart. Peck's suspected for years that Markless are too desperate, as a group, to be trusted. He's learned how to stay away from enemies and friends alike."

"Then what's the plan?" Erin asked. "Assuming your source is right, when do we move in on Logan? How do I know you're not just gonna kill him? And how does any of this fit with finding Peck and the Dust?" She looked at the two men nervously, but Mr. Arbitor was grinning now.

"Well, sweetie . . . that's where you come in."

5

Hailey arrived home just before sunset to the sounds of her mother in the bathroom upstairs, coughing and wheezing out the nanodust piled up in her lungs.

Growing up, Hailey's mom was always home while Mr. Phoenix

worked long hours as the head manager of a nanomaterials plant outside of town. But that changed when Mr. Phoenix passed away, and ever since, Hailey's mom had made ends meet by working her own long hours on the same factory floor once managed by her husband. Though Mrs. Phoenix never once complained, Hailey knew that her mother's job was a difficult one, made worse by the constant exposure to nanodust, which had given Mrs. Phoenix an awful, chronic cough.

Tonight, Hailey went straight to the kitchen sink, turned on the faucet, and let the white noise of the running water drown out the spasms of her mother's dry choking. She stood there for a full minute, hands braced against the countertop, just staring out the kitchen window. Finally she grabbed a pot and lit the stove to boil some water for lentils to eat with her mother. But when she put the pot on the stove and turned the faucet off, the familiar coughing again filled the empty, quiet space.

"My favorite," Mrs. Phoenix said when she sat at the dinner table twenty minutes later. "Thank you, honey." She chewed and swallowed gingerly. "So how's Erin? Any news?"

"Erin's good." But Hailey put her spoon down. "Suspicious, though. She's careful, no doubt about it."

Mrs. Phoenix nodded. "And how was your walk?"

"Refreshing," Hailey said, and Mrs. Phoenix knew what that meant. She extended her hand across the table and put it lightly on Hailey's.

Each of them knew that these days, anything they said might very well be used against them, given Hailey's connections with the Dust. They'd never found evidence of bug tape (an electronic adhesive used to record and transmit sound to DOME's headquarters), but their house was dusty enough that a bit of surveillance powder was always a possibility. So Hailey and her mom had long ago decided that their mother-daughter conversations were best kept as vague as possible, and it was a rule they'd yet to break.

"Thanks, Mom." Hailey said, smiling just slightly. "Hey, I'm starting a new sculpture tonight."

"Oh yeah? That's great! It's been a little while."

"Yeah," Hailey said. "Figured it's time to get back into it."

Hailey was a gifted artist, particularly with sculpture. She could turn garbage into anything, and this was good, since in Hailey's neighborhood, garbage was just about all she had to work with.

"Any idea what you're going to make?"

"Yes." Hailey winked. "But you'll just have to wait and see."

"I'm very proud of you," Mrs. Phoenix said, unable to say more for fear of who might be listening. "You're doing just great. I want you to know that."

"I'm not sure I am, Mom." Hailey sighed. "My team's down for the count, and I still don't see a way not to lose."

"You'll find it," Mrs. Phoenix said.

But Hailey shook her head. She no longer believed that was true. And in her frustration, Hailey decided finally to break her own household rule. "DOME's winning," she said. Then she laughed, and her mom watched wide-eyed as Hailey leaned far back and said loudly into the powdery air, "You hear that, DOME? You're winning."

Mrs. Phoenix couldn't stop coughing after that.

THREE

THE SETUP

1

THE SMELL IN THE STABLE WAS STRONG AND natural, a far cry from the smells of Slog Row, where the Dust used to live. Jo opened the doors, and Blake scrunched his nose as he and the others filed in.

"This it?" Eddie asked, shuffling through the straw stalks on the ground.

"This is it." Jo nodded. "Welcome to our new home."

Already Tyler had made his way onto the upper beams of the enclosure, tiptoeing across one of them with his arms out. "New game!" he called, faltering a little and waving his arms wildly to keep his balance.

"So, what? We all just pick a horse and bunk up?" Eddie walked to a stallion at the stable's end and waved his hands in its face.

"Pretty much," Jo said. "The livestock'll throw off any heat detectors or satellite pictures, and their noise should distract long-range mic surveillance from picking up any of your lousy snoring."

Behind all of this, Tyler quietly lost his footing and fell into a pile of hay.

"You all right?" Blake asked without much concern.

"I won." Tyler groaned.

"Let's just try not to kill ourselves before DOME gets the chance, hm?" Jo said, checking to make sure Tyler was okay. "You'll ruin everyone's fun."

"Speaking of which." Eddie pointed to the door as it swung open. "Whaddo you suppose we do with *him*?"

Meg walked into the stable, dragging by his feet a man who lay slack and splayed on the ground. His head rested sideways, bouncing a little as it slid across the dirt. His arms followed behind, stretching up and over his head, and for the moment he was deadweight. Knocked out. Harmless.

That would change, of course. The DOME badge on his shoulder promised it.

Blake closed his eyes and composed himself. "I give Mr. DOME Agent here another hour before he comes to. Tops." He sighed. "There's a stream down past the corn field. Have you seen it?"

Meg nodded.

"Put him in faceup."

Eddie took hold of the man's hands, and he and Meg turned to head out the door.

"And hey—" Blake called after them, "make sure he floats before you let go."

"Whoa, whoa, what happened here?" Dane asked, eyebrows raised as he entered the barn.

"Another scout," Blake said.

"He make it all the way to the farm?"

"No, they still don't know we're here. This guy was just tromping through the woods when Meg found him. Then she . . ." Blake paused. "Well, I dunno. Meg, what'd you do to the guy? Clobber him?"

Meg smiled and nodded.

Blake turned to Dane. "Meg clobbered him."

"Yeah, thanks. I'd gathered that much," Dane said. He sighed and dropped his bag to the ground. "So they really aren't letting up, then."

"On the contrary. They're closing their grip around Hailey as we speak. She'll lead them right to us with these daily messages between her and Peck."

"Nah, she won't," Dane said. "Peck's system is good. It's safe. And besides . . . we'd lose her completely without it."

"*Dane's* in love with *Haaai-ley*," Tyler sang from the hay.

"Will you shut it? This has nothing to do with me," Dane said. "Right now Hailey's our only contact with the outside world. We can't find Logan without her."

"And, wait—I'm sorry," Eddie said sarcastically. "Could someone, anyone, please remind me *why*, exactly, we're still risking everything for that traitor? Because I've forgotten."

"It's not about Logan anymore," Jo said, no less annoyed. "It's about Lily. Peck and Logan are obsessed with saving her."

Dane sighed. "She was Peck's best friend, Jo. And she's Logan's sister. It's hard to blame them."

But Eddie just laughed. "He's out there again, isn't he? Peck. Right now. Leaving yet another message for Hailey."

"Yeah." Blake rolled his eyes. "Right now."

"*Man*," Jo said. "Night after night after night! What will it take to get through to that tightwad? He's gonna get us all caught—or worse!" Jo shook her head as an awkward silence settled over the stable.

"Hoooooooo-*wee*, are we in trouble!" Tyler laughed abruptly. "Welcome to the big leagues, kiddies!" He rolled out from his spot in the hay and lay flat on his back, arms folded over his stomach. "And all thanks to our good ol' friend, Logan Langly! Three cheers for that guy! Wherever you are, ya skinflint! To good health! To long life! To happiness!" He looked around playfully.

But no one else was laughing.

2

Logan waited with his hood up and a scarf over his nose and mouth. He waited at the farthest edge of the huddle. He didn't let a single tightwad out of his sight.

He'd spent the whole day this way, scared and indecisive. He knew it was a risk to show his face anywhere downtown. He had planned to see his aunt and uncle, to visit their safe, public, well-lit bakery, to ask them for help because he simply didn't know where else to turn . . . but what if Bridget was right? What if the Mark really did trump family? What if they turned him in no matter what?

And yet, how much safer was it to stay where he was now? Bridget *had* returned that morning, just as Andrew said she would, shortly before the huddle began waking for the day. No DOME officers in tow, no magnecuffs, no "Gotcha, ya filthy, stinkin' beggar!"

But she wasn't exactly forthcoming, either. Logan had pretended to be asleep when she arrived. He had pretended not to notice when she slipped silently under her blanket before making a big show of waking up after "a great night of sleep." But he *had* noticed, and he couldn't help but wonder what Bridget was hiding.

For the moment, Logan decided to risk it and stay at least one more day with the huddle. He needed the rest anyway, and time to plan. But he kept his distance all the same.

"You're quite the social butterfly," Bridget joked, walking over to Logan. "Making lots of friends, I see."

"Just, uh, don't wanna be in the way," Logan said.

Bridget smiled. "You're not. Here—let me show you around. It's not much, but it is our home. And it's yours now too, if you want it to be."

She brought Logan to a pillar at the edge of the huddle's space in the underpass. At its base was a row of boxes, each labeled with something along the lines of "Fiction A–F," or "History O–Z." The flaps of each box hung open invitingly.

"Books?" Logan asked. "Printed books?" Outside of museums, this was only the second time in his life that Logan had seen so many.

"You bet," Bridget said. "Gotta keep the mind sharp somehow. And we Markless sure ain't gonna be reading off tablets and plasti-screens anytime soon."

"But where'd you get them?" Logan asked. "*How'd* you get them?"

"There's been a book circulation for years now among the Markless in New Chicago. Who knows what the source was. There's rumors it was this kid Peck . . . but people say a lot of things about that guy." Bridget shrugged, looking over the collection. "Anyway, this is what's left after all the raids. We all took what was most valuable to us and ran." Bridget smiled. "Usually, that was our huddle's stash of books."

Logan flipped through some of the yellowing pages in front of him. "Any recommendations?" he asked.

"Oh, lots," Bridget said. She passed a thick one his way. "This one here'll keep you busy for a while."

"Wait a second," Logan said. "Is this—"

"A Bible. Yeah," Bridget said.

Logan stared at it.

"We have all kinds of religious texts here, if you're interested. Not to mention philosophy, politics . . . any of that sort o' stuff. It's all banned, so naturally it's pretty popular among the Markless." Bridget winked. "If it'll get you arrested, we probably have a copy somewhere."

Logan looked through the book, scanning the columns of tiny type on each page. The pages were so thin they were almost translucent, and they made a soft crinkling sound as he flipped through them.

"Just don't get caught with that," Bridget warned.

Logan looked up at her. "Thanks."

And Bridget walked on. "Over here's our clothing station. You ever need dry socks, a new sweater . . . this is where you'll come."

"You mean I can just take anything?"

"Well, we certainly don't expect you to be able to pay for it." Bridget laughed.

As they walked, Logan began to appreciate what the huddle had done. The surrounding streets were crumbling. The buildings were falling down, and the sidewalks were charred and split from long-ago gunfire and explosions. But the underpass was different. The underpass was bright and warm, like a home. All around it, there was art . . . finished paintings just lying on the concrete, sculptures scattered about, a shortwave radio chattering in the corner, tapestries hanging by string, poems graffitied onto each rusting pillar . . . all of it as if out of another era entirely.

"We still have time on our hands," Bridget said. "In fact, it's pretty much *all* we have. So we draw, or we write . . . we do whatever we can to contribute to the huddle."

Logan stopped for a moment and listened to an older woman

strumming a battered guitar and singing a song to a small circle of Markless surrounding her.

"Michael, row the boat ashore," she sang. "Hallelujah . . ."

"We sing a lot around here too," Bridget said. "It keeps our spirits up."

Logan looked at her, silent for some time. "Where'd you go last night?" he asked finally.

"Nowhere." Bridget frowned. She wouldn't look at him as she said it.

"I know you snuck off. I watched you come back."

"I didn't sneak off. Maybe you dreamed it—"

"I didn't dream it," Logan interrupted. "You're hiding something from me."

"*I'm* hiding something? From *you*? You won't even tell me your name!"

Logan clenched his teeth and swallowed hard. In the background, the woman sang her gentle refrain, but it did nothing to cut the tension between the two of them.

Bridget sighed. She looked away, disappointed. "You're really gonna make me say it, aren't you? You're really gonna ruin the surprise."

Logan narrowed his eyes, and he waited for Bridget to explain herself.

"Okay, okay." She laughed, easing up a little. "Tomorrow morning. There's a landfill half a mile north of here. If you still wanna know, meet me there when the sun comes up."

Another night in the underpass. A secluded meeting place. Just thinking about it, Logan's palms began to sweat. "How do I know I can trust you?" he asked.

"You can't," Bridget said with a wry smile. "But if you really wanna know so bad what it is I'm hiding from you . . . well, then I guess you're just gonna have to risk it." She shrugged. Then she turned to sing with the other Markless, leaving Logan in the dark.

彐

In the morning, the sun shone brightly through the windows and cracks of the barn, but none of the Dust were awake. Meg and Dane slept soundly in two of the three empty stalls not occupied by horses. Blake slept sitting up, his back against a wall, next to a pile of hay where Rusty was sleeping soundly and sucking his thumb. Eddie dozed on a stool beside the stallion's stall at the far end of the stable, swatting idly as the stallion leaned over to chew on his thick blond hair. Jo slept beside the barn door, intending to keep watch. And Tyler lay smack in the middle of the barn, laughing in his sleep.

Mama Hayes stood in the entryway, taking inventory and shaking her head. "All right, kids. If you're gonna stay, you're gonna work." She spoke over a chorus of groans and mumbling. Tyler rolled over and said something about rest for the wicked, which Mama Hayes ignored on her walk past. "Come on," she said. "Everybody up."

Mama Hayes was not a farmer herself. Until recently, she spent her days maintaining an abandoned convenience store out on Slog Row, where for years she and her husband, Papa, stocked black market food and supplies for the Markless living in Spokie. It was only after the Slog Row raid in September that the Hayeses fled to the farm, and only last week that the Dust finally heard about it, after nearly a month of following the vague leads and best guesses from stray Markless in the area.

The field between the stable and the farmhouse was wide and patchy with hard, gray ground and untouched snow. Withered cornstalks from the summer still stood against the monochrome backdrop, and Tyler and Eddie made a point of kicking each one they passed.

Inside, the farmhouse smelled like oatmeal and cinnamon. The Dust filed in through the front door, kicking off the dirt and snow from the tatters that remained of their shoes. Blake leaned in and whispered to Tyler and Eddie, "Behave, or you're sleeping outside tonight."

But Tyler was too focused on the kitchen to respond. His mouth hung slightly open, and his eyes were wide, as if the smell of the food were good enough to see.

"Good morning," Peck said, waiting patiently at the dining room table to everyone's left. "Please, join me. Breakfast is served."

Not many words were exchanged among the Dust over the course of their meal. It was all Blake, Joanne, Tyler, Eddie, Meg, Rusty, and Dane could do to sit, chew, and listen while Mama and Papa Hayes discussed the latest news with Peck.

"You're in quite a pickle," Mama said. "I don't envy it."

"It's true things are . . . a little out of hand at present. I'll admit to that," Peck said.

"Peck mentioned that you kids spent these last few weeks in the woods. Couldn't have been easy with this weather."

"It wasn't," Blake said.

Jo frowned. "The weather wasn't the problem. The problem was DOME. They have scouts everywhere now."

"Well, you're safe here," Mama said. "And we want you to stay. At least until you're able to find that Langly boy."

Eddie snorted. "Can we all just admit right now that waiting around for Logan is a terrible idea? Please? This is getting ridiculous."

"We'll find him," Peck said. "I know Hailey can do it."

"Hailey. I remember her. The girl who'd visit the Fulmart, evenings and weekends," Mama said.

Peck nodded. "That's right. She was with her mother when DOME ambushed the warehouse, so she's still in Spokie. Goes to school, walks around town . . . they haven't arrested her yet."

"Yeah, because DOME's hoping she'll lead them straight to us!" Blake said.

Peck shrugged and spoke again to Mama and Papa Hayes. "Never underestimate DOME. That said, I believe we've covered our tracks well enough. There's nothing Hailey's doing that would bring DOME to the farm. I actually think there's a good chance DOME will lead *us* to Logan."

"Peck, *snap out of it!*" Jo said.

Peck smiled at the Hayeses. "My friends here aren't too excited about my plan—"

"Because it's suicide," Blake interrupted.

"—but I've requested that Hailey befriend Erin Arbitor, the daughter of the man who was brought here to capture me."

Mama Hayes nodded, considering this.

"With their resources, DOME *will* find Logan," Peck continued. "And I have a feeling Erin will be the first to know about it when they do. If we can get Hailey close enough to her, we might just be able to latch onto DOME's investigation—and beat them to the punch."

"Keep your friends close and your enemies closer," Papa Hayes said.

"And hope in the meantime that Logan isn't too far behind."

"Okay, and *then* what?" Eddie demanded. "The kid's a walking DOME magnet."

"He's in danger. We are helping him."

"Yeah, and we *tried* that already. It nearly got us all killed."

Blake put his spoon down. "Eddie has a point, Peck. Sticking our necks out for Logan after what he's put us through . . . I just don't see what good it does us."

"Lily," Jo said, bitterly. "How many times do I have to say it? This whole thing's about Lily. Peck, why won't you just admit that?"

"It's bigger than Lily," Peck said.

"No, it isn't! So just say so! You and Logan are exactly alike—you'd both happily trade every last one of us to have her back!"

"I would not!" Peck said.

"Admit it!"

"That's enough!" Papa hit the table with the palm of his hand. "This is *exactly* what DOME wants you to be doing. Chancellor Cylis has taken our rights, our freedom, and our dignity. He has divided us against our own families and friends with nothing more than a Mark. If we turn on each other now, what do we have left?"

The room was still for some time.

Finally, Mama Hayes pushed her chair out from the table, collected the breakfast plates from everyone around her, and said, "The day is wasting. There're chores to be done."

4

Logan's head swam with exhaustion. He'd spent the night out on his own, sleeping in a gutter several blocks from the huddle, just to be safe. He didn't know if he could trust Bridget. But he had to know what she was up to. He had to know what he was up against. Only then, he told himself, could he properly decide what his next steps should be. Off to the bakery? Back to the woods?

The landfill was below him. Logan was lying flat against hard rubble, peering just slightly over the edge of an old building, through a gap in a crumbling wall on its third floor. It was a good vantage point, and well hidden. If this really was a trap, he'd at least be one step ahead of it.

Bridget arrived just after daybreak, just as she'd said she would. She was alone. Logan watched for some time, waiting for even the smallest suspicious movement or sound. But there were none. There was only Bridget, sitting at the top of a garbage heap, playing with a broken yo-yo, and growing increasingly impatient.

"I'd just about given up," she said as Logan stumbled toward her through the trash. "Thought you bailed last night."

"I did," Logan said.

"But you're back."

Logan shrugged. "Chalk it up to bad judgment."

Bridget turned her mouth down and nodded.

"So what's the big secret?"

Bridget laughed. "I never said it was a big secret. *You* said it was a big secret."

Logan glanced nervously around the landfill. "Look. You have about thirty seconds to tell me what's going on here, or I'll leave, and you'll never find me again."

"You're not gonna wanna do that," Bridget said.

"Oh yeah?"

She shrugged and took Logan by the hand as she led him down to the bottom of the trash hill and along a narrow path between the mountains of garbage, where she sighed and pointed to it— her big secret. "It's a bike," she said. "I found it here a while back. Never thought I'd have a use for it. But after talking to you two nights ago . . . well . . . I figured you might want it."

"I don't understand." Logan ran his hand over the seat.

"You're Markless now. Markless look out for one another." Bridget frowned. "Your aunt and uncle can't get you to Beacon. You'll never make it on foot. But with a bike . . . with a bike, you might stand a chance." She was staring at the handlebars now, too shy to look at Logan any longer. "I know it doesn't look like much. I wanted to fix it up first, but . . . well, here we are. It rides well enough."

At first Logan didn't know what to say. "I've never seen a bike in real life," he admitted, finally. "Growing up, everyone I saw on the streets just used rollersticks."

"Then everyone you saw on the streets was Marked." Bridget smiled. "I'm afraid you're gonna have to lower your standards."

Logan wiped a nervous hand against his forehead, trying to imagine how this bike changed things. "Don't get me wrong," he said. "I'm grateful. I just . . . how will I even ride it?"

Bridget laughed. "You'll manage. It's not hard."

Logan pumped the brakes a little, testing them.

"My mom was a big cyclist," Bridget said. "Rode everywhere

with a bike she found just like this, since it was the only free way to get around the city. Things were easier then, of course. Wasn't a crime, yet, to be Markless. Just inconvenient. But Mom would always brag about biking forty, fifty miles a day, so I gotta figure you'll be able to handle that, easy, once you get the hang of it. You'll be sore at first, of course, but I bet that's a reasonable pace."

"Okay . . . ," Logan said.

"Well, that means you're only looking at twenty days' travel if you can stick mostly to the old pre-Unity highway system. It's all torn up, but bikeable, I'd imagine, and a whole lot easier than dirt or grass or ruins."

"Twenty days . . . ," Logan repeated. "I never dreamed I'd make it there that fast . . ."

"I know," Bridget said. "It's doable."

For a while, the two of them didn't speak. And then, in his excitement, Logan swung right onto the bike, smiling and determined, pushing hard off the ground with one foot, and balancing the other on its pedal. He laughed and whooped as he wobbled down the winding path, past hills of garbage, the sickly sweet landfill air blowing back his hair and rushing in his ears.

"That's it! You're a natural! Just keep it straight, Logan—you've got it!"

But immediately Logan froze, jamming the breaks, screeching to a halt. He fell forward, stumbling as the bike slid out from under him.

Bridget's eyes went wide as she slapped her hands to her mouth. She knew the mistake she had made.

He'd never told her his name.

"What do you know about me?" Logan said, his heart now thumping so hard it made his arms shake.

"Nothing," Bridget said. "I . . . well . . . I know you're the kid who escaped DOME. I know they want you pretty bad."

Logan took two angry steps toward her. "How? *Who told you?*"

Bridget frowned. "No one told me, Logan. It was an easy guess!"

"So what? You went to DOME? Is that it? Is that why you're being so nice to me? Trying to keep me around just long enough for you to collect a fat reward for your huddle?"

"No!" Bridget said. "I'm trying to help. That's all . . ."

"*Help?* Why would you help me? I know as well as anyone the trouble I've caused—you've every reason to turn me in!"

"It's true." Bridget nodded, quickly, nervously. "Lots of Markless are angry with you. You're right to be suspicious. But, Logan—I'm not one of them. I . . . I want you to make it to Beacon."

"Why?"

"Because you're fighting back. Because you're the only one who is." She stepped forward. Slowly. Cautiously. "Please. You're making history, Logan—whether you realize it yet or not. Just . . . just let me be able to say that I helped."

Logan picked up the bike and gripped the handlebars tight, preparing to take off at any second. But he knew he wouldn't get far without practicing first. And something about the look on Bridget's face made him want to believe her.

"No more secrets!" Logan said.

Bridget nodded. "No more secrets."

"I leave today."

"Tomorrow," Bridget revised. "Practice today. Get a few hours rest before you head out. The last thing you need's a broken arm only five miles into your trip."

Logan stared at her.

"You know I'm right. Come on. Just let me have the afternoon. I can scrounge up a week's worth of food for you in that time."

"Tonight," Logan bargained. "If not today, then tonight."

"Logan, don't be stupid about this. I'm giving you your ticket to Beacon. You could at least give me a few hours' trust in return. Haven't I earned that much?"

Logan wasn't sure.

"Come on," Bridget said. "What's the worst that can happen?"

5

It was midafternoon. Tyler and Meg were chopping wood like maniacs while Jo supervised. In the stable, Eddie was feeding the horses and talking to the stallion, updating it on the morning, as if Eddie had made a new friend. Rusty and Dane were in the coop, gathering eggs and giving fresh water to the chickens. And in the barn across the cornfield, Mama and Papa Hayes were showing Peck and Blake how to milk the farm's only cow.

"I hope you know how much it means to us that you've taken us in. It's been a rough month," Peck said. And he and Blake shared a look while Blake switched his full bucket for an empty one.

Papa Hayes nodded and gave the cow a little pat. "It's been a rough month for all of us, Peck. But for you especially, we know."

"You kids were helpful in looking after the Fulmart," Mama Hayes added. "We always did appreciate that, and we're happy to repay you for it. Besides—we sure can use the help around here."

"Of course," Peck said.

Blake brushed his hair back with his forearm, taking a break from the milking and looking disgustedly at his hands. "You know . . . Mama . . . I'm happy to be doing this . . . or whatever," he said, clearly not happy with it. "But I just have to ask . . . I mean . . . what exactly are we doing here? This farm's pretty meager. It isn't even yours . . ."

"It's for show." Mama nodded. "The corn, the animals . . . in case DOME comes looking. Jean would much rather do without the hassle, but, well . . . Jean doesn't much like taking chances, and having us around is risky enough even with all of this here as distraction."

"Jean?" Blake asked.

"The owner of this land. She's Marked. But she's on our side."

Papa leaned down and examined the milk bucket. Then he gave Blake a nod, and Blake didn't hesitate to stand up and be done with it. "Jean never was much interested in farming," Papa said. "This farm was her husband's love, but it was his alone."

"Papa and Robert were in the States War together," Mama said. "Fought many battles, side by side."

Papa nodded and untied the cow from its post.

"But when Lamson took over, they took . . . different paths."

"Proverbs 2:12–13: 'Wisdom will save you from the ways of wicked men,'" Papa said distantly. "From men 'who have left the straight paths to walk in dark ways.'" Papa laughed softly to himself. "Robert, you old fool . . ."

"You have to understand," Mama told Blake. "This here was a family farm. How many generations, Papa? Three? Four?"

"Four," Papa said.

"Four generations. This land belonged to Robert's great-great-grandfather. You have to understand how *long* that had been . . . the *history* there . . ."

"Oh, stop making excuses for him! The man chose poorly and that's that. Ain't no accounting for life's poor choices."

"Well, anyway," Mama said. "When Lamson came along . . . when he teamed up with Cylis like that . . . it was either take the Mark or lose the farm."

"'Can't sell crops without a Mark,'" Papa recited. "'Can't own land, can't sell crops'. . . . How many times did I listen to those excuses?"

"Jean never wanted it," Mama said to Blake. "Like Papa and me, Jean knew something wasn't right about Lamson, about Cylis, about their whole scheme . . . didn't sit well with any of us. But this farm meant the world to Robert. So he and Jean Pledged, along with just about everyone else."

Papa sighed. "When Robert died a couple years back, Jean found us out on Slog Row. Said she had some ideas on how we might be able to use this land to help the Markless after all."

"Help the Markless?" Blake laughed. "With what? *Milk?*"

Papa was smiling now. "Come," he said. "Gather your friends. I'd like to show you something."

Outside the farmhouse, two large oak trees stood, bigger than any the Dust had seen in Spokie, and bigger than any of them normally imagined trees to be. Peck had rounded everyone up, and the group looked at those trees now.

"What's the biggest advantage the Marked folk have?" Papa Hayes asked.

"Money?"

"Nuclear weapons?"

"No, no!" Papa said. "Simpler than that. Think—what was *our* biggest advantage, back on Slog Row?"

"The Fulmart?"

"Canned food?"

"*Community!*" Papa said. "The Marked have *community*. Boil everything else down, and that's what you're left with. That's what they have right now that we don't.

"And it's no small thing," Papa said. "To be able to talk with one another, to stick together, to share ideas, to plan . . ." Papa Hayes walked toward the trees now, placing his hand on one of the trunks. "DOME's driving us apart. They're spreading us thin. Just look at you: you used to be inseparable, and now all you do is fight."

The Dust looked around at one another sheepishly.

"We're helpless without organization," Mama added. "But that's exactly what makes our work here on this farm important." She pointed to the branches in front of them.

"Trees?" Tyler asked. "You . . . you want to start a new society in the trees?" He began to laugh until Jo punched him on the arm.

"Look closer, Tyler. What's *in* these trees?"

The Dust looked more closely.

"Sap?" Eddie guessed.

"A birds' nest." Tyler pointed upwards.

"Wire," Jo said, squinting up at the branches. "They're strung up with wire."

"That's right!" Papa told her. "Antennas. The fact is, kids, this ain't really a farm anymore. It's a radio station."

"A *what?*"

"A Markless radio station! Shortwave. With our equipment, we can broadcast all over the globe. They've been doing it in the countryside for years . . . but ours was the first in the New Chicago area."

Dane, the one musician of the group, was visibly excited. The rest of the Dust just stared.

"Shortwave?"

"Radio?"

Somehow the idea of it didn't immediately light their imaginations on fire.

Papa Hayes laughed deeply. "I'm showing my age, aren't I?" He clapped Blake on the back. "I know, I know, not exactly cutting-edge. But, kids—that's the whole point. You don't need tablets to hear a radio broadcast. You don't need fancy computers or the Internet at all. No power, even! Just a foxhole radio made from junk you can find on the ground. Wire for the antenna and the tuning coil, a clothespin, a rusty razor blade . . . that's all it would take for you to hear our broadcast anywhere from here to the other end of the city. Get a little fancier, maybe upgrade to a crystal radio or a vintage radio, like the kinds they used to sell in the pre-Unity days, and with the power supply we have on this farm, you'd be able to hear our station halfway across the country."

The Dust looked up at the tree.

"So we can communicate," Blake said. "Even with no money, no shelter, no tech. We can still organize."

Papa Hayes nodded. "You kids didn't need to worry about this stuff back on Slog Row. But trust me. It's worth worrying about now. And with all their fancy equipment and satellites, shortwave is the last place in the radio spectrum DOME would think to listen."

"Can I have my own radio program?" Dane asked, thinking back to his glory days as lead singer of the Boxing Gloves. "Please?"

Papa laughed, and for a moment, it even looked like he might have been considering it.

"Finish your chores," Mama said. "Then we'll see."

ᄂ

Another lonely day had passed at Spokie Middle. The final bell had rung, and Erin sat alone on the floor against the wall of the Arctic Wing, watching students file past under the slow, pastel ribbon dance of the aurora borealis. Behind them, simulated icebergs crashed and fell into the sea. Erin studied each splash, imagining the glacier water spraying out of the screens and into the hall, imagining each student drenched and sopping wet and freezing with it, stranded in the real Arctic as lonely and miserable as Erin was now.

"Oh dear. We mustn't be sitting in the hallways, please, Erin," Ms. Carrol said.

Ms. Carrol was the school secretary at Spokie Middle. Erin hated her as much as everyone else in this stupid town, but she stood up all the same.

"Sorry, Ms. Carrol." She waved, and left school for the day.

Three times on the walk home, clusters of Spokie Middle students accosted Erin, pressing her for updates on Dane and Logan.

"Have you heard anything?" they asked.

"I heard it was your fault Dane got kidnapped."

"I heard you've been arrested."

"I heard your dad works for DOME."

"I heard your mom works on Barrier Street."

"I heard . . ."

"I heard . . ."

"I heard . . ."

Finally, Erin swung around, her classmates piling up on top of one another as they stopped short in the line that was following on her heels.

"It *was* my fault Dane got kidnapped," she said. "I *was* arrested the night of his concert. And my dad *does* work for DOME. I was there the day DOME raided Slog Row; I was there the day Logan flunked his Pledge. And I have *no idea* if we'll see either of them ever again.

"You all treated Logan like dirt when he was at this school, and you've never treated me much better. So stop acting like this is all some personal tragedy to *you*, like your own stupid lives are the ones that have been ruined, and leave me alone before I give DOME *another* reason to arrest me *right now*."

She stood facing the group for some time, nothing but heavy breathing between them.

Then one of the girls in the back of the group started giggling, and the giggles slowly spread among the clique. Eventually those giggles turned to laughter, and then the laughter turned to jokes among the friends.

Erin turned from the group, walking away with her head held high, too quickly for any of them to hear her sniffle once and then again a second time.

Minutes later, Erin passed Wright Lane, Logan's street, with its familiar buildings and shrubbery. She blinked a few times to see it through the mist in her eyes.

"Thinking about him?" someone said.

Erin jumped. "I didn't see you there." Hailey had a knack for showing up unannounced and starting conversations without saying hi.

Hailey is a great spy, Erin thought a little enviously. She really did respect that about the girl, even if she couldn't ever say so.

"Sorry," Hailey said.

Erin eyed Hailey for a moment. And suddenly she became very embarrassed, and she turned away quickly. "No, no, it's fine. And yes, actually. I was thinking about him. Logan was the only friend I had out here." She sighed. "He might have been the best friend I had *anywhere.*" And as soon as she said it, Erin knew that it was true.

"I get it." Hailey sighed. "I liked him too."

They shivered quietly for a moment.

"He was such a dork though," Erin said, laughing all of a sudden. "I mean, *man,* what a nerd."

"I know!" Hailey laughed. "He was the worst."

What was this? Were they really becoming friends? Erin didn't even know anymore how she'd feel about it if they were.

"You okay?"

"I'm fine."

Hailey frowned. "Anything else bothering you?"

"It's nothing," Erin said. "It's just . . . my dad's just making me do something I don't want to do, is all."

Hailey nodded, trying hard not to reveal too much of her interest. "It must be hard, just you and him out here alone."

"We're not alone," Erin said. "My iguana's out here too."

"Oh, that's right!" Hailey said. "I've seen him, haven't I? The little guy you had in the park when we first met. *So* cool. I'd forgotten all about him!"

In fact, Hailey couldn't have forgotten about Iggy if she'd

wanted to, after seeing him so many countless times through windows, after hearing him through walls, after talking about him with members of the Dust . . . her forgetfulness was completely fake. And yet Hailey's excitement wasn't. She really did think Iggy was amazing, and that Erin was pretty cool for having him.

"He keeps me company," Erin said. "But yeah, it is hard, since you mentioned it. Mom and I were pretty close."

"But you must still talk to her, right?"

"You'd be surprised. It's . . . it's hard. But you know a thing or two about that," Erin said. "I know your dad . . ."

"Dead. Yeah."

Erin nodded.

"And anyway, Mom's . . . she's not doin' so great herself. Sometimes I think I got the short end of the stick when it comes to family. Just a whole lot of bad luck." Hailey shook her head.

They'd found a bench now, at the edge of the park between Erin's neighborhood and Hailey's, and they sat for a while.

"My family is broken," Erin said, for the first time to anyone. "I think that's why Mom's been spending more and more time in the E.U. these last few years. I think that's why my dad took this transfer to Spokie too. They won't even tell me how they feel about it. They just blame it on their jobs and expect me to believe we're still a big, happy family, that we just happen to be separated by a thousand miles right now. It's like they think I'm stupid."

"No one thinks you're stupid, Erin. No one."

They were quiet for a moment.

"I'm gonna fix it, though," Erin said. "I'm bringing us all back together. I'm going to do it. That'll make it all better. I'm sure it will. It'll work." Hailey nodded, and Erin said it again, almost as if it was herself she was trying to convince.

"How will you fix it?" Hailey said. "If you don't mind my asking."

Erin frowned and looked down at her knees. "Hey, I gotta get going. I'll see you tomorrow, okay?"

"Sure," Hailey said. "Yeah."

And Erin stood suddenly and walked away.

Hailey sat for another moment. "Hey, you forgot your—" But Hailey stopped herself. On the bench was Erin's tablet computer, left behind. When Hailey picked it up, she saw a message from Erin's father displayed in the corner of its screen.

DOME BREAKTHROUGH.

MARKLESS GANG

RUINED SECTOR

UNDERPASS

Hailey cleared her throat. "Your tablet," she called. "Erin, you forgot your tablet!" And she quickly held it out.

Erin turned around, her face going very red. "Thank you!" she said, and she walked back to the bench and took the tablet from Hailey's hands. "Boy . . ." Erin glanced at its screen. "*That* would have been a bad thing to leave behind."

꒕

Hailey opened the door to her house and sneezed twice when she stepped inside.

Dusty in here, she thought. *Worse than usual . . .*

"You home?" Mrs. Phoenix called from upstairs.

"Yeah, it's me," Hailey said. "I'm going for a walk."

There was a pause. Hailey winced at the awful rhythm of her mother's coughing. "Another one? You've been out all night."

"I know." Hailey frowned. She sat at the kitchen table and ran her hand across its surface. "I want you to come with me on this one."

"Hailey, it's too late. I'm already in bed."

"Well, then you'll have to get up," Hailey called. She looked at her palm. It was white with chalk.

And a strip of clear tape lined the edge of her chair.

〓

"Put it *out*."

"*Make us*."

Joanne and Eddie had been arguing about the campfire from the moment Tyler lit its first twigs.

"There are *agents* in these *woods*," Jo said.

"And, yeah, I'm sure the first thing they'd assume about a totally reasonable amount of smoke coming from the private farm of an honorably Marked citizen is that a band of skinflints is responsible for—"

But Jo had already dumped a mound of snow on the fire, snuffing out the flames. "Great," Eddie said. "I was hoping tonight would be the night I'd finally freeze to death."

The two of them stopped arguing when Dane and Blake entered the circle and sat on a nearby log.

"If you were hoping for ghost stories and marshmallows, you can forget it," Eddie said. He kicked at the soaking firewood.

But Tyler looked at what Dane was holding and said, "Hey, whaddaya got there?" immediately forgetting about the fire.

Dane held it up for the three of them to see. "A radio," he said, almost as if it were a question instead of an answer. "Papa gave it to us. Told us to bring it by you guys and tune in. I guess he's broadcasting right now."

"How do you work this thing?" Tyler asked. He'd come over and was leaning down, looking closely at the device Dane held in his hands. It was old plastic, pre-Unity for sure. There wasn't any touch screen, nothing that lit up or glowed. Just a boxy black thing with a long, stiff antenna, two knobs, a strip with a bunch of numbers on it, and a grid of holes covering some crummy old speaker. Out of the back dangled two wires, stuck to a potato with copper and zinc clips.

"Papa said to turn it 'til this little needle points to thirty-nine hundred kilohertz."

"*Man*, do you have to wind it up too? I'm surprised it's not made out of a rock." Eddie laughed.

"Is that a potato battery?" Jo asked. "We learned about those in, like, first-grade science class."

Blake nodded. "Papa warned us this tech was old. I guess it's supposed to run off batteries that don't even exist anymore. He said this rig here was the best he could do."

"How is a Markless supposed to find one of these things?" Eddie asked.

"They aren't. This is the fancy version." Dane laughed. "Believe it or not. Papa says for the most part people listen in on that foxhole kind he was describing, with the wire and razor blades, however *that* works."

Tyler turned the first knob on the radio and jumped back when a static *click* erupted from the speaker. Then Dane turned the second, and the little needle moved across the number strip. When it passed over the thirty-nine hundred kilohertz mark, the static lessened, and a voice took its place. Like a lonely face emerging on a foggy street, Papa Hayes's voice came through the old speaker, fuzzy, but loud and unmistakable.

" . . . can't help but be reminded of the story of Exodus. 'But the more they were oppressed, the more they multiplied and spread; so the Egyptians came to dread the Israelites and worked them ruthlessly. They made their lives bitter . . .'"

"Whoa!" Tyler yelled. "It's Papa! Guys, are you hearing this?"

"Keep it down." Eddie laughed. "We're hearing it, we're hearing it . . ."

But suddenly Dane's face went blank with surprise and disbelief. "And not for the first time," he said.

Blake looked at him. "What do you mean?"

"I've heard this before," Dane said. "Papa's voice on the radio. For years now, I've been hearing it. I can't believe I didn't recognize him sooner!"

"How?" Jo asked. "Dane, what are you talking about?"

"Back home. My family had a Markless servant, George. I always liked him, and he and I . . . we'd hang out sometimes, at night, you know?" Dane spoke slowly now, lost in his memories. "How many times did I walk in on him listening to this? I can't even remember. They were stories—a different one every night. Like, ancient history stuff. About people suffering or celebrating or doing awesome things . . . George *loved* it! He listened almost every night on this big antique thing that sat on the floor of his room—I guess . . . well, I guess it must have been a radio. It was a present my parents gave him. The only thing he ever asked for. I never thought anything of it. But hearing this now . . ." He laughed. "I can't believe it . . ."

Jo chuckled, fixating on an earlier point of Dane's story. "A Markless servant . . ."

"Oh. Yeah . . . ," Dane said uneasily. "Sorry. I know that's . . . not too cool . . ."

Jo was quiet for a minute while they listened to Papa Hayes coming through on the tinny speaker. "Must be tough for you," Jo said, sincerely. "Adjusting to all this. It's not exactly Old District out here."

Dane frowned. "To tell you the truth, it's a bit of a relief," he said. "I never much liked it in that stuffy house. My parents are definitely what you guys would call hotshots. Moguls. Tycoons. Marked and rich and proud of it." He shook his head. "All I ever wanted to do was play music. I don't even think they liked me much. George was cool, though. You could say I miss George."

"I miss *my* parents," Jo said. "Every single day."

"What happened to 'em?"

Jo looked down at her hands. The wet logs were still steaming in front of her. "I grew up on the Row," she said. "In one of the abandoned brownstones, with my folks. They refused the Mark as soon as it became a thing. There was an adjustment period, I guess, while they relearned how to survive, but I was too young to remember it. Things weren't too bad yet for Markless back then, of course. Living without the Mark was more of an inconvenience than anything else. The A.U. was brand-new, and we were still transitioning out of war money—you know, the paper kind—which my parents still had plenty of. Anyway, we made our way to Slog Row, and that's where they raised me. I went to school in Spokie like anyone else until I turned eleven, and I lived a pretty normal life.

"Then, one day while I was at school, some DOME officer caught my mom and dad swiping a few cans of beans from a Spokie store. I was growing up, I guess, and the rations from the Fulmart weren't cutting it anymore. DOME charged my folks with petty theft, which was accurate enough. Should've been no big deal. But at that point Parliament had already passed its stupid zero-tolerance law. Even a misdemeanor, by then, was enough, if you happened to be a Markless. . . . The case was closed before it was even opened. I haven't seen them since."

"That's . . . awful," Dane said.

"Well, I found Peck pretty early. He made it easier on me. It would've been tough without him. That would've been real tough . . ."

Blake and Tyler and Eddie were on the other side of the fire pit, their ears to the radio speaker, listening intently. "Are you listening to this?" Tyler asked Jo. "Now Mama's talking too! They're famous . . . the Hayeses are *famous*, Jo!"

"How about them?" Dane asked, pointing to the others as they sat distracted by the broadcast. "What's their story?"

"Well, the whole group is Peck's doing, of course. Soon as he realized DOME was using the Pledge to swipe troublemakers, he swore he'd never let another Spokie kid risk flunking. So Eddie, we kidnapped," Jo said. "Like we did you. I don't know what's wrong with him." She laughed. "Just a problem child, I guess. I mentioned to Peck one time how much trouble he was always getting into at school. I'd seen him around, growing up, even though he was a couple grades below me—he was just notorious." She shrugged. "So Peck red-flagged him, and a couple months later, he was living with us.

"Same with Meg, pretty much. Peck heard there was a girl in

town with autism, and he knew from the patterns he'd seen that this made her a target. So we headed that off at the pass.

"Tyler, on the other hand—he grew up orphaned. Lived in huddles all his life, out on the Row." She laughed again. "Poor kid never stood a chance." Jo stared at Tyler now. He was still listening to the radio, mouth open, enthralled by the pre-Unity tech. "Amazingly, after all that, Tyler still planned to Pledge. Wanted to 'turn his life around.'" She shook her head. "*Man*, he would've flunked so fast . . ."

"So you kidnapped him too."

"Well, it wasn't much of a kidnapping, taking some beggar orphan from a huddle. We just popped in one day and started hanging out with him. Soon enough he was living with us. He'd forgotten all about his big plans."

Dane nodded.

"Blake was another easy one," Jo recalled. "He ran away from home on his own, just before his Pledge. Good instincts, I think. As good as Peck's. He knew something was wrong about the whole process. He and Peck met at the Fulmart back when Peck could still show his face around town. They hit it off right away. And they've been friends ever since. Best friends, until all this."

In the background, Papa's voice was soothing through the static of the airwaves.

"Logan's not a bad guy," Dane told Jo. "I want you all to know that. He'd never have wanted to put us through all this."

"Yeah, well, he did," Jo said. "Everyone here's had it tough. There's no excuse for what he's done."

"Peck seems to think there is."

"Then Peck's an idiot."

Dane frowned. "So what if we find him? What if Hailey really is able to bring Logan here? Are you all just gonna stop being friends? After everything you've been through?"

Jo stared into the pit, mesmerized by the sizzling of the last few ember pockets in the wood. "We'll see," she said. "But we probably won't ever have to deal with that."

"You mean . . . DOME . . ."

"Yeah," Jo said. "Between you and me? Logan doesn't stand a chance."

ᗡ

Hailey and her mom dusted themselves off and walked out past the outskirts of Spokie, past the abandoned six-lane expressway, past the ghost town of Slog Row and the charred remains of the old warehouse, deeper and deeper into the woods beyond.

"The house is bugged even worse than before," Hailey said. "Surveillance powder everywhere. Bug tape . . ."

"And you're surprised? After your little outburst at dinner yesterday?" Mrs. Phoenix smiled.

"I know," Hailey said, and she took her mother's hand.

"So when are we gonna talk about those clothes?" Mrs. Phoenix asked.

"We're not," Hailey said. She looked down at the dressy coat she was wearing. It covered a blouse, skirt, and leggings that screamed middle-aged.

"You look about forty." Mrs. Phoenix laughed, and she coughed a little when she did.

Hailey shrugged and adjusted the heavy purse on her shoulder. "I'd hope that's about right," she said.

Her mother sighed. "This is it, isn't it? The endgame."

Hailey's dress shoes clapped against the hard snow. "I need to know if you can take care of yourself after I'm gone."

The two of them walked for a long time under the branches and the clouds and the stars.

"I don't want you to think about any of that," Mrs. Phoenix said finally. "I am . . . hardly what's at stake here."

"It's important to me," Hailey said simply. "I need an honest answer before I go."

Mrs. Phoenix stifled another cough. "So you've found him, then?"

"I think so," Hailey said. "I think Erin finally slipped up. It's urgent, Mom."

"So why are you wasting your time on me?"

They came upon a cave in the woods and Hailey stopped abruptly, just outside of it. "This is where I'm going," she said. "Can you read it?"

Mrs. Phoenix knelt down. "Yes," she said. "I can read it."

"Good. Also . . ." Hailey reached into her purse and pulled out an old wooden board covered with little odds and ends. "I wanted to give you this. It's a sculpture to remember me by. I finished it today."

"That was fast!" Mrs. Phoenix said. "It's beautiful."

"Might be my last one for a while. So take good care of it, okay?"

Hailey's mother nodded, sniffling once.

"Do you know what it is?"

Mrs. Phoenix examined the object, but at last she said, "No. I'm sorry. I don't."

"Okay." Hailey looked nervously over her shoulder, into the depth of the woods around them, listening carefully. "Well, when the time comes, I'm sure you'll figure it out." And she decided not to say anything more.

"You'd better go," Mrs. Phoenix said.

"I can't walk you back."

"I know that."

Hailey nodded.

"But I'm not that fragile, Hailey. I'll be just fine."

The clearing around them was wide and grassy and glowing under the moonlight. A breeze picked up and cooled their skin. Hailey hugged her mom for a long time.

10

"I don't *know* what they were looking at," Erin said into her tablet, several minutes later. "It's sticks and rocks. There's nothing *there*." She pointed her tablet at the ground.

"Could you hear what they were saying?" Mr. Arbitor asked.

"Barely. This long-range mic you gave me's a piece of junk."

"Well, how about you tell me anyway, Erin? Humor me a little."

Erin frowned. "She knows. She's going."

"Okay," Mr. Arbitor said. "Then we'd better move fast."

11

The moon was fuller tonight, lighting the broken sidewalks but casting everything along the underpass into shifting shadows.

Logan had spent the day riding his bike around the ruins. He was steadier now, and eager to head east. He'd only come back for the food.

Across the way, Bridget rummaged through the huddle's "kitchen" to ration what little she could for Logan's trek. Logan watched nervously with one hand on his bike, biting his nails and pacing short steps back and forth at the edge of the street's darkness.

Come on, he thought, willing Bridget on. *What's taking so long?*

He was fiddling with his bike's gearshift when he first heard the footsteps stomping across the overpass above.

"*DOME!*" a voice yelled down. "DOME coming!"

Within moments, Markless were fleeing in every direction, tripping over themselves, crying, leading one another around the lightless space.

Bridget weaved her way through the commotion, spinning in circles and scanning the darkness. "Where is he? Where *is* he?" she said, stopping the Markless around her as they gathered their things and scattered into the side streets of the Ruins. "Has anyone seen him?" She cupped her hands to her mouth, whispering harshly now. "*Logan! Logan, where are you?*"

Logan gripped the handlebars of his bike, petrified, too scared in the moment even to flee.

Bridget. She'd really done it. She'd gone straight to DOME. And she was about to turn him in.

"Hey—!" A hand grabbed Logan's elbow from behind. Logan swung around wildly to shake it off.

"Whoa, whoa! It's me, Andrew." Andrew held his hands up. "We need to get you out of here."

Logan hesitated. Then he nodded.

"So get down," Andrew said, pushing Logan as he ducked behind the bike. "Stay low. She's looking for you."

"I can't see DOME," Logan said desperately. "Where are they? Andrew—where are they?"

"Come on," Andrew said. "I know these streets. I can get you out of here."

"But Bridget—"

"Forget Bridget! They're *here*. And who do you think brought them, huh? 'Cause I'll give you one guess."

He grabbed Logan by the wrist and ran with him away from the underpass and into the streets of rubble, Logan pulling his bike behind them.

"Is it a raid?" Logan asked.

"It's definitely DOME," Andrew said. "But I've been through street cleanings—and this ain't no raid. They're looking for someone." He glanced at Logan now, and it didn't make Logan feel any better, how nervous Andrew looked.

The two of them ran until the underpass was far behind them.

"I'm sorry about this," Andrew said.

"Are you kidding? You're saving my life."

They stood catching their breath in the open space of an old intersection. Four stoplights lay across the ground on dead wires, giving no signal. All around them the moon shone off shards of broken windows, a dozen sharp reflections lighting the road.

"Do you hear footsteps?" Logan asked.

"No . . . ," Andrew said. "We're safe."

"I think I can make it from here. I've got my bike . . ."

But at the intersection one block away, two men stepped out from behind an old brownstone.

DOME.

"Couldn't risk bringing them right to the underpass," Andrew said. "Too dangerous."

Logan looked at him, not understanding.

"Don't stare at me like that. You'd have done the same to me."

"Wait," Logan said. "*You? You* ratted me out?"

Andrew glared at him. "Do you have any idea what you've done to us, Logan? Things weren't great before you went and made DOME so angry, but they weren't awful either." He shook his head. "They don't care anymore who they hurt or how many families they tear apart—they're going to find you." Andrew looked down now, at his feet. "And it might as well be in exchange for my immunity."

"You and Bridget . . . you were working with her all along . . ."

Andrew laughed. "Bridget had nothing to do with this. She liked you. End of story."

"I *trusted* you!" Logan said. "You set me up!"

And Andrew couldn't even respond before Logan was on his bicycle and gone.

Logan pedaled fast, squinting and struggling to keep his bike balanced on the busted streets in the dead of night. Somewhere in the distance behind him, Andrew was yelling. And Logan knew DOME couldn't be much farther behind.

It was lucky that the chase didn't last long. Another few blocks and Logan would surely have crashed. But instead, a woman leaped out in front of him, and Logan slammed on the brakes, skidding gracelessly into an old trash bin.

DOME was far enough behind that they couldn't be seen, so

Logan picked himself up and waited anxiously for the woman to speak.

But she didn't speak. Instead, she came forward and lowered her scarf.

And she didn't have to say a word for Logan to be the happiest fugitive in the world.

It was Hailey Phoenix. She'd come for him.

12

There wasn't much time. Hailey tossed Logan's bike into the shadows and dragged Logan down the city block. She shoved a peacoat, scarf, and fedora into his arms. "Put these on," she said. "Stand up straight. And hope they don't get too close."

"Hailey, where'd you get these?"

"Never mind that," Hailey hissed.

"Marks up where we can see them!" DOME shouted.

Logan stared helplessly at the men at the end of the block. "Hailey—*what now?*"

"Just act natural," Hailey whispered.

"*Marks where we can see them!*" DOME repeated, standing now in the light at the end of the block. "*Right now!*"

Hailey raised both arms up high, holding the sleeves of her jacket as casually as possible so as not to reveal her wrist. Logan was hyperventilating now, but he managed to do the same.

The DOME officers walked toward them with their guns drawn, the green laser sights dancing on Logan's and Hailey's jackets. But they stayed on the opposite side of the street.

"We're very lost," Hailey said, dropping her voice and not

missing a beat. "We were taking the late train into New Chicago. I'm afraid we got off a stop too soon."

"Train doesn't stop in the Ruined Sector, ma'am."

"Is *that* where we are? Oh my!"—she hit Logan lightly—"I *told* you we were walking the wrong way! I've been saying that for hours!"

To this, the officers turned in toward one another, whispering for several moments. One of them made a call with a communication device he had wrapped around his ear. Logan watched through tunnel vision as the officer listened to some silent command on the other end. He nodded to his partner. Then the two of them turned back to Logan and Hailey, and Logan braced himself for the fight that was sure to break out. But instead, the first man frowned. "Nearest bus stop's about a mile that way." He pointed. "But we have reports of a fugitive teenager in the area. Unmarked. I can call for backup if you need an escort."

Logan couldn't believe his ears.

"Oh, no, officer, that won't be necessary," Hailey said quickly. "I feel plenty safe just knowing you boys are in the area."

The men lowered their weapons, the second officer dismissing them with a wave of his hand. "Next time pay attention to the stop announcements, will ya? And get home safe."

"Thank you, officer. We most certainly will."

Hailey turned in the direction of the bus stop, and the officers retreated to scour the streets closer to the underpass. Logan resisted the urge to rub his wrist as he watched them go. He was glad he hadn't been asked to speak.

It was all he could manage not to throw up.

At the first available moment, Hailey turned around to get Logan's bike from the alley.

"Nice job finding this thing. Can you ride it? 'Cause you're gonna have to."

"Why?" Logan asked. "Where are we going? And how in the world did that plan of yours work?"

Hailey shrugged. "I have no idea. And I can't tell you where we're going. I can't tell you anything. There's still a good chance we're gonna get caught tonight."

"And, what? You think I'd squeal?"

Hailey didn't answer. Instead, she walked Logan's bike to an intersection a block away, where she reached into the shadows and pulled out the rollerstick she'd ridden in on.

"Where'd you get a stick?" Logan asked.

"Same place I got the clothes."

Then she slapped the bike's old seat. "Hop on," she said. "And try to keep up."

FOUR

SHOT IN THE DARK

1

THE RIDE TO THE FARM WAS QUIET. THE fields were dark and still. But when Logan stepped into the stable, everything inside was noise and confusion. Tyler had made his way onto a horse that he'd let out of its stall, and he was trying to ride the old mare bareback, but she wasn't cooperating. Instead, she stood perfectly still, munching on hay while Tyler swung his arm above his head and shouted "Yee haw!" over and over. Meg and Rusty sat on the ground, watching, rolling around, laughing, and clutching their sides. Eddie threw straws of hay at everyone, trying to distract Tyler and throw him off balance. Blake and Dane stood on the sidelines, arguing about chores. And above all this was Joanne, pleading with the rest to quiet down and appreciate the danger they were in, but only really adding to the noise herself.

All of this stopped when the Dust saw Logan. Tyler fell to the ground. Eddie and Meg went rigid. Blake and Dane went slack. Joanne put her hand to her mouth. Logan cleared his throat, and it practically echoed in the silence.

"Hi, guys . . . good to see you."

2

There was one held breath of waiting before the shouting started again.

"Well, look who it is!"

"The beggar's back!"

"We thought you were dead!"

"We *hoped* you were dead!"

Meg growled. Rusty hid in a horse's stall. The rest circled around, shouting in Logan's face, closing in.

"—can't *believe* you went to Erin—"

"—almost got us all killed—"

"—after everything we did for you—"

"Blake, Jo . . . guys . . . come on," Hailey said, but no one heard. Dane just shrugged as if the whole thing was out of his hands.

"—Mr. Opened a Can of Worms—"

"—burned down the warehouse—"

"—your *fault*—"

"Enough!" Peck said, entering and standing above the fray. Immediately the group stopped, breathing hard. "Time is short, Logan. If you would?" Peck extended his hand.

The barn door closed behind them. The two had left without another word from anyone.

3

"She's in Beacon," Logan said. "No doubt about it."

"You heard this from your Marker? Directly? You're sure about this?"

"Absolutely."

Peck nodded. "Then we go to Beacon."

The two of them sat for a moment around the remains of Tyler's fire. The sky sparkled with stars above them.

"You realize, Logan, no Markless has ever seen farther into the Pledge process than you. You're the expert now. No one has gone deeper into the rabbit hole and come out intact. Anything you learned—anything at all—is of great value to us."

"I guess you're right," Logan said. "I guess I never thought of it like that." He frowned, thinking back on it. "Everything happens fast; I can tell you that much. They give you the nanosleep first thing. There's no choice about it." Logan laughed. "Believe me."

"And then?"

"And then they give you this shot straightaway—"

"A *shot*? A shot of what?"

"I'm not sure," Logan answered. "They put it right in your wrist. Erin told me beforehand it was to numb the area, but . . . the area never went numb."

"You let them give it to you, then."

"I was out of it from the nanosleep. It was all I could do to stay awake. Anyway, they've got you hooked up to the computer by this point, with little suction cups all over your head. A brain-computer interface, I think. But if it was, it's the only one I've ever seen; I couldn't really say for sure."

"So they read your mind."

"Pretty much," Logan said. "Or close enough to it. And while they do, they're asking all sorts of innocent-sounding questions—what do you want to be when you grow up, what do you like to do for fun . . . you know, that kind of thing."

"Probing for signs of trouble. Of individuality. Of dissatisfaction . . ."

"I think so. It lit up pretty good anytime I told a lie."

"Then I was right," Peck said. "About all of it!" He slapped his knee, showing some excitement for the first time that night.

And Logan nodded. "It seems that way. More or less. But that's as far as I got before the whole thing went into a frenzy." Logan frowned. "It was awful, Peck, getting out of there. Injecting myself with some kind of waking agent, attacking my nurse . . ."

"You had to."

"She was innocent. That's not the right way to fight back." Logan sighed. "It's not. But it got the Marker's attention. With the answers I'd been giving, I'm not sure I even would've seen him otherwise." Logan chuckled, remembering. "I flunked it real bad, Peck."

"Told you so." Peck smiled.

And the two of them laughed a little more.

"So what'd he say? Your Marker, when he arrived?"

"He said he couldn't tell me everything. Said even he didn't have all the answers. But you were right, Peck. Lily's a flunkee. And she is alive."

Peck patted Logan on the back. "You did well. None of us would've had the guts to do what you did."

"He told me flunkees are sent to a place with no hope. Said there're a few of these places in the Union, different locations . . ." Logan shook his head. "I'd've let them take me if there'd only been one. Just let them take me right to her, magnecuffs and all. But there was no way to be sure where I'd end up. And I couldn't let Lily down." He looked at Peck sadly. "I never wanted DOME to crack down on everyone like this. I never could've imagined they'd—"

"No apologies. You did the right thing, fighting back. Never take the easy road just because it isn't hard."

Logan nodded, smiling at his next thought. "My sister must've been a special case, Peck. Sounds like Beacon's place is for the big leagues."

And Peck smiled too.

"You know, I've actually . . . I've actually been thinking a lot about Lily's Pledge," Logan said. "About where she could have gone wrong. And I've started to think . . . I think maybe it was Grandma. That morning, on Lily's birthday . . . Grandma said a lot of things. Against the government, against the Mark Program . . ."

"I remember that," Peck said.

"She'd done it all our lives," Logan said. "Since as far back as I can remember. She never trusted Chancellor Cylis. Never trusted General Lamson either. I could never understand why Grandma always talked like that. Why she'd say those things. And especially that morning . . .

"'Why's Grandma like that?' I'd always ask, and Mom would always say some weird thing about conviction, and she'd just leave it at that. It frustrated me. How it just never fit."

Peck nodded knowingly.

"And then this exchange with the Marker last month . . . for the life of me I couldn't understand that either. Why would he help me? Why tell me anything at all? It was insane to think he would."

"And yet," Peck said.

"And yet." Logan nodded.

"He's an excluder," Peck said. "Like your grandmother. Like the Hayeses. Like me."

"A what?"

Peck smiled. "Cylis has done quite a bit in the name of peace and unity. Most would say he's achieved those things." Peck sighed. "But there's a freedom that was lost too, Logan. A freedom to . . . to choose and to come to our own conclusions. About patriotism, about family, about religion. About everything.

"You know, of course, about the Religious Inclusion? You grew up celebrating Inclusion Day, right? Honoring the day we all were freed from the boundaries of religion, from the differences of our beliefs?"

"Of course," Logan said. "Who doesn't?"

"Well." Peck smiled. "Excluders don't. I don't."

Logan didn't quite understand. "Peck—refusing the Inclusion is illegal."

And now Peck was laughing. "Logan! Name one thing you or I have done in the last few months that *wasn't* illegal!"

Logan laughed too. Peck had a point.

"You see, Logan, Cylis gave the world the easy path, and the world took it. Can't blame anyone for that, really—we'd had it pretty hard up until then. War, famine, plague, a devastated economy, environmental destruction . . ." Peck was quiet for a moment. "The things we fight for . . . have fought for, throughout history . . . they're the liberties. The right to speak your mind, the right to be happy, the right to worship the way you want, to be treated equally . . .

"Dictators of the past *took* these freedoms away. And the world always fought back.

"But Cylis never *took* anything. He *offered*. Offered alternatives to freedom that made life so easy, who could turn them down?

"The Mark, the Religious Inclusion, the Global Union . . . they all share a single goal: to give us a life so easy that we *want* to surrender our freedoms. A life so easy that we want to hand over our individuality and abandon choice. Because to keep them is to take the difficult path." Peck sighed. "The world was ready for things to be a little easier. And choices are hard."

After he said this, Peck leaned forward and placed a dry log on the dying embers of Tyler's fire and blew on them until the log was aflame. Then Peck and Logan just sat by it for a while, listening to it, watching it, letting it warm their faces in perfect, thoughtful silence.

"There are many types of Markless, Logan. We all have our own reasons when we turn it down. But at the heart of it, each of us wants just one, fundamental thing: the freedom to choose."

The two of them watched the smoke rise.

"Beacon's a big city, you know. We're not just going to show up and see this place where Lily's being held."

"I know that," Logan said.

"Any clue beyond the city—anything at all—would be helpful."

"There is one thing," Logan said. "The Marker gave me a name."

"A name is good." Peck laughed. "I'll take a name."

But Logan frowned. "He called it Acheron. The place where Lily's being held."

The fire was burning brightly now.

"Listen, Peck. I can do this myself—"

"We go together, and that's the final word on it."

"I have a bike," Logan said. "It would get one of us there, I think. But not all of us. I don't have a plan that includes the Dust."

"Don't worry about that."

Logan stared down at the logs in front of them. "Your friends hate me. They'd tear me apart before we even made it past the Great Lakes."

"They'll come around—"

"But why should they? I don't mean to sound ungrateful.

DOME would have had my skin several times over by now if it weren't for you, and I know that. I know that I owe you. But I can't let you in on this. Let's face it. I've left a blazing trail of destruction behind me everywhere I've gone. The group's right—you're better off without me."

"I *will* be a part of Lily's rescue," Peck said. "DOME and I have a score to settle. Please try to understand that."

"But they won't agree to it, Peck! I know these guys look up to you, but it's asking too much! The Dust won't join us."

"They will," Peck said.

"What makes you think so?"

Peck shrugged. "Call it a hunch."

He turned around when he said it. The two of them had a visitor. Behind them, Papa Hayes stood, arms folded, standing against the black backdrop of the open field.

"So you're looking to get to Beacon . . . ," he said.

4

The farmhouse was warm with a yellow glow. The smell of the woodstove filled each room, and inside, Logan and Peck and Mama and Papa sat comfortably in the candlelight of the dining room, hunched over the long wooden table, sipping tea.

"A cross-country trip is hard enough, even for the Marked," Papa said. "Flying's impossible, electrocars wouldn't make it more than a hundred miles, and electrobuses don't run past the city power grids . . . not even sure they have 'em out in Sierra yet. Magnetrains are government-run. Can't get anywhere near 'em without a Mark, and even then, it's checkpoints all along the way." Papa shook his head and said it again. "No. Cross-country trip is hard enough for the Marked. For Markless like you?" He exhaled hard and clucked his tongue. "Impossible."

But Mama smiled now, leaning forward, her face dancing with deep shadows in the light from the woodstove. "Or at least . . . it *would* be . . ." And the boys leaned in too, hanging off the Hayeses' every word. "If it weren't for the River."

"The . . . river?" Logan asked. "Mama Hayes, there's no river from here to Beacon."

"Not *a* river, Logan. *The* River. The *Unmarked* River. The network of Markless."

Papa grinned. "Members of the River, we call ourselves fishers. Our sea is the American Union. We are the fishers of men. We wait in the shadows. We find one another. We help one another. And we're growing in strength."

"No one knows the whole River," Mama added. "We can't risk that. But there are paths, all the same. And all along them, there's always a fisher who can point you in the right direction."

"That's it?" Logan asked. "That's all fishers can do? *Point?*"

Papa nodded. "'Fraid so. Now, that don't mean you're on your own, though.

"We've a system in place. Know the system—know the way."

Logan and Peck nodded, uncertain, waiting for him to continue.

"This here shows the path," Papa said. "You find this carved in a tree, or on a post, or on a stone . . . you know you're on the right track." He drew a symbol onto the wooden surface of the table, in thick lines with a piece of chalk.

"You just look for that, all along the way, and you'll never be far from help.

"Now, this here? This anchor?" He sketched it in three quick lines.

"It's a place to rest your bones. You see one of these carved into the countryside, you know there's a safe place to stay nearby. It might be a cave or it might be a mansion—you won't know 'til you see it. But if you can find an anchor, you can trust it, absolutely."

"Wait a minute. A mansion?" Logan asked. "What kind of Markless owns a mansion?"

And Papa grinned at him. "My boy, fishers aren't just among the Markless. This here?" He drew again on the table.

"This here is a lifesaver. Means a Marked man or woman has opened their lives to our cause."

"Lifesavers are crucial," Mama said. "We couldn't survive without them. You see one of these in front of a store some-where, you know you can ask for a loaf of bread, or a drink of water, or a shirt. They'll give it to ya. You see one in front of a home, you'll have a place to wash up, maybe a meal in exchange for a day's labor around the house. And if you see one next to an anchor, you go right ahead and feel safe spending the night, Marked host and all."

"Now this," Papa said, "looks kinda like a boat, don't it?" He scrawled a quick half circle next to the other symbols.

"This means you've found yourself a captain. See one next to a school? You better believe some teacher in there knows the way. You see one on a sidewalk? You can trust there's a shop owner offering more than goods. Find one by a house or a farm? Well," Papa said. "You get the idea.

"Look hard for these, though. They're few and far between. But folks with these symbols will do more than show you the way forward. They'll *take* you there, far as they can go."

"Who else knows the exact routes? Besides the captains?" Peck asked.

"No one. You look for waves or you look for a boat. You go too long without seeing either . . . you're lost."

Peck sighed. But he nodded for Papa to continue.

"Now, it ain't all nice out on the River," Papa warned. "I suppose you don't need me to tell you that, but, well . . ." He drew another picture on the table.

"Keep your eye out for this one. Hooks are danger. You might be offered help, or you might see another symbol in the area, but don't trust it. Because it's only bait. And it'll be the end of you if you don't take care.

"DOME hasn't cracked our code yet and they don't know our routes, but DOME does know of the River. And they'll do anything to stop it."

"So, what?" Logan asked. "In the morning we're just supposed to head out onto the River and hope to find some signs? Hope we don't get caught? Hope it takes us to Beacon?"

"That's about right," Papa said. "Though you left out some steps." He laughed. "Most of them, in fact. Starting tomorrow, you kids are gonna walk, run, swim, crawl . . . this River's full of surprises. Don't think you'll spend the whole time on foot. Because you won't."

"What does that mean?" Peck asked.

Mama shrugged. "I wish we could tell you. But we only know our leg of the trip. Anything beyond it, we'd be guessing."

"Wait a minute," Logan said. "*Your* leg of the trip?"

"Oh, did we forget to mention?" Papa smiled. "Mama and I . . . we're captains."

"You?" Peck said.

Mama laughed. "Well, how do you think we got supplies for the Fulmart all those years? You think everything in there was pre-Unity?"

Papa stood now. "But enough planning. Tomorrow we head east. There's an anchor at the southern tip of Lake Michigan, and another captain not far beyond that. I have a raft for us on the stream out in the woods. We'll be able to take it most of the way."

Mama smiled. "You're in good hands, kids. This part of the River is ours; Papa could get you there with his eyes closed."

When Logan and Peck left the farmhouse, Peck walked past the trees strung up with antennae. On one of them, a boat was carved in the side. On another, an anchor. He hadn't noticed them before.

Papa chuckled from the farmhouse's doorway. "Good eye," he said. "Now you're getting the hang of it."

Peck sighed. "I'd better be. After tomorrow, these little drawings are all we get."

"Ah! Not quite," Papa said, stepping off the porch. "There's one more trick I have to show you." And Papa swung his foot out in front of him, making a long arc in the dirt. "Any time in your travels, if you want to find a fisher among the people you're talking to, you just do this, real casual-like."

"Okay. What's it mean?"

"Nothing on its own. That's the whole point. Just a fidgety leg and an arc in the dirt. Not even DOME would bat an eye. But if you're face-to-face with a fisher . . ." Papa carved a second arc in the dirt now, overlapping it with the first at one end. "They'll do the same. And do you see it?" He pointed down.

"A fisher will always have a fish."

"There's just one problem," Logan said. "There's still no way the Dust is gonna agree to come with us."

"Don't worry about that," Peck said, erasing the lines of the fish with his foot. "I'm telling you, they'll come around." Then he smiled and turned to walk back to the barn.

Logan hurried to follow.

5

Erin rode the elevator to the top of DOME's New Chicago head-quarters, known throughout Spokie as "the Umbrella." It was nighttime, but the doors opened to a full and bustling space.

The main floor of the headquarters was one big room, fifty stories up. It was glass on all sides, including the floor, with desks circling around the building's tall, central spire. Right now, hundreds of DOME agents shuffled about, preparing reports, ana-lyzing holograms, sorting documents on each desk's touch screen.

Mr. Arbitor stepped out of the crowd with a large cup of steaming nanocoffee and handed it to his daughter.

"It's not fresh," he warned.

Erin sipped it anyway. It was bitter and stale and her nose crin-kled when she tasted it, but nanocoffee never went cold, and the warmth helped after so many hours of following Hailey in the woods.

"Come," Mr. Arbitor said. "Time for an update."

The two of them walked to the outermost ring of desks. Mr. Arbitor swiped his Mark to unlock his tabletop, and he began pull-ing up documents for Erin to see.

"At twenty-two hundred hours, two of our men approached the underpass in New Chicago's Ruined Sector, where Logan Langly was identified. According to plan, our informant led Logan away from the group, leaving him vulnerable and alone."

Mr. Arbitor pulled up a series of night-vision stills and video feeds so Erin could see what he was talking about.

"At twenty-three hundred hours, Hailey Phoenix arrived at the scene, thanks to your good work this afternoon."

"Amazing," Erin said enviously. "How did she find him? Do you know?"

"That was your brilliant wording, Erin. The cryptic note you 'accidentally' left visible on your tablet. Nothing more. She came right to the underpass and headed Logan off early on during his escape. After a brief encounter with our agents, Logan and Hailey were identified, and the two of them were allowed to leave."

"Logan didn't find that . . . strange?"

"They had a plausible enough means of escape." Mr. Arbitor smirked. "Disguises and alibis and all that. It was cute, I'm told."

"But Logan didn't even catch on that he being was followed? That doesn't sound like him . . ."

"Ah. He *wasn't* followed," Mr. Arbitor corrected. "Once we had his initial coordinates, we were able to lock on by satellite surveillance." He pulled up another few files now, dragging them across the tabletop with his fingers. With a series of double taps, he zoomed in from an orbital shot all the way down to a close-up on two teenagers biking and riding a rollerstick through the woods.

"Wow . . . ," Erin said, amazed and a little scared by the technology of it.

"I know. Tastes good to be on the winning side, doesn't it?" Mr. Arbitor winked at her. Erin took another sip of nanocoffee and gagged on its bitterness. She didn't answer her father. "Anyway, Hailey played right into our plan," he continued. "She's already led us to a farm where some pretty interesting things are going down. It's legitimate—Marked—owned by a woman named Jean Meloy."

"You think they took it over? Or do you think Jean Meloy is a traitor?"

"Hard to say. Regardless, it appears Hailey and Logan have, at last, led us to Peck. And his band of misers. Exactly as you predicted."

"So what now?" Erin asked. "What's next?"

She looked around the Umbrella as she asked it. Agents across the floor were suiting up in full DOME-tech armor, strapping on vests, helmets, boots . . . loading weapons and holstering ammunition . . .

"Let me do this," Erin said suddenly. "You don't need all these people."

"We're not taking any chances this time, Erin. Everyone goes."

"But they'll see us coming. You'll scare them away!"

"Erin, no. We're through sneaking around now. We move in, and we take them. Brute force."

"You'll prompt a struggle. Dad, people could die."

"Beggars could die, Erin. *Beggars* could die."

Erin was frantic now, pleading. "Dad, listen to me. If you insist on bringing backup, fine, but send me in first. Alone. I can do this. I can talk to Logan. I'm sure he's scared. I'm sure he doesn't want any of this. I can . . . I can convince him. I can get you the Dust. Logan, Peck, and all the rest. I can get you everyone. Peacefully. Just give me the chance to negotiate, Dad. Let me *do* this."

"Absolutely not," Mr. Arbitor said. "The grown-ups are handling this now."

"But you grown-ups are making a mistake! The Dust aren't masterminds—they're kids. And I can get through to them. I'm sure I can!"

"Erin. Enough."

"Listen to reason!"

"Listen to *me*. You've played your part in this mission, Erin. You've played it very well. But your part is over now. And I'm not interested in your opinions on what to do next."

"It'll end badly," Erin said. "What you're about to do—it will end badly!"

"Nonsense. We're simply bringing these kids in for questioning. No reason for anyone to get hurt." Mr. Arbitor smiled. "Trust

me. This is a simple storm-and-capture operation. We want everyone alive just as much as you do."

But Erin couldn't help noticing that only one man among the
crowd was equipped with magnecuffs.

And he only carried two pairs.

ㅂ

It was no more than a *pop*, the sound that broke the December
night. It was distant . . . falling oddly flat against the farm's wide-
open field. Like a pebble dropped into a pond.

From where Peck sat looking out the stable door, it was nothing
but a little burst of light through the farmhouse window. It was a pin-
prick in the canvas of paint-black sky, easy to miss, easy to ignore . . .

It was the sound of a twig breaking, of a toe stubbed against a
table leg.

But the sound was a gunshot. It was the sound of Papa Hayes's
death.

Peck turned and looked over his huddle, all sleeping in the hay
and the dirt. "Wake up," he said. "They're here."

ㄱ

Erin stood in the doorway of the farmhouse, DOME soldiers flank-
ing her and signaling commands as teams of them secured each
room, one by one.

Mr. Arbitor smiled, his hand finding Erin's back and patting it
twice.

"You did this," he said. "This is thanks to you. You're a hero today, Erin."

But Erin didn't hear a word of that.

Instead, she was very far away, on her rollerstick with Logan. They were riding through the Spokie streets on a warm September night, and she was laughing as he held on tight and begged her to slow down, just a little.

She was in Logan's room, giggling in the closet while his dad came in and tucked him into bed, asking whether or not Logan wanted his night-light turned on before he went to sleep.

She was at an ice cream parlor, sharing a sundae with Logan and so relieved to hear that he was planning to Pledge the next day.

"No sign yet of the targets," one man whispered, snapping her back to the present.

"There was a shot fired," Erin said matter-of-factly.

"Just an old miser," the agent said. "But we'll keep looking."

Two men walked down the stairs now, carrying a man who lay limp in their arms.

And Erin closed her eyes. Tight. As tight as she could. Somehow not tight enough. And she was on the sports lawn at lunch, eating sandwiches with Logan, picking at the plasti-grass, sitting warm in the sun. She was not here.

She was not here.

目

"Who is here? Peck, *who?*" Jo hissed as she gathered her things and shook the others awake.

"DOME. They've found us. The Hayeses can't help."

"The Hayeses can't . . . Peck . . . Peck, *why can't the Hayeses help?*"

The voices came to Logan in a whisper and he rose, exhausted but on edge at the same time.

"Take the blankets."

So Logan rolled his tattered fleece tightly around his arm and slipped into his shoes. Immediately he was shivering.

"Leave the rest. Follow me."

"Peck, where are we going?"

"Away."

"But how will we know where to—"

"Don't worry about it."

And the Dust slipped out the open door. Blake ran first, carrying Rusty and whispering something about things being all right. Tyler and Eddie followed, laughing and flicking each other even now. Meg ran by, looking excited enough for all of them. Jo went next, shaking her head and setting the pace for Dane and Hailey behind her. Logan left last.

Four hours. He'd been given four hours of hope before DOME took it all away again. And he wondered, in that moment, what Erin might have thought of all this. He wondered about the plans she'd have for his daring escape, what she would have said to let him know that everything would be okay.

If only she were here.

And then Logan squinted through the darkness at the farmhouse across the field, and a horrible thought struck him.

What if she is?

It was hard to see through his shaggy hair, and his stomach grumbled and he worried about the noise it made, but the voices of the Dust all said, "This way" and Logan followed them blindly through the December-chilled woods. Tonight he would trust those voices. They were all there was left to trust.

Peck whispered now to all of them. "A shot was just fired in Papa's study. Most likely he's, well . . ." A gasp rippled through the Dust before Peck could say it. *Dead.* He was glad he wouldn't have to. "We have to assume Mama is in custody, or worse. But I have a feeling DOME's not here for them at all. I have a feeling they're here for us. Which means they'll be searching the farmhouse another few minutes before they expand to the rest of the perimeter."

The Dust looked at Peck expectantly. "Then what now?" Blake asked.

"There's a raft waiting for us on the stream in the woods. Tonight we take it as far as it'll go."

"Take it where?" Jo asked. "Peck, we have no plan!"

"We do have a plan," Peck corrected. "Once we're moving . . . I can explain everything once we're moving. Until then, just follow me. Stick together and everything'll be okay. All is not lost if we can stick together."

But just as Peck said this, Logan heard them, DOME, the officers, though they were trained for stealth. He saw in the corners of his vision the dancing laser sights and flashlights in the snow all around him. And he imagined the life ahead, locked up and forgotten . . . or tortured . . . or worse.

Immediately, the Dust scattered, running in half a dozen different directions.

Logan was alone again. And it was in that moment that he heard the scariest thing of all: Erin.

Erin was yelling in the woods behind him.

When Logan did, finally, reach the stream at the edge of the farm, he could not find the raft. He could not find the Dust. And behind him Erin was running, shouting, horribly, to the DOME agents trailing half an acre behind her.

"He's here!" she yelled. "I've got him right here!"

Logan was cornered.

And for some reason all of these things together simply broke Logan's heart. He realized, right then, that he did have something left to lose—the hope that Erin, somehow, somewhere, was still on his side.

He'd lost that now too.

"You were my best friend in the world," Logan said once Erin made it close.

Erin tried to speak and failed several times. What came out were short breaths and stutters. "Yes," she said finally. "But Logan . . . listen to me. This . . . it's—it's not what you think—"

"In what way, Erin? Huh? You've *killed* me, is what I think. You have *killed* me!"

"Logan, please—*just hear me out!*"

In front of him, the broad stream was dark and freezing, with a filmy coating of ice over the shallower areas. Even standing at its edge he could feel the rush of cold sucking his body heat into its surging water. Logan guessed he'd have maybe twenty minutes to float, tops, before hypothermia killed him. If he hadn't drowned by then anyway.

How?

How has it come to this?

He jumped into the water.

He didn't feel a thing.

FIVE

THE AFTERMATH

1

THE MORNING ON WRIGHT STREET WAS QUIET
and still. In the house where Logan grew up, Mr. and Mrs. Langly
were eating breakfast, which today was toast, orange juice, and cereal.

But Mrs. Langly hadn't touched her plate.

"Not hungry?" her husband asked.

Mrs. Langly shook her head.

"Maybe today's the day. You know? We're bound to hear something eventually."

Mrs. Langly just shrugged.

"So how's, uh, . . . how's the research?"

Earlier in life, Charlotte Langly had been a meteorologist.
Before Lily failed her Pledge, Charlotte would spend hours up in
her study on the top floor of the house, tracking weather patterns,
charting storms, following cold fronts, heat waves, natural disas-
ters . . . she'd studied all of it at great length. She'd written op-eds
on the aftermath of the earthquake that destroyed the West Coast,
published articles about the changing weather patterns and the dis-
ruption that it would (and then did) bring, lobbied Parliament for
environmental action, led seminars in New Chicago, organized volunteer "nature cleanup" days in Spokie . . .

But the interest dried up when Lily didn't return. All of it just went away, right along with Charlotte's daughter.

Then, about a month ago, Logan went in for his Pledge, and once again the Langlys had a DOME visitor by supper.

"Security tapes show your son attacking his nurse," the agent told them. "You can see him here, also threatening his Marker."

The Langlys stood at their doorstep, watching the video feed on the man's tablet. Watching their own son assault an innocent nurse. Mrs. Langly watched with her hand over her mouth. Mr. Langly watched poker-faced. Both of them were silent.

"Fortunately, as you can see, your son's Marker was able to talk him down from his hysteria." The man pointed to the screen on his tablet. "And look at this. You see these four men arriving to take your son for questioning?" He shut the tablet off now and tucked it under his arm, looking Mr. Langly in the eyes as he spoke. "Six minutes later your son managed to escape."

"Escape?" Mr. Langly repeated.

"We lost him, I'm afraid. He . . . managed to evade our guards and somehow sneak off. We have our best people on it," the man quickly assured them. "But for the time being, your son is missing."

"Is he in trouble?" Mr. Langly asked.

"No trouble," the agent said. "We'd just like to find him, is all. So please—if you see or hear anything . . . if he happens to come home . . . do let us know. Immediately, if you would."

Mrs. Langly had already excused herself from the conversation. Mr. Langly looked back, noticing her absence, but she was nowhere in sight.

"We'll let you know," Mr. Langly told the agent. "And . . . likewise . . . were you to find him first . . . you'd, uh, you'd let us—"

"Of course. Right away, Mr. Langly."

"He's been . . . troubled lately," Logan's dad apologized. "We don't quite know what got into him."

"Let's just hope this all ends soon," the man said. "For everyone's sake."

Then the DOME agent left.

And Mr. Langly stood at the open door for some time, just staring at nothing, letting all the cold air come in.

When he'd finally found his wife, she wasn't in Logan's room. She wasn't in the living room or Lily's room or the master bedroom. She was in her own study. She had dusted and rearranged all of her old equipment, and she was sitting among it at her old desk chair, reading over satellite feeds for the first time in years.

"Honey?" Mr. Langly said warily.

"Yes, dear?"

"Do you want to talk about it?"

She looked up from her work. "Talk about what?"

Then she turned back to the monitor.

And she'd worked nearly every waking hour since.

2

"The results of my research are . . . odd," Mrs. Langly replied to her husband at the breakfast table. "Did you know we've lost a third of all ocean life since the time of the States War?"

"I didn't," Mr. Langly said.

"We have."

"That sounds . . . very tragic," Mr. Langly said.

"It is."

Behind them, the elevator buzzed. Mrs. Langly's mother stepped out into the kitchen. "What's tragic?" she asked.

"The oceans," Mr. Langly said. "Charlotte was just telling me about how they've been dying out."

"Of course they're dying out," Grandma said. "What'd you expect them to do? We destroyed everything else on this lousy planet. You think the oceans'd just tip their hat and walk away?" She laughed callously.

"Yes, well, I've never read anything about the oceans being in trouble," Mr. Langly said.

"Everything's in trouble as long as that mogul Cylis is in charge. You hear the rumors that they're moving up the vote on the G.U. treaty?"

"I didn't," Mr. Langly said awkwardly. "That's great."

"*Great?* It's not great, it's terrible! At least Lamson's finally owning up to the fact that this was his plan all along . . ."

"Sonya . . ." Mr. Langly cleared his throat.

Conversations like this were common these days in the Langly household. During Lily's and Logan's years growing up, Grandma had stuck close to her retirement home in New Chicago, where nearly everyone liked to complain about Cylis as much as she did. But when the news hit that Logan was missing, Mr. Langly decided that drastic measures were needed in order to keep his family together. So he invited Grandma to move in.

She and he both thought it might do Mrs. Langly some good. But so far all it had done was set the stage for bitter, daily arguments.

"You know, Sonya . . . maybe we've had enough trouble with DOME for one lifetime, don't you think? Maybe we oughta just focus on Charlotte, and each other, and—"

"Oh, give me a break," Grandma said. "Hey, Charlotte—you listening? DOME took your children away. You still glad you got that Mark when Lamson told you to? I know *I* am!"

"Sonya, please!"

But Mrs. Langly didn't flinch. "I noticed something else recently," she said.

"Oh yeah, what's that?" her husband asked gently.

"Plague. I've been reading disease reports—"

"Oh, have you?" Grandma said. "That's good, dear. That's real healthy. Just read about all the death you can—I'm sure that's helping to ease your pain."

"Sonya." Mr. Langly kept a lid on his frustration, but it was beginning to boil over.

"In any case," Mrs. Langly said flatly. "We seem to be facing the start of a plague in this country."

Mr. Langly stared at his wife, not quite understanding. "Honey . . . don't you think the news would have said something about that?"

"No." Mrs. Langly shrugged.

And Grandma nodded. "What have I been saying? How many times have I told you, Dave? It's the end of the world. You've got to expect plagues when it's the end of the world. Just like you've got to expect freak weather and war and famine and all the other stuff I've been telling you about for years! What did you think? It's Revelation! You want me to read it to you again?—I've got my Bible just upstai—"

"All right, that's enough!" Mr. Langly exploded. "I will not have this nonsense exclusionist talk in my house! We're in enough trouble with DOME as it is. Charlotte, it's winter. There's bound to be flu in the winter months. Sonya . . . I don't even know where to begin with you . . ."

Mr. Langly picked up his tablet and pulled up the morning reports, tuning his family out. And he read in this way for some time, through the global news and the national news (including articles on how the two sections would soon be one), and finally on to the local news, with Sonya and Charlotte just sitting there, silent.

Mr. Langly had always been pretty good about keeping up with the news, had always been casually interested in politics and economics and the general goings-on. But in recent weeks he'd become obsessed, watching every report he could, privately desperate to learn something about his son.

There was nothing, of course. DOME matters were never reported in the news. The surge in raids on the Markless, the ongoing search for Logan and Peck and the Dust, the attack on the Meloy farm last night . . . none of it was ever mentioned. Mr. Langly didn't even know what he was missing.

But there was one brief article buried deep down in the news feed this morning. One little headline that Mr. Langly couldn't keep to himself. He read it aloud when he saw it:

HAILEY PHOENIX MISSING, LOCAL SCHOOL REPORTS
THIRD DISAPPEARANCE IN AS MANY MONTHS

"Apparently it was the middle school secretary who called the authorities. Mrs. Phoenix 'acknowledged the absence but couldn't say where her daughter had gone, why she wasn't at school, or when she might return.'" Mr. Langly shook his head, shocked. "Says here 'there's no criminal investigation at this time, but local police are baffled.'"

Grandma sat frowning, listening closely now.

"I don't understand it," Mr. Langly said. "Why wouldn't Dianne have reported the disappearance herself?"

The Langlys knew Hailey's family well and had been friendly with them for years through Logan. When Lily disappeared, Mr. and Mrs. Phoenix had been the most supportive of anyone in Spokie. They often had Logan over for dinners and evenings with Hailey as he dealt with the loss of his sister. And when Mr. Phoenix passed away, the Langlys did their best to return the favor. But the families had grown apart in recent years as the friendship between Logan and Hailey had gradually fallen away.

"Maybe Dianne's like your wife," Grandma said. "Airheaded in her grief."

Mrs. Langly closed her eyes, but she didn't respond.

"Says here the mayor's imposing a town-wide curfew. 'No Mark, No Dark,' it says. Anyone on the streets after sundown will be brought in for questioning if they can't show a Mark—especially the underage." Mr. Langly sighed. "Three months too late, Mr. Mayor."

But Grandma narrowed her eyes, lost in thought. "If you'll excuse me . . . ," she said.

Mr. Langly waved her off, reading the article again to himself.

And Grandma retired to her guest room in the Langly house.

∃

It had a crimson red wallpaper that made the space feel heavy and claustrophobic. The only sources of light were two table lamps, and each had a lampshade so thick that even at their brightest, the place was still dim and stuffy. Grandma entered it now, her guest room: Lily's old bedroom on the ninth floor.

The clutter was everywhere, never cleaned or moved or even touched since the day of Lily's Pledge. On the bedside table were a paper plate and a fork with a piece of birthday cake still on it. The cake had gone black, its original remains rock hard and shriveled, but around it mold had sprung up so thick and lively that the whole thing looked a little like a potted plant. Once, Mr. Langly had tried to move the cake, to throw it away before the bugs got to it, but this idea upset Mrs. Langly so much that Mr. Langly worried for his marriage. The cake hadn't moved an inch since.

"It's horrible in here," Grandma had said when Mr. Langly showed her the space three weeks ago. "You people are sick."

But Grandma had respected the room all the same. She'd not moved or changed any part of it; she'd not touched a thing. And she never intended to.

Grandma stood by the mirror that hung over the chest of drawers, leaning close to see herself, but careful not to bump any childhood trinkets or pictures still resting on the dresser top. She primped her hair and made herself up, alone in the dim light and the quiet, just thinking.

There was something about that article . . . something about Hailey's disappearance so soon after Logan's, so soon, in turn, after Dane's . . . that struck her as too strange to ignore.

Grandma walked over and pressed the intercom on Lily's

bedroom wall, calling down to the kitchen where Mr. and Mrs. Langly still sat.

"I'll be taking a nap," Grandma said. "Don't bother me." And Mr. Langly acknowledged that he was happy to oblige.

But when Grandma turned from the intercom, it wasn't to the bed that she walked. It was to the outside stairway door. She'd made up her mind.

Grandma was sneaking out.

4

There was a room at the tip of the DOME Umbrella, above the central intelligence disk and above even the smaller floor of offices on top of that. It was small—spacious enough only for the most private of meetings—and empty, save for a single round table at its center. The only way in was through a spiraling staircase in the top section of the Umbrella's spire, which Erin's father was ascending now.

He climbed alone to a small platform at the top of the stairs and swiped his Mark at a scanner. The platform rose up through a hatch, lifting Mr. Arbitor into the room above.

One man sat at the table, looking over a few documents displayed on his tablescreen, paying no attention either to the 360-degree view of the distant New Chicago skyline and surrounding suburbs or to Mr. Arbitor as he approached and sat down.

Director Michael Cheswick was the head of DOME's entire Eyes & Ears Bureau west of the Mississippi River, and had been since its inception over ten years ago. This made him Mr. Arbitor's boss's boss's boss. He stood six and a half feet tall, but couldn't have weighed more than 140 pounds. His nose hung from his face like a long, slender beak, and a thick set of black bangs shadowed his face. To Mr. Arbitor, looking at him was a little like looking at a vulture with teeth.

After a moment, Mr. Cheswick leaned back, adjusting his glasses, and spoke slowly to Mr. Arbitor.

"I've read the reports," he said. "But I wanted to hear it from you."

Mr. Arbitor cleared his throat. "Well," he began. "First of all, I'd just like to say—we made real headway last night. Major strides toward the apprehension of Logan Langly and Peck and their gang of Dust."

"Is that right?" Mr. Cheswick said.

"Johnson and I and our team downstairs came closer than we ever have to the full, definitive capture of—"

"That's twice, now, Charles, that this gang has evaded DOME. Twice. Teenagers. In one month."

Mr. Arbitor cleared his throat nervously. "A little more than one, actually." He made a teeter-tottering motion with his hand. "Six weeks. Give or take."

Mr. Cheswick laughed, his chin down and his smile not visible to Mr. Arbitor. "Do you have any idea how this looks?" he asked. "I'm honestly curious. Do you have any sense at all of what Markless throughout New Chicago must be thinking? What *Lamson* must be thinking?"

"Surely General Lamson won't need to know about—"

"Charles, you were brought here from Beacon because of the unique promise you showed in tracking down Markless."

"And I will make good on that promise, sir. I will—"

"*Twice. One month.*"

"Sir, to be fair, we did manage to apprehend a known Markless organizer, Meredith Hayes—"

"I didn't want *Meredith Hayes* in my Center this morning, Charles—I wanted *Peck*. We've *had* Meredith here before—she refuses to speak to us, and you know it."

"Well, sir, yes, but we were hoping—"

"Oh, you were *hoping*, were you? You were *hoping*? Charles, from what I gather from this morning's reports, we can't even prove whether or not Meredith was *aware* of the Dust's presence in that barn!"

"I don't buy that, sir."

"And *who*, in the name of Cylis, was the idiot who shot this woman's husband? I want a name."

Mr. Arbitor stuttered for a moment.

"Sloppy, Charles! This is sloppy, miserly work. Unacceptable. You couldn't even track them by satellite once you had them in your sights! How is that possible?"

"Sir, by the time we'd—"

"Save it." Michael sighed angrily. "It was a mistake bringing you out here. I can see that now."

"Mr. Cheswick, sir, please—"

"You're a family man, Charles. We knew that. To be away from your wife, watching over your daughter here alone . . . better men than you would be distracted by it." He frowned. "This is our error. I blame myself."

"Mr. Cheswick, I'm really close to a breakthrough here. I just need a little more time—"

But Michael flicked at the glass of the tabletop before Mr. Arbitor could finish, and a virtual document slid across the screen of the table's surface. It came to a stop in front of Mr.

Arbitor, and he read it, disbelieving, mouthing the words to himself as he did.

"Transfer? You're transferring me back . . . already?"

"It's been three months," Michael said. "In that time we've had kidnappings, we've had DOME equipment stolen from right under our noses, we've had an escape from the Pledging Center, and we've come no closer to catching any of our prime suspects among the Dust." He laughed under his breath. "In fact, Charles, our prime suspect list has managed to *grow*.

"Three months *is* enough time. It's enough time to know when you've made a mistake as big as this."

Mr. Arbitor looked again at the document in front of him.

"I didn't call you in here for an update, Charles. I called you in here for your swipe." He held his hand out, expectantly. "Please, if you would. Just swipe right there on the line. The sooner you do, the sooner we can put this big, failed experiment behind us. And the sooner I can forget about the whole miserly thing."

5

Logan woke up with the sun on his face. He was lying up to his neck in a tunnel carved into a mound of snow, his fleece blanket wrapped around him, and he was shivering.

"Lips are still blue," a voice whispered above him. "Not a good sign." It was Dane. Logan squinted up at him, into the sun.

"Well, look who's awake," Hailey said.

"Where are we?" Logan asked. His head ached violently, and immediately he felt himself fighting back a powerful wave of nausea.

"Still in the woods, a few miles downstream from the farm, I'd guess." Hailey was whispering. "We should keep moving now that you're awake. There're sure to be DOME agents around here looking for us."

"Where's everyone else?" Logan asked.

Hailey looked at Dane uneasily, then back at Logan. "We don't know," she said.

"You don't *know*?"

"We never found the raft. It looks like . . . like they left without us. It was lucky enough that Dane and I found you."

Dane nodded. "You were stuck on a log in the stream. Just lying there unconscious when we swam by. You'd've died, dude."

"And DOME never caught up with us?"

"Well . . . we don't know for sure about the rest. But no, they didn't get near the three of us. I guess the agents weren't too keen on jumping in the stream after us, and there was no way they could keep up on foot."

"They're out here, though, right now," Logan half asked and half stated. He rubbed his eyes. Blurry vision. Headache. Another wave of nausea.

"Most definitely."

"Then let's go," Logan said. But as soon as he stood up, he regretted it. Outside the shelter of the tunnel, the wind cooled his still-wet clothes, and immediately he was overcome with a paralyzing shiver. Hailey stepped forward and touched his neck.

"He's freezing," she told Dane.

"I can see that."

"Logan, how do you feel?" Hailey asked.

As if in response, Logan suddenly lurched forward and fell to his knees, resting his hands on the ground and propping himself up, but just barely. "Not great," he said. "Sick, I think. I'll be fine in a minute."

But the expression on Hailey's face said otherwise. "Logan," she said. "I'm not sure you will . . ."

"What are you talking about?"

"You have hypothermia, Logan."

Logan squinted at her, confused.

"We're losing him," Hailey said to Dane. Then she took Logan by the shoulders and began quickly rubbing his arms. "Logan, you were in the water a long time last night. When we dragged you out, you were unconscious. You've been in those wet clothes all night. Your body's past the point of being able to keep itself warm."

"That's okay," Logan said, closing his eyes. "I don't mind."

Without another word, Hailey took Logan's wet jacket and sweater off and wrapped the fleece blanket tightly around him. She led Logan back to the enclosed space of the snow tunnel, putting her arms around him and shielding him from the wind.

"He needs help," she told Dane, already sensing how uncomfortable this made him. "I don't like it any more than you do. Just . . . be useful, okay? Please?"

"We gotta find the River," Logan said.

"No, Logan. We need to stay away from the river. The river's too cold."

"Not the river. The River. We need to find the River."

"He's delirious," Dane said.

But Logan shook his head. "Papa Hayes," he told them, slurring his words a little and closing his eyes with a frightening indifference. "He told me. About the River. We're gonna make it to Beacon, you guys. I just know it."

┗

Grandma knocked softly on the house's front door. When there was no answer, she walked to the ground floor window, peeked into it, and knocked on that too. Several minutes passed with no sign of life.

"Come on," Grandma said aloud. "I know you're in there."

Then Grandma heard the coughing.

Mrs. Phoenix opened the door.

"I knew I recognized you," Mrs. Phoenix said. "It's been years, though. Three? Four? I've lost track."

"About that," Grandma said.

Inside, the house was filled with an oppressive, wet heat. A hot shower was running upstairs, and the kitchen faucet was turned on to as hot as it would go. The humidity hung in the air and condensed on the walls and countertops.

"Who's here?" Grandma asked, pointing up.

"Oh. No one," Mrs. Phoenix said, waving a sponge she held in her hand. "I'm just cleaning." And she set upon the kitchen table, scrubbing it with soap that spilled off the sides and dripped onto the floor.

Grandma frowned. "Not any kind of cleaning I've ever seen. Feels like a rain forest in here."

Mrs. Phoenix coughed a few times. "Uh. Sonya? Can I get you anything? I'm afraid I don't have much to offer in the way of food or drink . . . perhaps a glass of water, though?"

"No." Grandma stood where she'd entered, making no attempt to get comfortable.

Mrs. Phoenix smiled uneasily.

"I assume you know why I'm here," Grandma said.

Mrs. Phoenix shrugged, politely.

"You read the news this morning?"

"Oh." Mrs. Phoenix laughed nervously, and this made her cough again. "If you're referring to the article about Hailey—the whole thing is a big misunderstanding. She's running some errands today, that's all—I'm sure she'll be back in just a matter of—"

"Then why aren't you at work?" Grandma asked. "You work at the nanomaterials plant, don't you? They run a pretty tight ship over there."

Mrs. Phoenix didn't answer.

"I'm not a stupid woman, Dianne."

Mrs. Phoenix stopped scrubbing.

"And I think you know a lot more than you're letting on."

The two of them moved to sit at the kitchen table, the humid air sparkling strangely around them. "DOME bugged the house," Mrs. Phoenix whispered. "Surveillance powder. Get this place humid enough, though . . . the stuff shorts out pretty quick." Mrs. Phoenix was fiddling with a ball of clear tape that she'd crumpled up and soaked in soap. "And this, too—bug tape. Sends anything it hears straight to them for record keeping." She laughed. "Unless it's been submerged in water, of course."

"Sounds like you and the little one got these moguls pretty riled up," Grandma said.

Mrs. Phoenix smiled. "Hailey," she said. "She deserves all the credit. I'm just the proud mom."

"I always knew you didn't like that Mark on your arm any more than I liked the one on mine. I could tell that about you. You're one of the sane ones."

"I wouldn't go that far," Mrs. Phoenix said.

Grandma sighed. "Dianne. My grandson's missing. My grand-daughter's dead. My daughter's a wreck. Please. If you know anything about what's been going on these last few weeks . . . please tell me."

Mrs. Phoenix crossed her arms. "How do I know you're not another one of DOME's tricks? How do I know they didn't send you?"

"Dianne, I hate Cylis more than anyone! I've been saying that for years! You've heard me!"

"They could've forced you."

"How? What do I have to lose that they haven't already taken? DOME can't make me talk."

"You wouldn't need to talk. Strap a wire on you and—"

"You think DOME would strap a wire to an eighty-year-old woman?"

Mrs. Phoenix frowned. "I think there's nothing those bigwigs wouldn't do."

And suddenly Grandma smiled. "You know, Dianne? I think this might be the beginning of a beautiful friendship." And she walked to the kitchen sink. She turned on the cold-water faucet and cupped her hands under the running water. She splashed the water onto herself until she was soaking wet. And then she pushed her dripping hands through her hair.

Mrs. Phoenix looked on in shock.

"There," Grandma said, standing in a puddle on the floor. "Now, even if I were wired—which I'm not—it'd be shorted out."

Mrs. Phoenix tried to speak, but failed a few times.

"I want to know what happened to my family, Dianne. I want to know, and I want them back."

Mrs. Phoenix looked down at the table for some time, seeing

pieces of herself in the rainbow reflections of the soapsuds on its surface. "Then we start at the beginning," she said, and she held her breath.

"Go on. Out with it already."

The two of them stared at one another for several tense moments. Then Mrs. Phoenix said it, all at once. "Your granddaughter isn't dead. Lily's very much alive. Logan's gone to find her. And my daughter has decided to help."

Grandma narrowed her eyes, holding her breath, stepping forward . . . the short-circuiting powder still sparkling all around her . . .

"You heard of the Dust?" Mrs. Phoenix asked.

"I've heard whispers, in my retirement home. Kids we exclusionists call 'the great hope.' I always thought it was nonsense."

"It's not," Mrs. Phoenix said. "They are the great hope. And they're led by Daniel."

"*Lily's* Daniel? Daniel Peck?"

"That's right. Good friends, I remember."

"*Friends?* Those two kids were crazy about each other! Anyone could've seen that."

Mrs. Phoenix nodded. "When Lily flunked, it sent Peck over the edge. He started believing the worst, started looking for conspiracies . . . and wouldn't you know it?" Mrs. Phoenix laughed, stifling another cough. "He actually found one." She scrubbed the table a few more times, absently. Grandma looked on. "When Hailey's father died, she took it pretty hard. There were a lot of changes around here, as you know. I had to Pledge, I had to work . . . and about that time—I don't know if you know this—but about that time, your grandson and my daughter had a bit of a falling-out. Something to do with their friend Dane."

"Three's a hard number," Grandma said. "Someone's always left out . . ."

"Anyway, Hailey was looking for support and not really finding it anywhere. With me at work so much and no one left for her to turn to at school . . . she eventually found the Dust. Found them out on one of those long walks of hers, on Slog Row.

"I was worried at first about the influence they'd have on her. But I didn't mind that they were Markless." Mrs. Phoenix smiled. "I understood the reasons for that well enough."

"You mean to tell me," Grandma said, "that your daughter is a member of this Dust I've been hearing about?"

"That's right. Since last year, she's been friends with them, though for the most part she wasn't participating in any of their . . . activities. That changed fast, though, as Logan and Dane got close to Pledging age. Peck started fearing the worst for them, and . . . well . . . for months, now, Hailey's spent all her time over there on the Row, doing anything she could to help protect them. One thing's led to another. And now here we are."

"So what's the conspiracy?" Grandma demanded. "What did DOME do with my granddaughter?"

Mrs. Phoenix sighed. "Sonya. You'd better sit down."

⌐

The sun was almost at its highest point in the sky, and the Dust was still riding on Papa's raft. By now, Peck had explained to them the idea of the Unmarked River, had described its symbols, its system, and its people to the Dust.

"I don't like this game," Tyler had said. "Too many ways to

lose." But under the circumstances, each had agreed there was no better way forward. So throughout the night, the Dust took turns steering their new raft with a long stick, determined to ride until they found some sign of the next "anchor," whenever that might be.

It was Eddie who broke the day's silence. "After all that," he said. "After *all* that, we're just leaving Logan behind."

"We're not leaving anyone behind," Peck said, pushing the raft around a cluster of rocks and trying hard to fight his exhaustion. "Logan will make it to Beacon. I know he will. Hailey and Dane too."

"But not with us."

"No. Not likely with us."

"And yet *we're* still going to Beacon. Even though this is *Logan's* sister we're talking about here."

Peck looked at Eddie sideways. "You got a problem with that?"

"*I* do," Jo said. "You gonna use your little power trip on me too?"

"I'm not using a power trip on anyone, Joanne. This isn't up to me anymore."

"Well, then who's it up to, huh?"

"No one! Think it through, Joanne. Where else can we go? The Row is out of the picture. New Chicago's swarming with DOME, all of whom are looking for us. And the farm's been discovered. What else do you expect us to do? Beacon's our last safe bet."

Blake had been lying back on the raft, hands behind his head, looking up at the treetops and the sky passing overhead. But he sat up now, a strange look in his eyes. "You knew, didn't you?"

Peck turned to him. "What are you talking about?"

"You knew they would come for him. For Logan. You knew that he'd lead them right to us. That as long as Logan was a part of the Dust, DOME would always be just one step behind. . . . You *wanted* it . . ."

"Why would I want that, Blake? Why?"

"To drive us off the farm! To take away our safe house. To keep us on our toes—always on our toes! Because you knew we wouldn't follow you any other way!"

All of the Dust was looking on now, in a sort of stunned silence.

"And what if you're right?" Peck asked.

"Dock the raft. I'm getting off."

"You *can't*, Blake. DOME's out there. They'll find you and kill you."

"You're *using* us!"

Suddenly Peck drove his stick very hard into the streambed, and the raft veered dangerously to the right. It swerved and crashed hard against the bank, jostling everyone and throwing Blake to the dirt.

"We are *in* this, Blake. *Together.* You knew what you'd signed up for with the Dust. You knew it was the hard road. Since when have I ever promised it would be easy to bend history toward justice?" Peck shook his head. "I'm ashamed of you right now."

And now Peck spoke to the group of them, to everyone on the raft.

"There is a place in Beacon where kids are sent to suffer for crimes they may or may not ever commit. Now, I don't know about any of you, but when I hear that, it makes my blood boil. So I am going to Beacon to do something about it. Do I need you kids to come with me? No. I don't. So any of you who wants out, now's your chance. Here we are. Final stop. But you'd better make it quick. Because DOME *is* on our trail. And because *I've* got work to do.

"Why do I want you with me on this? Because we're a family. Because I love each of you. Like brothers. Like sisters. The same way I love Logan. And Dane. And Hailey. And Lily.

"But we're out of time, Blake. So if you—if any of you—feel differently about me—about any of this—then leave now and don't look back."

Overhead, a soft wind whistled in the empty tree branches. A few lost birds chirped in the distance. The rushing water of the stream lay a blanket of comforting sound around them. And the sky was blue and inviting.

Blake stood up at the spot where he'd fallen off the raft. The Dust looked around at one another. Jo. Tyler and Eddie. Meg. Rusty.

And Blake stepped back onto the raft. "Push off," he told Peck, defeated. Not looking him in the eyes. Not looking anyone in the eyes. "Come on, already, will you? Let's go." And he leaned over and shoved the ground hard, sending the raft back onto its journey himself.

☐

Logan's grandmother tiptoed up the spiraling staircase outside the Langlys' home, still in shock over everything Mrs. Phoenix had said.

Kids taken by DOME. Imprisoned for signs of doubt in Cylis. For dangerous thoughts they didn't know they had.

And at the same time, Grandma felt large. Larger-than-life. Ballooned up with a level of pride she'd never before imagined.

Her grandson. Logan. Throwing everything away to stand up against it.

As she changed into dry clothes and ran a towel through her

hair, Grandma thought very hard about ways she could help. There had to be something. She would find it.

But the Langlys couldn't know. David, Charlotte . . . they'd never allow it. Would they even believe it? They'd never listened to her before . . .

Grandma sat on the bed for a long time, holding the charm on her necklace and praying that she might find some way to help her grandchildren soon. Praying for something, for any little thing to point her in the right direction. She twisted the small, silver cross in her fingers and thought, *I'm listening. I'll hear it.*

Eventually Grandma walked to the elevator, to find her son-in-law and lie to him about her long nap and her wonderful dreams.

Tomorrow would be another day. Mrs. Phoenix would be waiting. And Grandma had a feeling she'd better get good at coming up with alibis.

9

Erin was surprised to find her father home when she returned from school. She'd expected him to work late after the disaster at the farm the night before.

"What are you doing here?" she asked.

Mr. Arbitor shrugged, not looking up from the mug of nano-coffee he held between his hands on the kitchen table.

"School's a mess," Erin said. "Between the kids whispering about Hailey's disappearance, and that ridiculous secretary, Ms. Carrol, running around talking to reporters like a chicken with her head cut off, the whole place is chaos." She dropped her bag and sat across from her father.

"That's nice, dear," Mr. Arbitor said absently.

"You should have listened to me," Erin said. "I'd have found him. I'd have checked the barn before running around blowing people's heads off like a maniac. Logan would have talked to me if I'd shown up alone. He'd have protected me from the Dust, and he'd have talked to me. You could have moved in anytime, and you'd have caught them. And we'd know what Logan knows. And I'd have my friend back."

Mr. Arbitor stared intently into his mug.

"Are you hearing me, Dad?" She waved her hand in front of his face.

"We're moving back to Beacon," Mr. Arbitor said. He sipped his nanocoffee, still not looking at his daughter.

"Wait. We are?" Erin's eyes lit up. "When? Dad, that's great! Have you told Mom?"

"I was demoted," Mr. Arbitor said. "Cheswick demoted me. Said I was incompetent. They're calling it a transfer. But I was demoted."

Erin was quiet for a moment. Then she shrugged. "Well, what do you expect, Dad? You are incompetent. If you'd have listened to reason, we'd have caught the little misers by now. We'd have Logan Marked and on our side, and maybe you'd be getting a promotion instead of . . ." Erin trailed off. She was still trying to start a fight. But Mr. Arbitor wasn't biting. And this scared her almost more than anything. "Dad. Come on. There's a silver lining here. We get to be with Mom again!"

"You're right," her father said. "You won."

"What? No, Dad, I—this isn't about me."

"You sneaked into DOME and stole our supplies. You helped Logan escape while he was in our custody. You set this whole mess into motion. All because I dragged you out here. All because you wanted to go home. And now we are." He finally looked at her. "So you have won." Erin's father pushed the nanocoffee away with his forearms. "We leave the day after tomorrow. Better start packing."

Then Mr. Arbitor put his head down on the table, resting his cheek against its surface. And Erin slipped quietly away.

10

It was in the afternoon that the Dust saw it: the sailboat lying on bone-dry ground in the middle of nowhere, half an acre away from a lone house in the distance. They'd made it out of the woods, riding the stream deep into the wastelands, with not a person in sight—and yet here was this house, all by itself. With an old sailboat fifty miles away from the nearest lake.

"A boat," Jo said. "A boat is a captain's symbol . . ."

"I thought we were supposed to be looking for an anchor," Eddie said.

Tyler scoffed. "*I* thought we were supposed to be looking for drawings. Not the real thing."

But Peck smiled.

The Dust disembarked from the raft and walked across the scrubby field.

Through the window, Peck could see a man sitting in a rocking chair on a dirt floor. It was a one-room house, nothing else in it but a fireplace, a card table, and a vase on the windowsill, with two dead flowers inside.

"Who's there?" the man called out.

"Just us, sir." And Peck poked his head inside the open front door. He motioned for the rest of the Dust to follow. "We don't mean to bother you. But we couldn't help noticing the boat on your property." He stepped toward the man, close to the rocking chair.

"Yeah? What of it?"

Peck shrugged, slyly arcing the toe of his shoe through the dirt.

The man looked down. He stared at the ground for some time.

Then the man drew a line as well.

The arcs came together.

The fisher's symbol lay on the ground.

11

Dane was nearly a mile away by now. He hadn't truly believed Logan's story about the Unmarked River, but he'd agreed to look for it all the same, if only for an excuse to walk off his jealousy over Logan and Hailey.

Except, the last several minutes, Dane hadn't been walking at all. He'd not been even been moving.

There, on the tree ahead of him, carved into the bark, were the waves of the Unmarked River. He'd never have noticed them if he hadn't been looking. But beside that tree a thin trail branched off and wound its way out of the woods, revealing the path forward. Dane had to laugh. *I guess the Markless have a few marks of their own after all*, he thought. And he turned to run back toward his friends, filled with hope for the first time in weeks.

He was just beginning to feel better about his luck and everything else in his life when Dane thought again about his two closest friends hugging. For warmth. It almost sucked all of the hope right back out of him.

Dane walked loudly in his final steps toward them. He cleared his throat when he arrived.

"How's he doing?" he asked, trying hard to hide his jealousy.

Hailey turned toward him. "Warmer," she said. "Not so out of it anymore. But Dane . . . he's still claiming there's this thing called the Unmarked River."

"There is!" Logan insisted.

"I know." Dane had to smile, despite himself. "You're right. I've found it."

SIX

THE RIVER CODE

1

THE COVERED WAGON WAS STUFFY AND uncomfortable. Up front, the captain sat, holding the reins and urging his two horses onward. The Dust hid cramped in the back, leaning forward under the canvas, sitting awkwardly on the hard wooden platform, hay strewn about, legs all tangled, arms pushed up against one another's.

No one complained, though. Peck's little stunt with the raft had made sure of that.

"Been a while since I seen a group this big," the man up front said, looking back over his shoulder. "I expect to see more comin', though, the way DOME's been chasing us out. Am I right?"

"I think that's right," Peck said. And they rode along quietly for a while.

"So where y'all hoping to get?" the man asked.

And before anyone could stop him, Rusty said, "Beacon."

The man sat up straight, surprised. "Beacon, huh? Don't see many Rivergoers headed all the way out there. Usually folks give up 'fore then. Stay country-side." He nodded. "Nice community, though, if you know where to look."

"Oh yeah?" Peck said.

"So I hear."

"Whaddaya know about Beacon?" Peck asked.

The man shrugged. "Fair bit."

And Peck hesitated. "You ever heard of a place called Acheron?"

Immediately, the captain pulled up on the reins. His wagon came to an abrupt stop, jostling the Dust about in the back. "What've you kids got to do with Acheron?"

Jo cleared her throat. "Nothing, sir. Or . . . not yet, anyway. We're looking for a friend."

The captain turned and eyed each of them.

"All my years on the River, I only ever heard one story that mentioned the name Acheron."

The Dust leaned in.

"And it ain't much of a story, really. More of a legend." He sighed deeply. "From what I hear . . . lookin' for a place like that is just lookin' for trouble. 'Cept trouble's a lot easier to find."

"All the same," Peck said uneasily, "what've you heard?"

"Almost too horrible to say," the man said. "But if I might could water it down for ya . . . well . . . I captained a woman one time— hundred miles or so—farther than usual, for any normal group o' Rivergoers. Anyway, she and I got to talkin'. Talkin' about this, talkin' about that, and . . . well . . . sooner or later she said somethin' 'bout her Markless brother turned around and right killed his wife one day. Claimed some act o' betrayal or something . . . but that ain't no excusin' it, though."

"No sir," Peck said.

"Anyway, I got 'round to askin' that poor woman whatever happened to him. The murderin' brother—Giovanni, man's name was. Provided I'm rememberin' right.

"Woman hemmed and hawed. Didn' much wanna talk about it. But I got the story outta her. That was a long ride, 'tween her and me. Finally, she star's cryin'. Said DOME caught up with him on account of it being a Markless crime. Woman said he right disappeared. But she wouldn't leave it at that, no, sir! Woman kept diggin'. Come to think of it, that mighta been how she found herself on the River . . .

"In any case, poor woman dug up some whispers she mighta wished she hadn't found. Whispers o' her brother being frozen alive. Kept in some refrigerated cell. Just frozen there to think 'bout what he'd done. Hidden somewhere no one's ever been found." The man shook his head. "I don't remember much else 'bout that story. But she did call that place Acheron. I do remember that."

"So it is a prison, then," Blake said. "We weren't sure . . ."

The man shrugged. "Ain't no prison I ever heard of. Not outside that tall tale, anyway. I do wonder, though, where Markless go, when DOME decides they won't be comin' home. They sure don't go to any Marked jail—that much is certain."

"What makes you say that?" Peck asked.

"You kiddin'? What gave you any illusions of Markless bein' treated fair by DOME? Ain't no Markless can call himself an A.U. citizen. Ain't *none* of us citizens. You kids know that—that's the whole point."

"Yes, sir," Peck agreed.

The man shrugged. "Gotta be an A.U. citizen to stay in an A.U. jail."

"But . . . we've had Markless friends taken by DOME," Blake said. "I've never heard of any special Markless prisons."

"Your friends ever make it past the Centers?"

Blake thought about it.

"Centers are another matter. Them's holding places. Markless come and go from Centers all the time, sometimes for questioning, or sometimes 'cause DOME can't make even the smallest accusations stick. But if there's a crime, and if that criminal's a Markless . . ." The captain raised an eyebrow knowingly.

Blake knew he was right. Joanne's parents had disappeared without a trace. Others had done the same. Some went into the Centers only soon to be released. But had there ever been a story of a sentenced Markless landing in an A.U. prison? Blake couldn't think of one, and neither could anyone else.

"Sure, no one much talks about it. DOME don't want any o' its Marked thinkin' we misers are bein' mistreated. Not yet anyway. But A.U. prisons are an A.U. right. And you and me ain't got none o' those."

"Still," Blake said. "If that's true . . . how come Acheron isn't mentioned more often? You'd think it'd be talked about among the Markless . . ."

The man laughed. "How? Any poor miser who goes in ain't ever comin' out! If DOME won't mention it, and if no one else ever lives to tell about it—well, then there ain't all that much to talk about, now, is there?" The man shrugged. "*Or* might could be Acheron don't actually exist." Then the man looked back at them, over his shoulder. "But whaddo I know? I'm just a crazy ol' captain, chartin' boats on *the driest* river man has ever known." He shook the reins, and Blake watched out the wagon's back as the man's horses made waves all along that dusty trail.

2

That night Erin was supposed to be packing. But she wasn't. Instead, she lay on her bed, staring up at the ceiling and thinking about how much she wouldn't miss this place.

She wouldn't miss the town.

She wouldn't miss the school.

She wouldn't miss the apartment.

She wouldn't miss not having any friends.

She certainly wouldn't miss being stuck with her lunatic father a thousand miles away from her real home and her mother in Beacon.

She wouldn't miss the lonely skyline.

She wouldn't miss the cold weather . . .

Erin sat up and walked to the cage her iguana was in. She didn't let him out. She just stared at him, her face pressed against the glass.

"I know how you feel in there," she said. "But we're not trapped anymore. We did it. We're going home." She frowned. "And that was the goal all along, wasn't it? Wasn't that all we wanted?"

Erin waited now for Iggy to respond.

He didn't.

You're right, Erin thought, not able to say it out loud. *That wasn't really the goal after all, was it? Not by the end.*

The goal was Logan. And he's as far away now as Beacon was then.

Erin lifted the lid on Iggy's cage and picked him up. He waved his tail and flailed his arms as she carried him over to her dresser, where she set him down and let him pace nervously from one side to the other.

"I'm out of options, little guy. I'm out of ideas. With Logan around there was always a next step. Visit Slog Row. Spy on the Fulmart. Sneak out to the baseball stadium. We were always thinking one move ahead in the chess match." Erin sighed. "But I'm lookin' at a checkmate here. I don't know where Logan is. I don't even know where he's headed." She petted Iggy for a moment, and he didn't particularly seem to mind.

"Well, sure, I know he's trying to find his sister. But that's a pipe dream, right? I mean, she's dead. She has to be."

Erin looked at Iggy and narrowed her eyes, speaking slowly and thoughtfully. "Except . . . you don't think that's true, do you? You don't think she *is* dead. But why don't you think so, Iggy?" Erin frowned.

"Because you know Logan. You know him too well to be fooled by the things you take for granted. And you know Logan wouldn't go through all this trouble unless by now he had some type of evidence that truly convinced him." Erin nodded slowly, looking up at the blank wall, staring at nothing. "That's smart, Iggy. That's very smart.

"But when would he have gotten that evidence, little guy? He didn't have it when we went for ice cream that night after he met Peck. So that means . . ."

And it dawned on Erin, how dense she had been up until this moment. How blind.

The Pledge, she thought. *What if he really did learn something from that Marker after all?*

It seemed impossible.

But was it?

Already Erin was at her desk, tablet computer in hand. She typed furiously at the screen.

Ξ

Logan, Dane, and Hailey had been walking all evening, keeping to the signs on the River. Now that they'd found the path, it seemed every few miles was another symbol to guide them on their way. Carved onto rocks, laid on the ground with rope . . .

But it was hard to get excited. The tension among the three of them was so thick it was almost visible. Dane hadn't said a word in hours, and all morning he'd walked just a few too many steps behind.

"Look," Hailey said, pulling Dane aside while Logan pressed on ahead. "You need to get over this me-and-Logan thing. Because it doesn't exist. All that stuff you thought was flirting back at Spokie this fall—I was *spying* on him, Dane. I had to get close enough to bring him to Peck. You should know that by now."

"You can say that all you want," Dane said. "Just like you can say that this morning was—"

"This morning was about saving Logan's life! Hypothermia could have killed him, Dane. He was *dying*."

"Right. Exactly. You can say that and whatever else you feel like saying. But that doesn't stop me from seeing it in your eyes when you look at him. You still like him, Hailey. You have since the fifth grade."

Hailey sighed, looking down at their feet. "I'm not going to stand here and deny it," she said. "But Dane, whether or not you're right—it's not on my mind. It's not what's important here. You get that, right? That this is bigger than any of that?"

"Yeah." Dane nodded, sarcasm dripping from his voice. "I get it. Logan wants to go to Beacon. That's certainly bigger than anything I happen to think or feel. Much bigger. You're right."

"That's not what I mean," Hailey said.

"Listen, just run off to him already, will you? I know that's where you'd rather be, and I don't need the company back here."

Hailey stared at him for a moment, hurt.

"So . . . do *you* get *that?*"

"*Hey, guys!*" Logan called, off in the distance. "*Guys! You'll never believe it!*"

Hailey frowned. "Fine," she said coolly. And the two of them ran to Logan.

"Train tracks," Logan said, pointing to the ground. They stretched out across the barren land as far as the eye could see in either direction. "These aren't magnetrain rails either—look." He knelt down. "It's just an old-fashioned steel-and-wood track. And here—" Logan smiled widely now, his hand running over the cold metal. "Right where the path meets it. A lifesaver. Carved in the rail as clear as day."

"You don't think . . . ," Hailey said.

"Yeah," Logan said, sitting down happily to wait. "I do."

4

The last time Erin hacked anything was during Logan's Pledge—and she really outdid herself that time. Breaking into the DOME Center security system? Commandeering each Markscan throughout the building? Reprogramming the map? Planting a worm to attack the electrical board just as soon as anyone swiped an interior scanner? You could retire after a hack like that. Erin had figured she would.

And yet here she sat now, back in the game after only a few weeks off, shuffling through the inner save files on DOME's security system hard drive. She was looking for video feeds. She was looking for one very specific video feed. She was looking for the recording of Logan's Pledge.

Erin had seen it before, of course, practically as it was happening—the video of Logan attacking his nurse, threatening his Marker . . . but she hadn't been looking for clues. She had been looking for guilt. So what had she missed the first time around?

The feed was buried deep. But eventually she found it.

"Good work, Iggy," she said as her iguana watched blankly from the dresser.

The video was silent. Sound wasn't recorded in the Center's Pledge rooms, so Erin couldn't hear what was being said. A month ago, she'd just assumed it was a litany of charges and punishments. But what if Logan's Marker actually *had* felt something for the little flunkee? What if Logan's Marker had decided to help? Might that behavior also look something . . . like this?

Erin was no lip reader. But the last word spoken by the Marker was clearly of some great importance. Erin watched the clip on a loop: the Marker leaning in, annunciating so clearly, directly into Logan's ear . . . but what was it he said? The way his mouth moved . . . it didn't fit with any word Erin had ever heard. It looked like nonsense. Three syllables, she could tell that much. But what were they? The first looked like an *ah*. And the word ended with an *on* sound. Or was it an *ot*? *En*? No—definitely an *on*. With a *kuh* in the middle? A *chuh*?

She just couldn't place it. But it looked—it really looked—as if the word that the Marker was saying . . . was *Acheron*.

5

The old-fashioned freight train arrived late in the night, running off its own electric engine, chugging along with a chain of double-door boxcars behind it. Logan and Dane and Hailey stood when they saw it coming, and they waited just a few steps away from the track.

The train slowed when it came upon them, its conductor leaning out the front window.

"What're you kids doin' out here?" he yelled. "It's dark out. Get outta here!"

But Logan and Dane and Hailey stood their ground, and all three of them held their hands up as though they were waving, casually showing their Unmarked wrists.

The conductor cut the engine and set the brakes, and still the train rolled on for some time. But when it stopped, he hopped out, no hesitation about it. "You lost?" he asked.

"No, sir," Logan said. He looked the conductor in the eyes. And he drew an arc in the ground with his foot.

"Well, I'll be . . . ," the conductor said. He held out his Marked hand, and Logan shook it. "Name's Arnold." He pointed to the boxcar beside him, his smile wide and inviting. "Where you headed?"

"As far as you'll take us," Hailey said.

"These tracks go south to a little town by the Gulf. But they'll veer east a while first."

"That'll help," Logan said. "Where's the next place you'll cross the River?"

"Long ways. 'Bout five hundred miles, at the track's closest point to the Potomac."

"The Potomac?" Hailey asked, intrigued.

"That's right. But folks only risk that route if they mean to take their chances in Beacon. I wouldn't recommend it. Most Markless prefer the quieter destinations down south. It'll make a nicer life for ya."

"Well," Logan said, hedging for safety, wanting to avoid revealing too much. "How 'bout we sleep on it? What would you say to that?"

In answer, the conductor doffed his hat and waved it toward the train, like a kid finally getting to play his favorite game. *"Allllll aboard!"*

⊔

It was warmer a little farther south. The old captain let Peck and Jo and the rest of the Dust off by an arrangement of rocks he'd found in the middle of a vast, empty prairie. They filed out of the wagon, and he gave each of them a bit of food as they did.

"Head this way," he said, pointing into the darkness. "In the morning, just follow the sunrise. You'll hit ruins, eventually, and you just keep going, now, when you do. It's a long haul, for sure. But from right here, you just head exactly due east, and you'll hit the next anchor in about one day's time." He shrugged. "Can't help you farther than that. This here's as much as I know."

"We can't thank you enough," Peck said.

"And you'll never have to." The man turned his wagon around and rode off the way he had come.

It took them a little while to settle in, but the Dust now sat on the cracked, dry ground, circling a fire they'd built using dry grass and bush twigs. They sat with a full can of refried beans each. Tyler was playing a game where he'd wait for Eddie to scoop out a handful of his own beans to eat, and then Tyler'd pounce, knocking the back of Eddie's hand and sending the glop flying.

"Knock it off!" Blake said. "Tyler, you're eating that off the ground. Eddie, you can take your next scoop out of Tyler's can."

"You can't tell me what to do," Tyler said.

But Blake snapped back, totally out of patience. "If Peck can force the lot of us out to a city halfway across the country that none of us wants to live in, you'd better believe I can force you not to waste the first meal we've had in two days."

Peck looked on silently, and Tyler stuck out his tongue at Blake until Eddie smacked him on the chin and sent Tyler's teeth clamping up on it.

"Thweet!" Tyler lisped around his swelling tongue. "That wath thuch a good one, Eddie!"

"We have to think," Peck said soberly. "*Think* where this prison could be. Acheron. *Acheron.* That's what Logan called it. The captain all but confirmed he was right. But how do we find a place we don't know anything about?"

Jo spoke quietly into her can. "We know it's where we're all gonna die, if we actually go through with this crazy prison break attempt."

"What was that?" Peck said.

"Nothing."

Rusty was asleep already, curled up by the fire. Meg was off on her own in the dark of the wide prairie stretch, trying to catch whatever animals she could find in the nighttime dirt so they might have breakfast in the morning.

"Well, we know the place is cold," Eddie said. "Captain definitely said something about refrigerated cells. You remember that? Maybe that's a clue right there."

"I think you're right," Peck said. "Thank you, Eddie."

Eddie smiled, a little shy to have helped such an unpopular cause.

And Meg came back and dropped a huge spider on Jo's head.

It was a good thing they were so far out into the wastelands. Forget surveillance powder—any closer to civilization, and DOME would have heard that scream by ear.

No one saw Jo again that night.

And privately, Peck wondered, *What have I done? What mess have I dragged us all into now?*

He went to sleep with tears in his eyes.

It was so late that it was early. Logan sat with his head against the cold metal of the boxcar, looking out through the open side door at the countryside rolling past.

Dane sat at the other end with his legs dangling off the edge, and Logan listened to Dane's griptone singing softly through the empty space, just barely loud enough to hear over the wind and the rumble of wheels on tracks.

"He's pretty good at that thing," Logan said to Hailey, who sat beside him in the shadow of the boxcar wall.

"He'd better be; he plays it enough."

"Whatever," Dane said, with a shrug neither one of them could see. "I can hear you, you know. I'm right here."

"I just said you're pretty good, is all. Sheesh." Logan rolled his eyes. The two of them hadn't exchanged a friendly word since the hypothermia scare in the woods.

"Hey—comin' atcha," Dane said, and he threw the griptone to Logan.

It was the size of a lemon, and squishy, with a little hole at its two ends.

"Just speak into it. Anything you want."

Logan held the ball to his mouth. "Twinkle, twinkle, little star," he said, and the words came out of the griptone as a perfectly tuned low C note.

"Okay," Dane said. "Now squeeze it lightly, just a little bit, when you say the second twinkle."

Logan did and the griptone let out a painful squeal.

Dane laughed. "Lighter than that. Maybe try pressing one finger at a time. You can get a little more nuance that way." And Logan tried it. The second "twinkle" came out as a higher note than the first. "That's really all there is to it. Once you get a feel for it, you can sing anything, just by speaking. It's connected to the network too, so you can even download songs or text and make your own melodies with them."

"Can you communicate with it?" Logan asked. "Over the network? Long distance?" He tossed the griptone back to Dane.

"I guess you could receive a message." Dane shrugged. "If someone hacked into it or something. But I've never heard of anyone doing that."

"Of course not," Hailey said. "How silly to think that this piece of junk might actually come in handy."

"Well, Hailey," Dane said, turning caustic. "I sure am sorry I don't have my wailing mitts out here to impress you with. Or was that just another fake interest of yours?"

"It was fake," Hailey said. "An excuse to scope out your house."

"Guys, will you drop this?" Logan said. "Please?"

"You know . . . you never did apologize for the way you and the Dust bagged me," Dane said. "Sneaking around like that, crashing my concert, knocking me out with chloroform . . . that last part especially," Dane said. "Thanks for that."

Hailey inched out of the shadows into the moonlight shining through the boxcar doors. "I saved you," she said. "You'd be a flunkee right now if it weren't for me. Besides, you sure didn't seem to mind the attention at the time."

Dane turned away, looking over the amber ground rushing past, letting the wind tousle his shaggy hair.

The boxcar was silent for miles and miles.

"Whatever happened to us?" Hailey finally asked Logan. "There was a time when I thought we were the best friends in the world."

Dane picked up his griptone again, ignoring her. Logan laughed nervously.

"Remember Underbrush Woods?" Hailey asked.

"Underbrush!" Logan said. "*Man*, that place was great! Best sleepaway camp ever—I still believe that."

"It was awesome," Hailey said. "Like, so great."

"Those camp counselors were the worst," Logan said.

"Are you kidding? They were the best!"

"Our parents thought they were the worst," Logan corrected. "They didn't watch after us *at all*."

"No, that's true. Remember that night we slept out on the lake, in the canoe—"

"And they sent the search party out to find us—"

"But not until, like, two o'clock the next day!"

"That's what I loved about the place," Logan said. "Cause as much trouble as we wanted."

"Some things never change, I guess." Hailey laughed.

Behind them, Dane hummed some song he'd written for his old band, the Boxing Gloves, louder and louder, doing his best to tune out his two old friends.

"Hover-dodge league too," Hailey said. "We could've gone professional if we'd stuck with it just a little longer." She laughed.

"Whatever," Logan said. "That was all Dane. You and I were always just trying to keep up."

"Yeah, right," Hailey said, and both of them laughed.

"I remember the day all three of us skipped school," Logan said. "You guys remember that?"

"Come on—how could I forget?"

But still Dane didn't respond.

"Spent the whole day in that playground at Spokie Central Park," Logan said.

"That was the greatest playground." Hailey sighed.

Logan nodded. "Then the Dust met me there for a show-down in September," he said. "I've never thought of it the same way again."

"Well. All I remember about skipping school is how much trouble I was in when I got home. I don't think my dad had ever been madder." Hailey frowned. "He hardly ever got that way. But it's funny how you remember the low points."

"My parents too," Logan said. "They took away my tablet for a month."

"I remember that! And Dane and I would sneak up to your

window at night since we couldn't message you!" Hailey slapped her knee. "Man. Whatever happened to *that*?"

"Nothing," Logan said, turning to face Hailey and Dane both. "We're the same as ever."

Dane rolled his eyes. "You're kidding yourself, Logan."

"No. I'm not. You think we aren't still the best friends in the world? Look at us!" Logan laughed now—a genuine, hearty laugh. "We gave up *everything* for one another. We had it *good* in Spokie, guys! We had it really good! And we threw all of that away without batting an eye. Didn't even flinch! The time came when we needed each other, and we threw our whole lives out the window to answer the call. If that doesn't make you two the best friends in the world to me, then I don't know what does. And you're both crazy if you don't see it." Logan looked back out to the countryside now.

A minute later Hailey put her hand on Logan's shoulder. She patted it twice. Dane finally turned toward them, and he frowned from his side of the boxcar.

The three of them sat like that, just staring out at the world rolling by, and they watched the sun rise.

日

The next morning, Erin's apartment was empty. Not just sort of empty—*truly* empty. The movers had come first thing and taken every last piece of furniture, trinket, and decoration that had once been in the space.

Her father was at work, gathering his belongings there to take with him as carry-ons on the train ride back. And it would have been a school day for Erin too, if she hadn't already been pulled from Spokie Middle.

As it was, she'd never have to set foot in that miserly school again.

So Erin sat on the open floor of her abandoned apartment alone, basking in the white light reflecting unimpeded off the blank walls, and delved into hacking territory so deep that it was unfamiliar even to her.

The memo system in DOME's mainframe computer was heavily protected, vast, and shockingly unorganized. All morning, she'd been searching high and low for some appearance—any appearance—of the word "Acheron" in any of DOME's files. She had just about given up hope of it being a word at all—much less of it being a word within DOME's database—when, finally, she found it. A single memo from Mr. Michael Cheswick, the man who demoted her father:

PROJECT TRUMPET CONTAINED

ACHERON IMPS SUCCESSFUL

TARGETS ELIMINATED

DETAILS TO FOLLOW ON PAGE

It meant nothing, as far as Erin was concerned. She read the thing over thirty, forty times. She dissected every last letter. The memo was gibberish.

And then the header caught Erin's eye.

"TOP SECRET," it said.

"FOR GENERAL LAMSON'S EYES ONLY."

And a wide smile spread over Erin's face.

On her second visit to the Phoenix house, Grandma didn't even bother to knock. She walked right down the sunny street, up onto the porch, and through the door without so much as a greeting.

"Sonya. You're back." Mrs. Phoenix was sitting at the kitchen table, hunched over a sculpture, hands pressed against her ears, coughing a little. She looked as if she'd been concentrating intensely.

"You skipped work again, I see," Grandma said.

Mrs. Phoenix frowned. "What can I do for you, Sonya?"

"I've been thinking about it. About Logan and Hailey. Dianne, we need to help."

Mrs. Phoenix looked at her and shrugged.

"What's the, uh . . ." Grandma waved her hands around the air. "What's the situation?"

It took Mrs. Phoenix a moment to catch on. "Oh!" she said finally. "We're good. DOME's not listening. No signs of surveillance right now."

"That's lucky."

"Well, with Hailey gone . . . I was never exactly their prime target."

Grandma nodded. "Then that's our advantage."

Mrs. Phoenix slumped down in her chair at the kitchen table, coughing for a while. "Listen, Sonya. Not that I mind the company these days, but . . . your coming here like this . . . I'm afraid I just . . . don't really see the point."

Grandma shrugged. "What's that you've you got there?" she said, pointing at the sculpture in front of Mrs. Phoenix.

"It's . . . well, it's nothing," Mrs. Phoenix said, pushing it away.

"Nonsense. I didn't sneak all the way out here just to get the runaround—"

"Oh, give it a rest," Mrs. Phoenix said. "It's a radio, all right?" She laughed. "An actual radio." She shook her head. "Can you believe it?"

Grandma sat at the table now, eyeing the sculpture. "A radio, huh? Doesn't look like any radio I've ever seen . . ."

"Well. It is one, all the same. AM-type. Shortwave."

Grandma narrowed her eyes. "Shortwave? Dianne, there hasn't been a shortwave station since pre-Unity days. Last ones went off the air before you were even born."

"I know," Mrs. Phoenix said. "It's all super high-frequency now. Satellite transmitters and computer receivers. This here's more like what they used . . . well . . . a long time ago. World War II, at least."

Grandma scoffed. "What do you know about World War II?"

"A lot, actually. History's always been an interest of mine."

"Fine," Grandma said. "Then where'd you get it? And what in the world are you listening to?"

"I'm not listening to anything right now," Mrs. Phoenix said. "That's the whole problem."

Grandma picked up the sculpture, ignoring the strong sense she had that Mrs. Phoenix very much disliked the idea of anyone touching the thing but herself. "I don't understand."

Mrs. Phoenix took her hands from her ears, pulling out the earphones she'd been wearing and laying them down in front of her. "Hailey made this," she said. "Gave it to me the night she left. I didn't recognize it at the time—thought it was just another sculpture of hers—but she told me I'd figure it out, and she was right. When I got home, I found some earphones, hooked them up right here . . ." She pointed to the end of a wire sticking up from the sculpture's surface. "Sonya. The thing works. And someone was broadcasting. The Markless are broadcasting on shortwave signals! Makes sense, I guess—it's the last place anyone besides them would bother to look. And you clearly don't need money or anything high-tech in order to listen in."

Grandma laid down the device and examined the earphones now. "Well, so what are they saying? What's the news?"

"I don't know." Mrs. Phoenix sighed. "The station went dead the night Hailey left."

"It hasn't come on since?"

"That's right."

"And yet Hailey definitely knows about it. Listens to it. For communication."

"Of course. That's why she made me this radio—so that I could listen too. Except her plan failed. The thing's useless now."

"Useless?" Grandma was standing now, one foot already out the door. "Dianne, don't you see what this means?"

10

Project Trumpet contained. Acheron IMPS successful. Targets eliminated. Details to follow on page. Erin ran the message over in her head, having easily memorized everything about it, right down to the font type (Courier) and time stamp (07:16:32, August 16).

She needed to find that page. It was that simple. Erin *needed* to find a copy of that page.

She rode her rollerstick to the Umbrella and parked it by the base of the spire.

In and out, Erin thought. *If anyone sees you, you're here to see Dad.*

And she swiped her Mark over the scanner by the elevator doors. *Just in and out.*

Except . . . the doors didn't open.

Erin swiped her Mark again. The scanner beeped and flashed.

She swiped a third time. The scanner flashed red.

Her father's transfer was already in effect. Erin was locked out.

Erin cursed and thought for a moment about what to do next. But she didn't hesitate. *Never hesitate*, she thought. And she unfolded her tablet.

It rang four times.

"I'm here to see you, Dad!" Erin said over the connection. "But the building won't let me in." She frowned. "Can you open the door for me?"

"Erin, I'm busy," Mr. Arbitor said. "Why can't it wait until I'm home?"

Erin frowned, the wheels in her head turning quickly. "Remember all those supplies I stole back in September?" she said.

Mr. Arbitor narrowed his eyes.

"Well, I brought them back! What's left of them anyway . . ."

"You told me nothing was left."

"I was lying," Erin lied.

Mr. Arbitor shook his head. "Fine," he said. "Might as well salvage some amount of my respect around here."

And with a swipe at his tablescreen, Mr. Arbitor opened the elevator doors.

Erin's heart raced as she rode the elevator up the fifty-story ascent. *In and out*, she thought. *In and out, in and out . . .*

The elevator opened and she stepped into the main disk of the Umbrella. Her father still stood by his desk at the other end of the room, busy with the cleanup of his space and distracted from noticing her entrance.

Erin didn't think twice—she dodged quickly around to the other side of the spire at the room's center, slipped into the stairwell door, and ran up to the very top. She reached the platform leading to Mr. Cheswick's office and swiped her Mark over its scanner just as she had the one at the Umbrella's main entrance.

It went red. Predictably. And Mr. Cheswick's face appeared on the screen above it.

"Erin," he said over the connection, not quite menacing, but certainly not friendly. "What can I do for you?"

"I just came in to return the supplies I stole. You know, back in September," Erin said. "I, uh, I put them back already, but . . . but I wanted to apologize to you personally before I left."

"Fine," Mr. Cheswick said. And like her father before him, the man buzzed Erin in. The platform began to rise.

Erin had to think fast. She had one shot at this. "I really am . . . very sorry," she said as she stepped off the platform and into the room. "Just . . . so sorry for all the trouble I've caused. And I wanted . . . I wanted to tell you that. In person. Myself. Now that Dad and I are leaving."

Erin tried to be casual about it as she scanned the room. There were no closets, no cabinets, no places to file paper of any sort. There was only the desk, off to the side of the small glass room. So where was this top secret page of his? Where could Mr. Cheswick's filing system possibly hide in an office like this?

"Well, I appreciate that," Mr. Cheswick said, fidgeting with something beside his chair. And that's when Erin saw it, the single drawer just under his desk.

Erin's goals, then, were simple: She had to get into that drawer. And Cheswick couldn't know about it.

Suddenly, Erin frowned, hard. "You just . . . you can't know how difficult it's been for Dad and me. Out here. By ourselves."

Dead puppies, she thought. *Lost kittens. Frown harder!*

"And now he's just . . . so sad . . ."

Iggy. Iggy being hit by rollerstick. Splat. On the ground. Iggy dying.

"And I just . . . I don't know what we're gonna do . . . and it's all my fault . . . and . . . and . . ." Erin sniffled.

There you go, she thought. *Yes. Yes—that's it!*

She sniffled again.

"And . . . I just . . . I know I let you down . . . and I know I let Cylis down . . . and my mom . . . and . . . and . . . everybody . . ." A tear! She felt a tear in her eye!

That's it, Erin! Keep it up!

"And now you hate me . . . and my dad hates me . . . and e-e-everyb-b-b-body h-hates m-m-me . . ." And bingo. Erin was crying.

The tears came fast now, and the hyperventilating, and the hysteria. Mr. Cheswick looked on in horror. Never having had a child of his own, he had no idea how to handle a situation like this.

"Erin. Erin, please. It's . . . it's all right, Erin. Honestly. I'm— I'm not mad at you. I . . . I promise! I don't hate you!"

But Erin only cried harder. Blubbering now. Uncontrollably. Inconsolably.

"Would you . . . would you like me to get your father?" Mr. Cheswick said.

"O-o-oh . . . kay . . . ," Erin said between sobs.

"Just . . . uh . . . just take a seat here, all right? Just . . . just sit right here, and I'll be right back." Mr. Cheswick moved swiftly from his seat at the desk to the platform in the middle of the room.

Erin made sure to look up at him, to look him in the eyes, with her blotchy red face and the snot dripping from her nose. She made sure he got a nice, long look at that face before he descended.

And then she was alone.

Erin wiped the tears on her sleeve.

She had to work fast.

11

It was midafternoon, and Logan, Hailey, and Dane were already exhausted.

"I'm not gonna make it 'til sundown," Dane said. "I can't walk much farther."

Earlier in the day, the three of them had hopped off the freight train just where they said they would—at the track's closest point to the Potomac River.

"Can't help you find a boat," the conductor had said. "But from what I've heard, you just follow this ridge twenty miles or so. There'll be a valley after that—green and inviting, right next to a bend in the South Branch of the Potomac. Don't know where or how you're likely to find a way to ride that bend, but fishers say it can be done." And the conductor rode his train on toward the Gulf.

"You can make it," Hailey told Dane now. "If I can, you can." They'd been on their feet for hours, hiking the difficult ridge of the Appalachian terrain.

"'Least it's warmer out here," Logan said. "Beats the lake weather in New Chicago; that's for sure."

Hailey shook her head, pulling a foot up out of her boot defiantly. "I didn't have blisters like this in New Chicago."

"Me neither," Dane agreed.

It was nighttime when the three of them finally came upon the valley.

"I'm never walking again," Dane said, basking in the rushing sound of the Potomac. But he was laughing. They had made it.

"I don't get it, though," Logan said. "It's just . . . grass."

But Hailey kept walking. She made it a hundred yards out before she stopped and saw it, the sign sticking up from the ground. It was wooden, waist height, propped up by two stakes in the dirt. "Village of the Valley," it read, and a little anchor adorned its face.

"Look here," Hailey called. "Says this is . . . a village."

Logan laughed. "Well, what is it? Invisible, then? There's nothing here, Hailey."

Hailey shrugged, looking very small against the wide field backdrop, the mountains all around them, and the stars in the clear, crisp sky.

But then something amazing happened. Behind Hailey, in the middle of fifty acres of grass and dirt, the ground popped open, and a man poked his head out as if it weren't anything out of the ordinary at all.

"What's the ruckus?" he barked, and Logan, Hailey, and Dane all jumped what felt like fifteen feet into the air. "It's nighttime! Don't you kids have manners?"

Hailey held up both arms, displaying her empty wrist. "We're a little lost," she said. "We didn't, uh . . . we didn't quite expect we'd be bothering anyone out here . . ."

"Well, didn't you see the sign?" the man asked.

Dane laughed. "Yeah, but . . . dude . . . there's no village here . . ."

"No village? Well, *that's* quite a thing to say!" And almost as soon as the man had spoken, all across the field, a dozen other people poked their heads up out of the ground.

12

Two hundred miles away, the Dust were developing blisters of their own. They'd been walking east going on sixteen hours, through street after forgotten street and who-knew-how-many ghost towns, and they'd passed now into an area so isolated that even the ruins were far behind them. Since sundown, they'd been hiking along an old, decrepit highway labeled "70" by the pre-Unity signs that had long since fallen to the ground. Every few miles, they'd pass a car by the side of the road, or sometimes right in the middle of it, abandoned, rusted, falling apart . . .

"We're gonna die out here," Eddie said.

"No we're not," Peck told him.

But two hours and four abandoned cars later, Eddie continued the thought. "I think we are. I think we're all gonna die out here."

"You're wrong," Peck said.

"No, I'm definitely not," Eddie mused, yet another hour later.

"Eddie! We *are not going to die*," Peck insisted.

"But I'm not so sure . . . ," Eddie said, well into their twentieth hour of walking.

This time Peck just shrugged. "Fine," he said. "Then we die free."

No one talked after that.

On their twenty-second hour, the Dust saw it, the mansion in the distance with a light in every window.

At first, Blake thought he was seeing things. He was sure he'd begun hallucinating.

But when everyone else saw it too, it became clear: the mansion really was there. It was the biggest they'd ever seen. And the lights really were on.

Someone was home.

At the end of a long, winding driveway, there was a post where a mailbox used to be, a relic left over from pre-Unity days, when paper mail still existed.

The post still had an address number on it, 2103, and it had something else too: a lifesaver drawn below the number, and an anchor drawn below that.

It was Tyler who pointed it out. The rest just stared, disbelieving their luck.

"Last one there's a rotten egg!" Tyler screamed, and immediately the Dust was running as fast as they could along that winding drive, tripping and shoving one another all the way.

They were elated and hopeful, eager for shelter, company, a meal, direction . . .

So much so that not one of them saw it when they passed by. They didn't even notice it in the corners of their eyes, scrawled on the picket fence just a little ways toward the house. But it was there. For anyone who knew to look.

SEVEN

HOUSE ARREST

1

Well, come on, then," the man said, and he motioned Logan and Hailey and Dane over.

When the three of them got to his hatchway, they could see that the man was standing on a staircase made of rock and hard-packed dirt below ground. They couldn't tell where the stairs led, but it was warm under there, with an inviting, yellow glow.

"Well?" the man said. "State your purpose. Out with it."

Hesitantly, Hailey responded. But it wasn't anything she said. Instead, Hailey feigned a yawn, and she motioned a big stretch with her hands out. As she did, Hailey made sure to sweep a wide arc with one arm, as if she were outlining a hill.

The man narrowed his eyes. He frowned for a moment. Then, with his hand, he made another wide arc, outlining a valley instead of a hill. The gestures were feet apart and drawn only in the air, but it was clear to the four of them: together, they'd made the fisher's symbol.

"River kids, are ya?" the man asked.

"That's right."

"It's a long ways from the nearest anchor. And it's late. You three must be tired."

"Yes, sir," Dane said. He was swaying a bit even as he said it.

"All right. Down you go, then." And the man slid the plank over and onto the grass. "*Rivergoers!*" he yelled to all the folks looking on from various other spots across the valley. "*We've guests tonight!* If you would," he said more quietly to Dane, who trailed the other two, and the man pointed to the plank.

He then turned and walked down the steps, Hailey and Logan and Dane following, and Dane replaced the cover behind him as he did.

"Weather's not safe in these parts. Hasn't been for years," the man said. "Plus we're not too far from the Beacon sprawl. Can't risk DOME's satellite eye, and anyway, can't abide the harsh climate. Hurricanes, hailstorms, heat waves, fires, frosts . . . you name it, we've had it. Don't know what to make of that, except that this community here is better off underground. Keeps us cooler in the heat, warmer in the cold, drier in the wet, and safer in any raid attempts.

"My neighbors and I," the man continued. "We're too old for this life of ours not to be at least a little less risky these days. Not like you kids."

The four of them—Logan, Hailey, Dane, and the elderly man—sat at a little wooden table with two burning candles on it. The room was carved right into the dirt of the ground, with floors and walls irregularly shaped around rocks that must have been too difficult to remove.

Through an archway at one end of the room, a woman entered, carrying a candle in one hand and a heap of blankets and pillows in the other.

"You Rivergoers get younger every year," the woman said. "Hard to believe." And she joined them at the table.

"Kids, this is my wife, Tabitha. Married thirty-seven years, now, Tabby and I."

Hailey smiled and held out her hand. "It's nice to meet you, Tabitha."

"Pleasure."

And Logan and Dane followed suit.

"My name's Hans. You can call me Papa if you'd like."

"Hans is good," Dane said. And the man shrugged and nodded.

"I'm Logan," Logan said. "These are my friends Hailey and Dane. We were told by our last captain that we might be able to use the Potomac branch that runs through here to make it the rest of the way to Beacon."

Tabitha frowned, nodding slowly. "That's true," she said. "It's only a couple hundred miles to the City Center hill. A few rough water spots along the way, but you can get out and walk past them if you really need to."

"We're experienced canoers," Logan said. "If that makes any difference."

"It does," Tabitha said.

"So . . . it's true, then?" Hailey asked. "You have boats here? Somewhere in this village?"

"No." Tabitha frowned. "But it's true that we make them, for fishers like yourself. If we're convinced Beacon's the right place for you to end up."

"It's not for everyone," Hans said. "Not in the least."

Logan frowned. He looked at Hailey and Dane, who shrugged in a "go ahead" sort of way. "Well," Logan said. "What do you folks know about Acheron?"

2

"*Acheron?*" Hans said. "What do you three have to do with a place like that?"

"You've heard of it, then?"

"Well, sure. You're not the first who's come through here looking for it. Place is the stuff of legends." He laughed. "You might as well be looking for the pot of gold at the end of the rainbow. Or the lost city of Atlantis. Or the Loch Ness Monster . . ."

"The Loch Ness Monster doesn't have my sister," Logan said.

And the man sobered up quickly.

"We think Acheron's the name of a prison. I went through quite an ordeal to get that information, so I'm inclined to believe it's *not* just the stuff of legend. Hans," Logan said. "We're breaking my sister out."

"No can do," Hans said. "No, sir. Nooo, sir. We've heard stories of folks who've gone *into* Acheron. Sure, here and there over the years. But nothing has ever been uttered of folks coming *out*."

"Hans . . . Tabitha . . . if you do know anything about the place . . . anything at all . . . it'd be a great help to us. We know a name, but . . ." Hailey looked at Logan and shrugged. "That's about it."

"Well, now, that's the whole riddle, isn't it?" Hans said.

"It's why we have trouble believing it," Tabitha added. "A city that dense, that populated, that famous . . . how does one *hide* a prison in a place like that?"

"But we do have stories," Hans said. "If you're determined to hear them."

Logan nodded that they were.

Tabitha sighed. "Acheron's a Markless prison. There're very few like it, far as we can gather."

"A.U. prisons, they're all over," Hans said. "But Markless don't end up in A.U. prisons, as I'm sure you've all figured out by now."

Tabitha nodded. "Markless—they have their own fate."

"So flunkees and criminals . . . they end up together?" Logan said.

"I don't know for sure about flunkees," Tabitha said. "But my guess is that they're no different in DOME's eyes, and that they're all funneled into the same handful of places. As you might guess, Beacon's is the biggest. They use that one for the people who are . . . how might one put it? . . . *special*, let's just say. One way or another."

Hans sighed. "Marked prisons, they're kind. Humane. Some tycoon's thrown in, serves his time in a little cell, does some community service, and he's done."

"But in Acheron?"

Hans shrugged. "I've heard different things. None of them fit. Hard to know what's true, if any of it even comes close."

"One man came through here once, whispering of a story he'd heard about Acheron poking the eyes out of its prisoners. Letting them wander around a whole big space, free to move about . . . but totally blind." Tabitha shuddered just thinking about it.

"That's so cruel," Hailey said. "Why in the world would they do that to someone?"

"Who knows? Another man came through here once, and *he* had quite a different take on it. Said Acheron keeps its prisoners in tombs. Said Acheron keeps those tombs hot. They suffocate the people inside—or practically, at least—with a fire all around them."

"Yet *another* story," Hans added, "is that Acheron dunks its prisoners in a pool of boiling tar and then feathers them. After that, the people are free to roam the prison, but . . . how free is that?" He looked at Hailey now. "Cruel . . . it would appear that *cruel* just barely begins to describe the stories of what Acheron does to its prisoners."

Logan was hyperventilating now, listening to this. Involuntarily, he laid his head on the table, sighing audibly and feeling light-headed. The thought of Lily being blinded, burned, tarred and feathered . . . it was too much. For the first time, he wasn't sure he could face what had been done to his sister.

"It's awful, no doubt," Hans said. "There's isn't much of a way to sugarcoat it. And Tabby and I . . . we have a feeling all this might just be the beginning."

"What do you mean, 'the beginning'?" Dane asked.

Hans sighed. "Warfare, environmental destruction, the Mark, the Inclusion, governments unifying under Cylis . . . any of that sound familiar to you?" He stood and walked to a side room, to a little library with a single shelf of paper books. He pulled one out and brought it over, laying it gently on the table. When Logan looked up, he recognized it right away. It was the same as the book Bridget gave him back at the underpass. It was a Bible.

"I expect you kids haven't heard much about what this book has to say. But it's all in there. Friends . . . I'd suggest it's time you start getting your things in order."

Logan's head dropped back on the table, a dizzying tunnel vision setting in.

"Hans, you're scaring them," Tabitha said gently.

And Hailey put a hand on Logan's back. "Hey, it's okay," she whispered. "I'm sure . . . I'm sure Lily's okay, all right?"

Logan nodded, but he didn't at all believe her.

"Come," Tabitha said, holding the pillows out. "That's enough stories for one night. Tomorrow . . ." She looked at her husband. He nodded. "Tomorrow we'll get started on that boat."

ヨ

Grandma knew she had to be quiet if she was going to get away with it. She led Mrs. Phoenix up the outside staircase of the Langlys' house, and then the two of them snuck into Mrs. Langly's study on the eleventh floor.

"My daughter's had this stuff set up for years," Grandma whispered. "Satellite dishes, meteorology tablets . . . and look here." She walked over to the corner, picking up a wire that fed out through the window. "A radio antenna. She uses it to listen to electricity in the air—to track thunderstorms apparently. But we"—Grandma grinned now—"I think we could use it for something else. Dianne—you and I could *broadcast*."

"I don't know about this . . . ," Mrs. Phoenix said. "Didn't you say your daughter's up here all the time these days? What if she catches us?"

"She won't! It's true Charlotte spends her days here, but at night she's out like a light."

"Even so . . ."

"Oh, *come on*, Dianne! This is our chance. Shoot—even *you* kept listening to that dead station all week! If Hailey's still tuning in, *this* is our way to reach her. We *have* to try! I can't even sleep at night, I'm so guilty over this thing. All those times we condemned that stupid Mark program . . . Dianne, *we're* the ones who turned these kids into rebels. And now that they've finally listened to us, we abandon them? No! We have to help! Don't you want to know where your daughter is? How she's doing?"

"Of course I do," Mrs. Phoenix said. "Desperately."

"Then let's do this. Let's tap into their network. My daughter and son-in-law are sick of entertaining me anyway—they'd *love* it if you came over each night. We'll just wait for Charlotte to retire each evening, and then we'll slip up here undetected. We can *do* this. I'll take us live, and you be the voice—it's perfect!"

Mrs. Phoenix was smiling now, picturing it. "I've always hated the sound of my own voice . . . ," she said.

And Grandma smiled too. "Any chance I can take that as a yes?"

4

The mansion at the end of the drive was even more inviting from close up. It was huge, sprawling out in a pre-Unity style, with shutters outside its windows, powder blue clapboard, columns on the front porch, and two chimneys, smoke rising pleasantly from each stack . . .

Tyler was the first one to the door. He rang the bell before the rest of the Dust had even caught up.

It was a short wait for an answer.

"Whoever could that be?" a woman's voice called from inside.

"I've got it," another voice said, speaking with an accent Tyler didn't recognize.

"But at this time of night?"

A man's face peered through the window. Then he smiled and quickly stepped to open the door.

"Well, blimey . . . ," he said. "Rivergoers, honey!" he called back into the house. "A whole group of them!" He grinned, and he let the Dust inside.

Peck, Joanne, Blake, Tyler, Eddie, Meg, and Rusty all sat at a dining table that could have easily seated ten more. It was long and ornate, a beautiful, polished wood with a shining gloss. The chairs were high backed and plush with red velvet on the seats and arms. The room by itself was bigger than the footprint of most houses in Spokie.

"Welcome to the Rathbone home," the woman said from across the table. "This is my husband, Mr. Rathbone, and our son, Winston. Say hello, Winston."

He did, though some part of him looked uneasy about it.

"Honestly, at sixteen you think he'd have better manners," Mrs. Rathbone said to her husband, and Winston rolled his eyes.

"We're so glad you've joined us," Mr. Rathbone said quickly, eager to change the subject and gesturing kindly to the group. But Tyler practically gasped when he did. Mr. Rathbone was a handsome, clean-shaven, middle-aged man, with dark hair, a strong chin, deep, dark eyes . . . but Mr. Rathbone was missing his right hand. He smiled and picked up his fork with his left.

There was food on the table, and lots of it. Fresh apples, oranges, grapes; a pumpkin and an apple pie; turkey legs and sliced turkey breast; juices and sodas and milk; a large salad bowl . . .

The Dust had never seen a spread quite like it. Meat was barely eaten anymore, ever since the collapse of the farming industry during the States War, and unless it happened to be in season and close by, fresh fruit was nearly impossible to find.

But not for the Rathbones.

"You'll have to excuse our appearance," Mr. Rathbone apologized. "We would have tidied up, had we known we'd have guests."

The Dust looked around, confused. The entire house was spotless.

"Your home is beautiful," Joanne said quickly. "We are . . . *so* grateful to you for taking us in."

"Well, there's plenty of room for everyone," Mrs. Rathbone said. "We have more than enough beds." And the Dust stared at her for a few long moments. It had been years since the group had had beds to sleep on, or even anything somewhat resembling a bed. Meg and Eddie had more recently come from homes, so they at least remembered the feeling. But for the others, the idea itself was a long-forgotten luxury.

"I get top bunk!" Tyler yelled loudly.

And Mrs. Rathbone laughed. "Oh my . . . there are no bunks here. You'll each have your own room."

Tyler sat with his mouth hanging open.

"We can't imagine how hard you all must have had it, making it here." Mrs. Rathbone said. "We are . . . a long ways from the nearest community."

"We know." Blake nodded.

"But I'm sure you've all thought enough about such unpleasantries," Mr. Rathbone said. "Where are our manners? Please. Everyone. Let us eat."

The Dust felt as though they'd stumbled into a dream. They'd never tasted such good food, they hadn't been so warm and comfortable in months, and they hadn't felt so welcome since their short stay with Papa and Mama Hayes at the farm.

"So how does a family like you end up in a mansion like this out in the middle of nowhere?" Tyler asked. Immediately, Joanne shot him a look, but Tyler only said, "What? It's weird. Am I not allowed to say it's weird?"

Most of the Dust looked down at their plates, embarrassed. Mr. Rathbone cleared his throat. Peck looked on with great interest.

"We'd hate to bore you with the details," Mrs. Rathbone said finally.

But Tyler just shrugged tactlessly. "I'm not bored; I'm curious."

Winston snickered over at his end of the table, though he stopped abruptly when his mother caught his eye.

After dinner, the Dust were shown to their rooms on the second and third floors of the mansion, and sure enough, they all really did have warm beds waiting for them. Several even had their own bathrooms off to the side.

"Food, hot showers, and beds—I can't believe our luck,"

Joanne said privately to Peck, just before the two of them retired to their own rooms.

"Neither can I," Peck said. And then he leaned in, looking quickly over his shoulder. "Really . . ."

5

Erin rested her head against the window of the train. It vibrated and shook with the motion of the wheels along the tracks. How much shaking would it take before she couldn't think as well anymore? Before she couldn't feel as much?

She had earphones on, and she was listening to music too loud, not even enjoying the songs, but savoring it all the same, since the noise made it harder to think.

What would it take to distract her from what she'd uncovered in Cheswick's office at the Umbrella? What would it take to slow her mind down, even a little, just the tiniest bit . . . to stop the racing—constant, furious, maddening—even for a moment?

Nothing would, Erin realized. *This secret will drive me nuts until it's uncovered, once and for all. Until the pieces fit. Until it leads me, finally, back to Logan Langly.*

She didn't know how it would. Not yet anyway. But on that cross-country train ride back to her home in Beacon, Erin became quite sure—this secret was the answer.

Logan *would* find Lily. Erin knew that now, in her heart. And Erin would be waiting for him when he did. No matter the cost.

Beside her, Erin's father sat reclining in his chair. Erin stole a glance his way, looking to see if his eyes were open. They weren't. But could she risk it?

Erin desperately wanted to open her folded tablet, to pull up the picture she'd taken of the paper she had found in Mr. Cheswick's office. To study it. To read it again and again. She almost couldn't believe the things it said were real. It was as if the moment she wasn't reading them, with the proof right in front of her, they didn't exist. Because how could they? It was simply beyond reality . . .

But her father was right beside her. The train was a public place. Should someone catch even a glimpse of that picture . . .

So instead, Erin bit her nails and leaned her head against the window.

She just had to make it home. To her old room. With her old door that locked.

It would be three days until she made it there.

Three miserable days.

On the way out to Spokie, DOME had splurged on a direct route magnetrain, so the ride had only taken a day.

But DOME wasn't feeling quite so generous this time around. This time they'd chosen, instead, a more "economic" route, outside of the magnetrain grid altogether. Layovers, transfers . . . the works.

Three days until she could read again and again the truth about the IMPS. Until that truth led her to Acheron.

Three days never felt so long.

ᄂ

That morning, Michael Cheswick entered his office as he did on any other day. He rode the elevator up to the disk of the Umbrella, greeted the many DOME agents already on the floor, ducked into the stairwell at the center of the room, walked up the two flights of stairs into the tip of the spire, swiped his Mark and rode the platform into his small circular room, sat at his desk, and sipped at a nice, hot cup of nanotea.

It was a clear morning. Bright. The sun shone cheerfully through the all-glass walls of the room, and Michael Cheswick spent his first few minutes in that delicious indulgence he so rarely afforded himself: admiring the view.

He had high hopes for Johnson, Michael did. He looked forward to the work Johnson would do, picking up where Charles Arbitor left off, picking up the pieces, tying all those loose ends. Logan and Peck and the Dust couldn't have gone far, and surely today marked the end of the troubles involving this case. The G.U. treaty would soon be signed, and Michael could look forward to a promotion once it was. He'd overseen the raids of every major Markless community in the city, had driven the misers out of every last one of their former strongholds, and he had done so with an impressive amount of control over the public's perception of the events. Surely all Michael needed now was to wrap up this one last pesky investigation, close the book on this one last file— *Peck and the Markless Threat of Spokie*—and he would be golden.

He could practically see it now: A transfer to the E.U. headquarters, perhaps. Holding court with General Lamson. A seat at the table with Cylis . . .

A man could dream. And Michael did dream.

Mr. Cheswick took another sip of nanotea and opened the day's briefing. He'd dealt swiftly with the setbacks of the past week, and with Charles Arbitor gone and Johnson in, it was sure to be a relaxing day.

And then the little blinking light caught his eye at the corner of his tablescreen. A message was waiting. He double-tapped the light, and a file expanded to fill the desktop.

It was an automated alert sent by the DOME computer network's security system. Yesterday a virus had been detected, after its introduction to the system one day prior. It was a harmless virus mostly, except that it compromised the encryption of some files here and there.

No big deal, Mr. Cheswick thought. Such alerts were routine enough, and they were nothing the mainframe immune system couldn't handle after a few days' time.

Michael scrolled through the full report, checking for damage or alterations made to any of the DOME system's documents. None detected. That was good.

But a handful of files had been viewed, it seemed, by an unidentified, external party. By an actual person.

Odd.

Disconcerting.

But still . . . no big deal. With the virus found already, the damage would be contained, and no further snooping would be possible, at least not without the introduction of an entirely new virus. So Mr. Cheswick simply needed to double-check which files had been viewed, and then he could get back to more important matters, like his daydream of sitting with Cylis at the head table over in the capital of the new G.U. . . .

But that's when he saw it. The last file named in the security log's report.

The memo. Four lines long. The memo that read: *Project Trumpet contained. Acheron IMPS successful. Targets eliminated. Details to follow on page.*

And Michael Cheswick dropped his nanotea onto the

tablescreen, shattering the mug and not even noticing as its dark liquid seeped into the cracks in the glass.

The day passed slowly for Logan and his friends. On the grass above, Hans and Tabitha and many of the village's neighbors were working on the canoe. Logan wanted to help, but after he and Hailey and Dane spent the morning gathering wood and tree sap and other natural materials for the construction, Hans and Tabitha both simply insisted that "the kids rest while the grown-ups work."

"Your journey will be long enough," Tabby had said. "And it can be dangerous on the Potomac. If you're going to make it to Beacon alive, you need to rest first."

So "the kids" had spent the last few hours underground, exploring the strange Markless house.

"Reminds me of Spokie Middle," Hailey said. "The way it hides underground."

"Yeah, but this place is bizarre," Logan said, brushing a spider from his back.

"Why is it any different?" Dane asked. Underground buildings were relatively common these days, given the space constraints in the suburbs and the unpredictable bouts of harsh weather throughout the country.

"Because Spokie Middle was high-tech," Logan said. "This kinda looks like some people just dug a hole in the ground with their hands."

The steps from the hatchway above were carved right into the rock and dirt, as were the walls and floors. Here and there a few planks of wood had been used to level the ground, but for the most part, it was a house made of earth. Roots stuck out of the walls and through the ceiling. Moss grew on the rocks of the floors.

The main room of the first floor was the kitchen area, with a table, two chairs, and an alcove for a fire, the chimney of which led straight up to a camouflaged hole in the valley ground above.

Two side rooms branched off from this main space: a "library," where Hailey slept last night in a chair with a single shelf of paper books by her side, and a "guest room," where Logan and Dane had slept under spare blankets on the hard dirt floor.

This guest room was funny though. The ground was slanted due to the formation of the rock bed beneath it, meaning the room itself also acted as a sort of long, slanted hallway; the lower level of the house began where it ended, and that was where Hans and Tabitha slept.

To Logan, there wasn't much of interest in the house beyond the strange architecture itself, so he'd spent the last few hours in the library, reading the tattered Bible Bridget had given him back at the underpass and trying to understand what made the book so dangerous.

Dane, meanwhile, sat in the guest room, happy to be alone, playing an old pre-Unity acoustic guitar that he'd found in the master bedroom, and filling the air with the sounds of his strumming and his griptone singing.

Hailey, for her part, was enthralled by something she'd found in the main kitchen area, on a shelf carved into the wall. She was sitting at the table, examining it, when Logan entered, antsy from the waiting and the reading.

"Whatcha looking at?" Logan asked.

Just then, Hans and Tabitha opened the hatchway from above, letting bright sunlight in, and they descended the steps.

"I see you found our radio," Hans said, sitting at the table beside Hailey.

"Hans," Hailey said. "Is this thing tuned to thirty-nine hundred kilohertz?"

Hans laughed. "'Course! Every Markless radio's tuned to that."

Hailey looked stunned.

"Well, how else do you expect us to communicate with each other? The villages around these mountains have been at this for years."

"Back up," Hailey said. "'Communicate'? What do you mean, 'communicate'? Radio's a one-way stream."

Hans looked at her like she must have been the densest girl in the world. "Well, certainly. That's why each village has a transmitter."

Hailey smacked her forehead and laughed. "Of course. It's brilliant! If everyone broadcasts on the same frequency, then that channel becomes one big nationwide conversation."

"Exactly." Hans nodded.

"Can I broadcast?" Dane yelled from the guest room, more excited than he'd been in weeks. "Can I have my own radio program? Please? Please?"

Tabitha laughed. "Well, I don't see why not," she said. "If you can find a time when the airwaves aren't too busy. But you kids'll be ready to head out of here in another couple of days . . ."

Already, Dane had run into the kitchen, holding the acoustic guitar and smiling eagerly.

"Hey, you guys didn't ever happen to listen to a radio broadcast sent out by a couple of people named Hayes, did you?" Hailey asked.

"Mama and Papa?" Tabitha asked. "Sure! They're on the air pretty regularly, in fact. Signal's always weak from them, coming in and out depending on the weather, but yeah, we like those two."

"Actually . . . ," Hailey said.

But before she could break the sad news, Hans had turned the radio on. Immediately, soft chatter filled the airwaves from nearby villages—overlapping conversations about remaining food stores, requests for clothing, announcements of village fairs, or Markless births, or Markless deaths. It reminded Hailey a little bit of being in the cafeteria hall at her old school: lots of voices here and there, but still easy enough to listen to any specific conversation over the din of the rest.

"Neat," Hailey said, smiling at Hans politely. But just as she was about to lose interest, one particular voice on the airwaves caught her ears.

"Testing," it said. "Testing, one, two. Is it on? The light's not blinking."

"It's on, it's on—go ahead!" said another, fainter voice.

"Uh . . . well . . ." The first speaker cleared her throat nervously. "Hello there, New Chicago. Uh . . . if you're Markless . . . then, um . . . well . . . then I guess this broadcast goes out to you . . ."

The fainter voice in the background said, "That's good, that's good. Go on—you're doing great."

"Um. Okay. Well. This is day two. Of our . . . experiment. For any of you listening, welcome to . . . well, your new favorite radio program! It's . . . a news show . . . New Chicago news . . . weather today is . . . cold, I guess . . ."

"Keep talking!"

"And . . . listen . . . Hailey . . . if you're out there . . ."

The woman on the radio broke into a terrible coughing fit.

"Anyway, you get the idea," Hans said, moving to turn the radio off.

"*Don't touch it!*" Hailey yelled. And that's when Hans and Tabby noticed the expression on their guests' faces. Slack-jawed, all three of them.

⊟

For dinner that night the Dust ate roasted duck with orange sauce.

"So who wants to go for a drive after we eat?" Winston asked.

"A *drive?*" Eddie said.

"Yeah. I do it all the time out on these old roads. I can teach you if you'd like."

"I'm sorry," Eddie asked. "A drive in *what?*"

Winston laughed. "A car, obviously."

The Dust were all speechless.

"We have a car," Mrs. Rathbone said finally, a little shy about it. Even in the context of a house like this, everyone was perfectly aware of what a rare luxury that was.

"Wait a second. You're kidding, right?" Blake asked.

"Not at all. See for yourself. Go on. Take a look," Mr. Rathbone said.

Blake stood up from the table, walking tentatively to the window.

"He's right," Blake said. "They really do have a car."

"Runs off oil," Mr. Rathbone said. "Early pre-Unity model.

Can't buy anything like it. Not for a century. And even if you did, where would you get the fuel?" He laughed. "It's not like those modern models. Nothing electric about it. That's a combustion engine, through and through."

"Where'd you get it?" Eddie asked. "*How'd* you get it?"

But again this question was met with shuffling feet and averted eyes.

"After dinner," Winston said, "I'll take you for a spin."

Eddie fidgeted nervously in the passenger seat while Winston revved the engine and put the car into gear. "See how that works?" he said. "It's very easy."

"Yeah," Eddie said. "Thanks for, uh, thanks for taking me out in this. I've never been in a car before."

"You must be wondering about my parents," Winston said, getting right to the point.

Eddie cleared his throat, unsure of what to say.

"Have you ever heard of diplomatic immunity?" Winston asked.

"Not really . . ."

Winston nodded. "And what do you know about the European Union?"

Eddie shrugged. "I know Cylis is the chancellor. I know the merger happened just after the Total War . . ."

"Indeed," Winston said. "And have you ever learned about the politics of that merger?"

Winston was driving now, weaving slowly down the mansion's long driveway.

"No," Eddie said. "Or if I did, I don't remember much . . ."

"Notice how the pedals work on this. See how I only use one foot for both the gas and the brakes?" Winston was driving faster now, having turned onto the highway. He zigzagged between the potholes and the wide cracks in the pavement.

"I, uh . . . yeah. Neat."

"Well, anyway, most countries, they fell in line right away. Everyone was bloody miserable after the war, and Cylis's promise of peace and Unity was more than enough to start the coalition." Winston smiled. "But not the British, though. The United Kingdom wanted nothing to do with Cylis's new deal at first. *Whoops!* Sorry," Winston said quickly as they lurched over a jagged bump in the road.

"No problem," Eddie said, though his knuckles were white as he gripped the door handle beside him.

"My parents were a part of what changed that. A big part. An unpopular part. Hard to believe these days, the way everyone worships him, but back then Cylis had to work hard for his support. It's not an easy thing, you know, bringing so many countries together peacefully. The States were always one country, so Lamson's job was a little less tough over here. But in Europe . . . it took quite a lot of strategy."

"I'd imagine so," Eddie said, unsure of where any of this was going.

"Tell me honestly—have you ever heard of the Rathbone family?" Winston asked.

"No . . ."

"No. I hadn't thought so. Well, had you grown up in the E.U. instead of here, you most certainly would have. The Rathbones are an important political family; have been for generations, leading right up to the Total War."

"Oh," Eddie said. "Neat."

"Now, notice how very little I have to turn the steering wheel in order to change the car's direction. Do you see that?" Winston glanced at Eddie expectantly. And Eddie looked back, trying hard to follow what he felt sure were two separate conversations that Winston was having with him at the same time.

"My father's support for the chancellor was a turning point for Britain, you see," Winston continued. "First Brits to be Marked, my parents were." He shook his head. "It made them none too popular in New London at the time, I can assure you. Their relocation here was a safety precaution back in the day. Though I rather think my parents have come to like having more . . . privacy."

"Well, why'd they do it in the first place?" Eddie asked. "Why support Cylis, if it was so unpopular?"

Winston laughed. "Because Cylis struck them a deal, of course! If they hadn't been the ones to take it, someone else would have. The E.U. was inevitable by that point, and my parents knew it. They figured as long as *someone* was going to reap the rewards of an early endorsement—why not them?

"This dial here will tell you how much gas you have left. That's very important. Do you see it?"

"I see it . . . ," Eddie said, his head spinning.

"I couldn't talk about it back in the house, but every bit of the wealth you've seen in the Rathbone mansion—the building, the food, the clothes, this car . . . all of it is in exchange for my father's support back in the day."

"But isn't it a bit . . . impractical? Living all the way out here?"

"Oh, tremendously! I'm sure Cylis would much rather not be sending his minions out here every other week with supplies and delicacies and what have you . . . but a deal is a deal, and my parents continue to take him up on it."

"*Him?* Wait, Winston, are you saying . . . do you . . . *know* Cylis? Personally?"

"Of course," Winston said. "He's visited many times."

Eddie wasn't even remotely sure anymore how much of this was true. "Sounds . . . nice," he said, finally.

Winston laughed. "But then, my parents . . . they are conflicted people."

"Okay . . . ," Eddie said.

"They never did feel quite right about the whole deal, to tell you the truth. Even the riches couldn't entirely settle their consciences. So they became lifesavers. Secretly, and at great risk to themselves, they turned Cylis's gift into a weapon against him; they turned his mansion into an anchor on the Unmarked River."

"That's . . . very nice of them," Eddie said uneasily.

Winston laughed. "It was," he said. "It was. And then . . ."

"What? What are you getting at?"

Winston slowed the car to a stop. It sat in the middle of the old highway, idling softly. "This conversation never happened, do you understand? If you bring it up, I'll deny it. I need to go on living here once you're gone."

"Um, okay. Sure," Eddie said.

Winston nodded. "I am certain that by now you have noticed my father's missing hand."

Eddie nodded slowly. Winston turned the engine off. He opened the car door.

"Where are you going?" Eddie asked.

"Nowhere. We're switching seats."

Eddie stared at him through the windshield, confused. "Winston—I can't drive."

"Haven't you been paying attention?" Winston said. "I've been teaching you this whole time." He walked around to open the passenger side door and handed Eddie the keys.

"But . . . but . . ."

"Not to worry. By my guess you have until sundown to figure it out."

"Sundown? Why sundown? Winston, I'm . . . I'm not a fast learner," Eddie warned.

Winston only shrugged. "You're going to have to be. Edward. I'm afraid your friends are in grave danger."

ꟼ

Dane, Hailey, and Logan had spent the rest of the day up in the village's radio hut by the tower on the ridge above the valley. Once Hailey had explained the situation to Hans and Tabby, the couple had wasted no time in showing the three of them the way to the station, as well as every last trick of how to broadcast.

It took nearly an hour of trying and listening and wading through weak signals and static—long enough that Mrs. Phoenix was about to sign off—before, finally, Hailey's voice seemed to make it through.

"Mom!" she said, across all those miles. "Mom! Can you hear me? We're okay. We're doing just great. You don't have to worry about us, Mom!"

For a moment, there was silence on the airwaves.

"Is my grandson with you?" Logan's grandmother asked.

"He's here," Hailey said.

"Good," Sonya said. "Tell him he's grounded!"

10

Winston said nothing more about his parents or Eddie's friends on the ride back. "I'd hate to worry you unnecessarily," he said. "There's still a chance that your friends are just fine. Eyes on the road," he added, noticing Eddie's furious stare.

In the end, Eddie did manage to drive the two of them back to the mansion by sundown. But Winston's guess was wrong. Already, no one was there.

"We're too late," he said.

"Too late for what? Winston, what's going on around here?"

Winston was only half paying attention. He dashed from room to room as he spoke. Eddie did his best to follow. "Edward. I'm afraid your group isn't the first to come by since my father lost his hand," he said. "I'm sorry to tell you, but my parents have become a . . . a bit of a trap along the Unmarked River. They take Markless in, fatten them up, give them hope, and then drive the hook straight into their backs."

"*What?* How?" Eddie demanded frantically. "What happens to them?"

"The men arrive. They call themselves Moderators. They take the Rivergoers away. And before they do, they indulge us with each one's stated crime. They sit my parents down, and they describe the impending punishment in awful detail. It's a tradition that began at my parents' request. By now it is simply routine. They force me to listen. They can't imagine why I wouldn't want to hear . . ."

"Why you wouldn't want to hear about what?" Eddie asked, trying to keep up.

"Acheron."

Eddie nearly froze still. *"Acheron?"*

"That's right."

"Have they . . . have they told you much about it?"

Winston laughed. "Every chance they get! That's the whole point! I don't want to hear about it anymore! I can't stand another round of it!"

Eddie swallowed hard.

"How would you like to spend the rest of your life in a pit getting bitten by snakes and lizards?"

"Snakes?" Eddie asked doubtfully. The idea sounded insane.

"That's what they tell me! But that's just a for instance. Acheron's the biggest prison in the world. Inside . . . it seems anything can happen. Torture so unimaginable . . . and it's a life sentence, every time."

"Well, has there never been an escape?"

Winston shook his head. "Can't be done. The whole prison's surrounded by hundred-foot thick walls."

"How is that possible . . . ?" Eddie asked.

Winston threw his hands up in surrender. "I've no idea! This is simply what they tell me! And the worse your crime, the deeper you're sent . . . into those walls . . . those awful tortures . . ."

"But there must be *some* type of entrance . . ."

Winston shook his head. "They brag about that. Say the place is an island. One single entrance so hidden and secure, it might as well be solid brick."

"Really?" Eddie said. "That's *really* it?"

Winston shrugged. "That and the power supply." But very

suddenly, Winston stopped talking. He looked wide-eyed over Eddie's shoulder.

And Eddie turned around.

Mr. Rathbone towered above him.

"Cheers, Eddie. Looking for anyone?"

"What have you done with my friends?" Eddie demanded.

Mr. Rathbone clucked his tongue. "Not to worry," he said. "We've been sure to treat them every bit as respectfully as you Markless have treated me."

"You're a monster!" Eddie said.

But upon hearing this, Mr. Rathbone exploded. "We were *kind* to you beggars! We brought you in! We fed you! For *years*, we were nothing but kind, asking for not one thing in return! We were *sympathizers. Lifesavers.* And how do you people repay us? *You cut off my Mark, hand and all! You take it in my sleep!* And you *run off with it*, to buy—what?—new shoes? A tablet? A *candy* bar?"

"That isn't us!" Eddie protested. "My friends and I—we're not like that."

"*You're all like that!* You're all the same! All of you skinflints! You think we're monsters? *We're* monsters? You people are a parasite on this Union! You should be stomped out like bugs!"

Eddie listened in horror until finally, behind him, Winston had had enough. He stepped forward, handing Eddie the keys to his parents' car . . . and he pounced.

Immediately, Winston and his father were on the floor, rolling around on the polished wood, knocking into ornamental tables, breaking vases, mirrors, clawing, struggling.

"There's only one place left for them to be," Winston gasped between receiving a few punches to the gut. "Outside—check the cellar!" He struggled to hold his father down. *"Run!"*

11

Things were quieter in the Village of the Valley. Logan and Dane sat in the cool grass as the Potomac streamed past. Hailey gathered her things from the house. The wind whistled over the hills. Somewhere in the field, a cricket was chirping.

"I can't believe she grounded me," Logan said.

And Dane laughed. "She did have a point. Your parents probably really are as worried as she made them sound . . ."

Logan frowned. "You ready?" he asked.

The canoe was finished. It was time for the final leg to Beacon.

"I'm not coming," Dane said.

And Logan looked at him, confused. "Of course you are."

"I'm not. I've already talked to Tabby and Hans about it. I'm staying here."

"Dane, you . . . you can't. We need you."

"You need me *here*. I've been thinking about it. I'd be helpful to you here. You know your grandmother's signal won't make it to Beacon. But mine might. Logan, I can be the bridge between you and Hailey and your families. Between you and Hailey and all of New Chicago, for that matter."

Logan shook his head. "Dane, you're not understanding me. I'm not leaving you here."

"Well, then you're either going to have to stay yourself, or you're going to have to drag me. Because I've made up my mind."

Dane sighed. "You and Hailey . . . you're the real team here. I'm just the baggage."

"You are not *baggage*, Dane. You're my oldest friend!"

"And I'll still be your oldest friend, Logan. Hailey's too. I don't need to travel to Beacon to be that."

"Dane. There has to be a better solution than just leaving you stranded here . . ."

Dane looked up, craning his head back. He took a deep breath, and a little cloud of condensation puffed out from his mouth.

"I like it here, Logan. Haven't you liked it here too?"

"Well . . . I mean, sure, but . . ."

"But you have a sister to save. I know." Dane frowned. "I don't, though." He gazed at the dark night sky, cloudy and cool. "Instead I have my friends—Logan, Hailey, and the Dust. And as I see it, staying here is the best way for me to help them. What if Peck and the rest of the gang are listening in somewhere? What if you need your grandmother's help down the line? Logan, this mission you're on . . . you need all the help you can get. We proved today that this valley's radio station is a unique advantage. And I think I can make a real difference with it."

"I can't agree to this, Dane."

"You don't have to. You and Hailey . . . you have a good thing going, and it's calling you to Beacon. Let me help you in the best way that I can.

"This was the Hayeses' vision. We owe it to them to see that vision through. I can do more good here than I can as a third wheel to you and Hailey." He frowned now, looking down at his feet. "Just . . . make sure to take care of her, will ya?"

Logan laughed. "She doesn't need taking care of, and you know it. She needs less taking care of than any of us."

Dane smiled. "You're probably right. In that case, I guess . . . make sure she takes care of you."

Hailey was waiting in the front of the canoe. "Where's Dane?" she asked.

Logan hopped into the back, picking up a paddle. "He's not coming."

"What do you mean, 'he's not coming'?"

Logan pushed off, paddling hard into the current, sad, frustrated, but resolved.

"I'll explain on the way. Come on," he said. "Lily's waiting."

12

Eddie saw the cellar door just outside, locked shut. There was banging from inside.

It took the biggest rock he could find to smash the lock, but the moment he did, the Dust came pouring out.

"Eddie!" Tyler yelled. "It's not safe here!"

"Yeah—I gathered that!" Eddie said, and he led them over to the Rathbones' car.

"Okay," Eddie said as the rest of them piled into the back and into the passenger seat. "Everyone just stay calm. I know all about how to use these things."

"Is that right?" Peck said.

"Well. Yeah, for the most part," Eddie said nervously. In the rearview mirror, he could see Mr. and Mrs. Rathbone pushing through the front door past their son.

Eddie turned the key in the ignition, and he checked the gas gauge, just like Winston had taught him to do.

Eddie smiled. It was nearly full.

13

Two nights and two days on the Potomac was a quiet ride without Dane. But they had made it. The Potomac let out straight into the Atlantic (Chesapeake Bay had long since been lost to the rising tide), and Logan and Erin sat now, bobbing on the ocean's waves, staring into the distance at Beacon City.

They could not arrive by boat. They knew that much. They could not risk such a high-profile entrance.

So instead they sat, and they braced themselves.

"You ready?" Logan asked.

"I'm ready."

And the two of them stood up, leaning hard to the left. The canoe tilted dangerously beneath them, the lip of it just kissing the ocean's surface. And then that surface broke. Water rushed into the boat, flowing over the edge, filling the bottom and submerging Logan's and Hailey's feet. They leaned harder now, until one whole side of the boat was hidden under the cover of ocean. And soon the front tip disappeared. And then the back.

The canoe sank beneath them. One last pocket of air bubbled to the surface, and it was gone.

"Well," Logan said, treading water and already shivering. "No time to lose."

And he and Hailey swam toward the horizon.

Toward Beacon. The capital. The city on the hill.

EIGHT

CITY ON THE HILL

1

THE FIRST THING ERIN NOTICED WHEN SHE arrived at her old Beacon apartment was the smell of home.

The pictures were all the same. The furniture hadn't moved. The white rug felt just as it always had against her feet.

But her father stepped in behind her and there was no "Honey, I'm home!"

Her mom appeared on the threshold of the kitchen and there was no "Oh, how I've missed you!"

Instead, there was the *thud* of suitcases hitting the floor and the gurgle of water boiling in the kitchen. That was all. And in that way, Erin's old apartment was *very* different from how she remembered it.

"You're late. Dinner's ready," Erin's mom said, sounding almost bored by their return, as if this were any other day. But she did come forward to hug and kiss her daughter, and then she turned and looked at her husband, nodding once. He nodded back. And Dr. Arbitor returned to the kitchen.

For months, Erin had imagined this moment—her first meal at home among a family reunited. She'd imagined the laughter, the storytelling, the warmth and smiles.

She'd imagined her father saying, "I'm sorry, so sorry, for taking that awful job in Spokie; I'm sorry for pulling our family apart; a mistake, entirely; a lapse in judgment; thank Cylis we're back together and it'll never happen again."

She'd imagined her mother saying, "It's my fault, dear; it's my fault too. Too many late nights, too many trips overseas, too many hours spent away from what's really important: from my wonderful family."

She'd imagined both of them turning to Erin and saying, "Thank you, Erin. Thank you for bringing us back together."

Instead, the food on the table was lukewarm and undercooked. The macaroni was crunchy. The cheese sauce was cold, chunky, pulled from the refrigerator and not reheated. The drink was tomato juice, watered down.

"I haven't been eating at home," Dr. Arbitor said, explaining such a plain dinner but hardly apologizing for it. "We're really not set up here for the three of us right now. You can go shopping tomorrow, can't you, Charles?"

Mr. Arbitor laid his fork down and smiled an empty smile. "Of course," he said. "I won't have anything else to do, what with my demotion and all. Come to think of it, they probably don't need me over there at the office at all anymore, do they?"

Dr. Arbitor shrugged. "I didn't say that," she said. But that was all she said.

"Erin, would you like me to throw your plate in the microwave?" Mr. Arbitor asked. He looked at his wife out of the corner of his eye. "Mine's already cold."

"I'm fine," Erin said.

"She has school tomorrow at 8:15. I'll need to be at work; can you get her up?" Dr. Arbitor asked.

"I can get myself up," Erin said.

"She's going to be behind in her classes as it is, given the sub-par education she's been getting in Spokie," her mother continued, as if Erin weren't in the room. "So the least you can do is make sure she arrives on time."

"I'll see to it, dear," Mr. Arbitor said. He stood up to heat his own dinner in the microwave.

Dr. Arbitor rolled her eyes.

And Erin pretended to sneeze, so that neither of them would think twice about it when she began sniffling, or when she went to wipe her eyes on her napkin.

She pretended to sneeze a second time.

No one said, "*Gesundheit.*"

2

After dinner, Erin sat on her bed with the door closed, dazed and still hungry. Her room was bare and she kept the light off, and nothing about the space was as she remembered it. With so many of her things still packed in boxes, Erin hardly even recognized the room as her own. Its size looked different. Its walls were blank. Its dresser was empty . . . .

She recognized that view, though.

The apartment was seventy-eight stories high; about halfway up the building. Out the window, two stories above, was the third layer of Beacon's multitiered road-and-sidewalk grid, and taxis and electrobuses whizzed by like the pumping of the city's blood.

Erin observed the swath of apartments opposite hers, some with their lights on and their blinds open. Erin could see one girl in a distant window five stories below, studying at her desk. Erin recognized that girl. She'd watched her study every night for years and years.

Beyond the apartments across the street, hundreds more buildings stood, poking up into the sky with neither tops nor bottoms visible through such an elaborate suspended network of streets and elevators and ramps and bustle.

And beyond all of *that* was the ocean. From this distance, its waves looked still, frozen in time, same as they ever were.

She'd thrown away everything she had in order to make it back to Beacon. She'd put it all on the line, and she'd succeeded. Her dad was right—she *had* gotten her way.

Her parents resented her for it.

And the city was indifferent.

∃

Down in the Water District, Logan and Hailey walked swiftly across the piers and pathways connecting skyscrapers that rose straight up out of the ocean. They tried their best to blend in, but it was tough since they were soaked to the bone—and sorely out of place. All around them Beaconers rushed by, heads down, casually ignoring the crowds and bright lights and the waves crashing below, but to Logan it was mesmerizing.

"Erin told me that outer Beacon refused to move when the ocean rose," Logan said. "But I never expected it to be this beautiful."

Hailey nodded, gazing up. "It's incredible."

Eventually the two of them made it onto the district's main boardwalk, and Logan and Hailey felt as though they couldn't possibly see enough of it at once. Street vendors offering food Logan had never heard of and souvenirs unlike anything he'd ever seen; Markless performers playing music and dancing and telling jokes and doing tricks; countless smaller side bridges jutting off the main drag; a steady line of water taxis crossing the waves below . . .

Ten blocks ahead, the boardwalk sloped up, running into City Center and rising sharply with the gradient of the mount. When he saw it, Logan stopped short, overcome suddenly by the gravity of what he was here to do.

"Well, what are you waiting for?" Hailey asked. She put a hand on his shoulder. "We here to sightsee, or are we here to find your sister?" She pushed him playfully toward the hill.

The two of them didn't look back after that.

4

In her apartment just up the hill, Erin Arbitor tried desperately to drown out the sound of her parents' ongoing argument. She'd come home to a nightmare. And the only escape was Erin's belief that with just a little more digging, she'd find the path back to Logan.

Erin had her earphones on and her music at full volume as

she typed furiously across the surface of her tablet, sitting cross-legged on her bed, delving deep into the files of DOME's servers with the help of a new worm she'd programmed just that night.

On a plastiscreen by her side, Erin kept her picture displayed—the one she'd taken of Mr. Cheswick's top-secret page. Every few minutes, she'd look back at it, scrutinizing each line, down to the finest details.

Project Trumpet. IMPS. Acheron. It was all a part of the same vast secret. She had scratched the surface. But it was time to dig a little deeper.

Find the connections, find Lily. Find Lily . . . find Logan.

There, buried deep in cyberspace, was a short routing index of a single troop of IMPS, corresponding precisely with the dates on Cheswick's page.

Nothing too useful about a routing index . . .

Except.

There. The first and last stops. The coordinates of the IMPS . . .

They were right here in Beacon.

First and last stops.

Home base.

Could this really mean . . . ?

Yes. It must.

Acheron is at those coordinates.

Logan's destination . . . all along . . . has been just a few blocks from my house.

She had to get outside. *Now.* To be on the front lines. To make her way to Acheron. She couldn't do it from a computer. She couldn't do it from her bedroom. So Erin folded the tablet and stuck it in her pocket. She opened her door and braced herself. She stepped into the hallway.

The argument was louder than ever.

"*Look.* I don't want this any more than you do. You think I *like* coming back here like this? In this way? You think I don't *know* that this wasn't part of our deal? Things *change*, all right? Stuff goes wrong. So can't we at least *try* to make this work? For Erin's sake? Please? I'm not asking for much here . . ."

"*You're* not asking for much? *I'm* not asking for anything! I shouldn't *have* to ask for the same basic respect I give to you! You're the one who told me to give up everything I've been working toward my whole life, right at the time I was needed the most! This G.U. merge is happening *now*, Charles! I should be in Europe tonight! Not *here*, arguing with *you*—"

Erin shivered, hearing her parents talk like that. She shook her head violently, as if to shake the words right out of her skull.

Forget about them, she thought. *You're on a mission now. You're finding Acheron. You're finding Logan. So just forget about all this for now.*

"I'm going out," Erin called. Her parents went silent for a second.

"Okay, honey," her mom said weakly.

And Erin was gone.

5

Logan and Hailey had made it up the hill, all the way into City Center. They held hands so as not to get separated, but the crowd wasn't the only thing contributing to Logan's and Hailey's sensory overload; the lights and sounds were overwhelming after so many years spent in the quiet town of Spokie.

On the sides of each building, from the ground floor to as

high as Logan could see, were advertisements—bright, flashing, skyscraper-sized screens, demanding that A.U. citizens buy the newest tablet or rollerstick or soyshake . . . compelling them to vote for so-and-so or such-and-such in the upcoming spring elections . . .

And in the midst of it, hundred-foot-tall projections of Cylis walked from one skyscraper to another, superimposed on top of all of the other ads, each building coming together to make a citywide video screen just for him, so the chancellor could address everyone all at once, and speak "one-on-one" about the myriad advantages of the Global Union merger.

Still other buildings displayed bar graphs showing which stocks on Barrier Street were rising and which were falling. And those buildings even seemed to have Markscans where they met the roads, so that anyone who wanted to could walk right up and buy or sell or trade stock as they watched the graphs shift in ten-foot increments overhead.

Standing in the midst of it, Logan found himself longing to share this with Erin. It should have been their moment, really, but nothing had worked out as planned. And Logan was past believing it ever would.

No substitute would replace her. Not ever, he knew.

"It's amazing," Hailey said, pulling him back down to earth.

"Almost too amazing," Logan replied.

Above them, a grid of streets and walkways five layers thick stretched up into the sky, connecting buildings at their fortieth, eightieth, one hundred twentieth, one hundred sixtieth, and two hundredth floor entrances, though only a handful of skyscrapers actually rose quite that high, and the network of streets in the grid thinned substantially in its upper two layers.

"We can't possibly see it all," Hailey said. "How do we even begin to look for a place like Acheron in all of this chaos?"

"I don't know," Logan said. And from a hundred feet up, that skyscraper-sized projection of Cylis looked down at Logan, and it laughed.

ᄂ

Erin exited her apartment building on the eightieth floor, onto the third-tier sidewalk of the Beacon grid, and for all her loneliness, it did feel good to be home. The crowded streets, the angry, late pedestrians, the endless line of cabs and electrobuses, the fast-moving sidewalk treads, the lights so bright you had to squint when you came out, even at night. . . . This was where she was meant to be.

And yet what Erin was about to do was as far outside her comfort zone as anything she'd ever dreamed of.

She had to bite the bullet. She had to ask a beggar for help.

For a while, Erin walked along that third-tier level, looking for misers on the street, anyone she could walk up and talk to. But this was delaying the inevitable, and she knew it—the real Markless kept to the lowest levels. If she was going to do this, she had to descend.

It took her nearly a dozen tries to find a Markless that would even so much as look at her, but Erin was determined not to give up.

As she strolled along the ground level of the Beacon grid,

Markless were scattered all about. But some part of Erin knew that this couldn't be the whole story. With the street cleanings DOME so routinely did each night, there simply had to be somewhere else for them to go. Somewhere they could hide. Together. Out of sight. In Beacon's shadow.

As she walked, Erin eyed a woman sleeping on the ground with a dog. The woman had covered herself with a sign that read, "Don't need your money. Don't want your pity. The meek shall inherit the earth. Matthew 5:5."

Up ahead, a man weaved in and out of the throngs of Beaconers, juggling trash and dancing a bit and singing some pre-Unity song, "When the Saints Go Marching In."

He's gonna get himself shot, Erin thought, *singing an exclusioner song like that right out in the open*. But to Erin's surprise, no one seemed to mind. In fact, every time the man sang a lyric, any Markless in earshot would sing it back to him, creating an informal chorus of call and response.

Had it always been this way? To Erin's memory, Beacon's Markless were nothing but scoundrels—filthy, begging, crazy, and dangerous. Had they always been so . . . harmless?

"I don't understand," Erin said, stopping the juggling man in his tracks. "Are you begging, or what?"

The man stopped in front of her, but he continued juggling his trash as he spoke. "Not begging, ma'am." He smiled. "Singing. Do you know the tune?"

"No . . . ," Erin said.

So the man walked on, shaking his head. "Oh, when the trumpet," he sang, "sounds its call! Oh, when the trumpet sounds its call! Lord, how I want to be in that number—when the trumpet sounds its call!"

It took a couple more encounters like this before Erin realized she needed a new strategy. She *had* to get one of these tightwads to talk. She needed their help if her plan was going to work, and to get that, she needed a way in.

So Erin bought a tempeh sandwich from a street vendor, swiping her Mark at the cart's scanner, as an offering for the next beggar she found.

But even that, it turned out, wasn't enough to strike up a worthwhile conversation. When she approached a kid a few minutes later, holding the sandwich out and saying, "It's yours, really—take it!" the kid just scoffed at her and ran away along the sidewalk treads.

Her entire childhood, Erin had grown up fearing these people, resenting them, thinking they wanted nothing more than to have what she had, than to be who she was.

Tonight, for the first time, it occurred to Erin that maybe they were who they were by choice, that maybe they saw her and her shiny Mark with the same mix of pity and contempt she'd always felt toward them.

It was a disorienting thought, on top of the head-spinning display of lights and sounds and advertisements all around her. After the months she's spent in quiet Spokie, the whole place felt a little to her now like a run-down funhouse—bizarre, distorted, dirty, and fake.

And then, down the block, at the corner under the shelter of some scaffolding, one Unmarked teenager caught Erin's eye. He sat hunched over a tablet, quietly typing away in a trance of intense concentration. *How did a Markless like him get his hands on a tablet?* Erin wondered.

"Whatcha doin' there?" Erin asked, standing over him and looking down.

"Nothing to you, Marky."

Erin laughed, and she leaned over to peek at his tablet screen.

"Looks to me like you're programming . . ."

The boy looked up, clearly annoyed to be disturbed. "You here for a favor?"

"A . . . what?" Erin asked.

"Someone recommend you?"

"N-no . . . ," Erin said. "Should they have?"

"You're darn right they should have. Got any transactions that need deleting?"

"*Huh?*"

"Transactions. Markscans." He pointed to her wrist. "Got any you need forgotten?"

Erin hadn't the slightest idea what this boy was talking about, so she decided to take a more direct approach.

"I'm Erin," she said. "I'm looking for help."

"Then you came to the right place. Shawn." And Shawn held up his Markless hand.

Erin shook it hesitantly.

"They call me the Tech Wiz."

"Oh really?"

Shawn nodded.

"So what's a Markless like you doing with a tablet?"

"Can't be the Tech Wiz without one." Shawn shrugged.

"And as a 'tech wiz' you are . . . ?"

Shawn smirked. "Providing my services. And it's not *a* tech wiz—it's *the* Tech Wiz. The one and only."

Suddenly a Beaconer stormed up to the two of them. "Hey! Tech Wiz! What's she got to do with our deal?" he whispered harshly.

"Chill out, man. It's done. We're cool. You're set."

The man glanced around uneasily. "How will I know it worked?"

"You'll know 'cause you'll never get caught, that's how."

Shifting on his feet, the man shot an uncomfortable look in Erin's direction but finally nodded to Shawn. "Fine. But if you're lying to me——"

"Man, how could I be the Tech Wiz if I went around lying to people? You trust the man who sent you here or not?"

"Yeah, sure I do——he says you're the best."

"Then I *am* the best," Shawn said. "So you got your end of the deal or not?"

The man handed Shawn a rollerstick, and Shawn handed him the tablet. "Thanks," the man said. "I owe you one." And he ran off without looking back.

Erin sat down beside Shawn now, making no attempt to hide her interest. A Markless hacker? It was too good to be true. "Okay," she said. "What in the *world* just happened here?"

Shawn smiled. "The Tech Wiz provides a very special service," Shawn said. "For a price, the Tech Wiz can wipe a Marked slate totally clean."

"What are you talking about?"

"Look," Shawn said. "What's the real purpose of a Mark, huh? From DOME's point of view, I'm speaking."

Erin shrugged. "To separate upstanding citizens like me from riffraff like you?"

"EEEH——*wrong!* Erin Ms. Marky, thank you for playing . . ." Shawn made a little bow to her, like the host of a talk show, and he waved her along.

"Hey, wait——seriously." Erin laughed. "I wanna know!"

"Listen, if *that's* all DOME wanted to do, they wouldn't go through the trouble of giving each person his own unique Mark." He picked up Erin's hand, and pointed to the tiny numbers in the lines of her tattoo. "No. No—the *point* of the Mark is that *with* it, DOME knows everything about you. *Think* about it. Every time someone buys a sandwich, what do they do? They scan their Mark. Every time someone enters a building, what do they do? They scan their Mark. Every time someone goes to the doctor, or approves a document, or gets on a Metrorail, or goes to a sports game, what do they do? *They scan their Mark.*

"It's all digital. And all those little scans—everyone's scans— they go straight into DOME's network, where they're logged forever. If you're Marked, DOME doesn't just know you're a citizen—they know what kinds of food you like, they know how you get to work each day, they know what kinds of movies you watch, what kinds of prescriptions you're on, where you've been, where you're likely to go next . . . for all intents and purposes, they know *everything* about you.

"It's control. The Mark is control. Over *you*. Does DOME invoke it much? Maybe not yet. But they could. And they will when it's useful to them. So of *course* DOME wants everyone to be Marked. To be Unmarked is to be off the grid! To be free!" He held up his own Unmarked wrists and smiled gleefully.

"Okay, yeah. I get it," Erin said. "But what does that have to do with whatever just happened here?"

Shawn smiled. "Whoever that guy was—he's done some things with that Mark of his—some things that, let's just say, he'd just as soon Cylis not know about. Maybe he . . . skipped work to go to a pro hover-dodge game. Maybe he did some stuff to help a Markless family member. Whatever it was, *my* job is to hack into

DOME's Marked network, and delete a few eensy-beensy little boxes in a database. Just here and there. On the dates this guy gave me.

"Then he loans me his tablet, I work my magic, and bada-boom, bada-bing: Mr. Marky Mark here's scot-free. DOME won't come looking; no one else'll come asking . . . Mr. Mark can sleep easy again."

"And for this he gave you a rollerstick?"

"Hey, look—if you're good at something, charge what you're worth. I start my fees high, and I raise them from there." He looked over at the rollerstick. "I don't even want this stupid thing. But it never hurts to have a commodity. A rollerstick like this'll barter for quite a fair price in the sublevel, once I crack the Mark lock."

"Hold up," Erin said. "Sublevel?"

"Yeah." Shawn nodded. "What about it?"

Erin frowned. "I don't know what that is."

Shawn looked at her as though she must have been messing with him. "Wait a minute . . . you're not kidding? You really don't know what I'm talking about? *Really?*" Erin shrugged, and Shawn exhaled powerfully in his disbelief. "It's where I live! Where you'd live too if you'd had enough sense to skip your Pledge."

Erin smiled. "I think you're talking about just the place I'm looking for," she said.

"*You?*" Shawn laughed. "No way. *No way!* Nuh-uh. Not a chance."

"Come on," Erin said. "Just point me in the right direction."

"Nope. No, siree. No, no."

Erin sat for a minute in the shadow of the advertisement lights. Finally, she turned to Shawn. "Must get pretty annoying, having to borrow tablets all the time from the people you're helping. Bet you sure could do a lot with one of those things if you had one all to yourself."

"You better believe I could," Shawn said. "But there's not a Marked in the city willing to barter one o' those." He laughed. "I'd have to find me a *felon* to get someone desperate enough to spend that kinda credit on a simple hack-erase."

Erin looked at him, smirking just a little. Then she pulled her own tablet out of her pocket.

"Take me to the sublevel," she said. "And it's yours to keep."

⌐

That night in Spokie, Michael Cheswick sat at his desk for a long time, not doing much of anything. He would have stared out the all-glass walls of his office, but it was too dark to see.

He would have shuffled documents or gotten a head start on this week's agent assignments, but he just didn't have it in him.

He knew what he had to do.

There was no avoiding it.

But he stared at that call button without pressing it for a long, long time.

🗗

A full week had passed since Logan and Hailey first set foot in Beacon. They slept in gutters each night, scrounged for food each day . . .

And they'd made no progress whatsoever in finding Acheron.

With hands hidden, they'd snuck all around City Center by this point, but nothing anywhere had suggested even the *existence* of a Markless prison, let alone the location of one.

"Maybe we should just get ourselves arrested," Hailey suggested at one point, exasperated. "Quick—steal something. We'll be in Acheron by morning."

"No," Logan said, refusing to find either the wisdom or the humor in it. "I had that option once already. It wasn't a good idea then and it isn't a good idea now. We enter Acheron on our own terms, or we'll never make it out."

"I'm just saying . . ." Hailey smirked. She and Logan stood now at the edge of the grid's fifth-tier sidewalk, looking out over the whole city. It was a bit darker up here since not as many buildings and wall advertisements made it up this high, and it was less crowded too. The air was thin and cold.

"It really is a beautiful place," she said. They could see for miles in all directions. An ocean on one side, colliding gracefully with the bridges and skyscrapers of the Water District; a vast urban sprawl on the other, sloping down past City Center, to the outer districts that lay with their shorter buildings all the way to the horizon. Little dots of light twinkled in the distance, and Hailey imagined each one as a window into a cozy home with a happy family.

"Maybe it isn't in City Center after all," Hailey said. "Maybe it's out in the lower districts, off the hill."

But Logan shook his head. "With all the stories we've heard? Of all those different types of punishments? Enormous tar pits? Huge rooms to walk around in, blind? No way this place is small enough not to be a skyscraper. And the skyscrapers are all on the hill."

"But we've *checked* these buildings . . ."

"We haven't checked all of them."

"Logan, you can't *hide* a skyscraper. They're *tall*. Face it: if a place as big as Acheron were on this hill, people would know about it. We could *see* it. It would have bars on it, fences around it, guards . . . I mean, you're telling me Beacon houses the highest-security prison in the world, and we can't find even one building with barred entrances or more than a couple sleepy guards? How would that even work? They just ask all their prisoners really nicely that it sure would be great if they didn't sneak out?"

"I don't know," Logan said. "If I knew, we'd have found it by now."

"Look, whatever," Hailey said. She slumped down against the railing of the dizzyingly high sidewalk and pulled her foxhole radio out from her jacket pocket. "Wanna listen with me?"

"Sure," Logan said. He sat down too, taking one of the earphones from her. They sat close, shoulder to shoulder, listening in.

"Good evening to all you Markless out there in the greater Beacon area. This is Dane-o-rino, comin' to you live at thirty-nine hundred kilohertz. The only station bringing you chart-topper after chart-topper of the Boxing Gloves' greatest hits—performed by yours truly, raw and unplugged."

"He is such a dork," Hailey said.

"Actually . . ." Dane cleared his throat. "We're the only station bringing you anything at all. So don't go away—because you can't!" He laughed. "Anyway, this next song's called 'Comet,' and it goes out to a special girl whose mom just wanted me to say she's thinking of you . . . and she hopes you're doing all right. Wherever you are."

And then, between bouts of static over those weak, shortwave airwaves, Dane strummed a few chords on Tabitha's guitar. And he began to sing.

Logan chuckled, listening to it. And he felt Hailey's shoulder moving up and down, too, so he looked over at her to laugh about it. Except Hailey wasn't laughing.

She was crying.

"Hey," Logan said. "Hey—it's okay. It's all right. Really."

"It isn't all right," Hailey said. "We're lost in a city with no one to help us. We have no idea how to find what we're looking for. I've given up my family, my school, my friends. . . . Logan. What were we thinking?"

Dane's strumming played on in the earphones. He paused to perform a griptone solo.

"Let me read you something," Logan said. He pulled out of his pocket the Bible Bridget had given him back at the underpass, which seemed like a lifetime ago now. "I've been reading this," he said. "A friend told me it was one of the more dangerous ones to keep on me, so . . . I figured there must be some good stuff in it." He smiled.

"What's it about?" Hailey asked.

"I'm not sure yet. Everything, it seems. But listen to this, from a chapter called Ecclesiastes." Logan read from it now. "Wisdom is a shelter as money is a shelter, but the advantage of knowledge is this: Wisdom preserves those who have it. . . . Wisdom makes one wise person more powerful than ten rulers in a city." Logan laid the book on his lap. "You and I? We're broke. We certainly don't have shelter. But Peck's told us all along—what we're really after out here is knowledge. It's not supposed to be a quick fix. It's supposed to be something we have to work for.

"You wanna know why I think this book was banned? Because it's *filled* with stories of people who took the hard path. People who risked everything to fight for what they knew was right. People who died for what they believed in. Just like Peck is always saying." He grew excited now, flipping through the pages.

"Hailey—maybe the *reason* Cylis and Lamson are scared for us to talk about pre-Unity history and religion in this country is because history and religion are true and *inspiring*! They show us that people can stand up for something real. They give us something to believe in. These stories really happened and they remind us that it's okay if we're not here right now to finish everything. Because we're *definitely* here to start something. *Big.* And maybe that's enough. Things weren't always like this. We have to start making it right."

He held Hailey's hand, and the two of them looked out over the sidewalk's railing, out to the city below, out past the hill, to the dark horizon, with its twinkling lights that bled right into the stars of the sky. Dane's music played on in their ears, and Hailey still cried, though her tears grew gentle and calm.

Somehow, in that moment, Logan knew. That he would find Lily. That he would find her soon.

9

It was late in the evening when Logan and Hailey were awoken from their sleep against the sidewalk railing, earphones still in, heads drooping, legs stretched out across the pavement . . .

"Street cleaning!" a Markless whispered as he ran by. "*Street cleaning!*" And he tapped Logan and Hailey's feet as he passed.

The pair stood quickly, Hailey grabbing her radio and Logan his book.

"Come on," the Markless called, several paces beyond them now, heading toward the grid-system elevator. "Not safe up here."

So Logan and Hailey followed, hoping that this stranger knew what he was doing.

The three of them made their way onto the elevator just as the doors were closing. They made the two-hundred-story descent in silence, crammed in with a mob of Marked Beaconers, hoping not to draw too much attention to themselves.

When the elevator doors opened at the ground level stop, the man they'd followed slipped quickly through the crowd and into the busy streets.

Logan and Hailey ran after him, trying not to think about how much danger they might be in. DOME didn't have its eye out for them here the way it did in New Chicago, but that didn't mean they'd likely survive a sweeping.

The man led them far past the main streets and deep into the dark side alleys of City Center's edges. *"Hurry,"* he whispered, propping open a door with an "Employees Only" sticker on it and waving frantically for Logan and Hailey to catch up. Beyond the chain-link fence at the end of the street, the hill dropped off sharply, and for the briefest moment, Logan paused, absorbing the view. He could just barely make out the tops of the Water District buildings below, where the ocean met the sky at the horizon, and he whispered, "It's still beautiful" just before Hailey yanked him hard through the open door.

10

The man ahead of them gave no explanation of where they were going; it was as if he assumed they already knew.

They traveled through the cold, metal hallways of the building's back entrance, down a silver, grated stairway and into a dark basement, well beyond the dim light from above, well into the thick black of a tunnel. Logan walked with one hand tracing the wall, using touch as his sight, while all around him, a faint, ominous hum filled the air.

Finally, the three of them made it to another door; when the man opened it, a soft light and a blast of air flooded the tunnel. They entered, and descended further.

"What is this place?" Hailey whispered.

But as soon as she said it, it was clear. The stairs led to a steel mesh catwalk, fifty feet or so above a cavernous industrial space with concrete walls, tile floors, and enormous padded tubes running along the floor. Emergency work lights lit the room with a red glow that bounced softly from the hard, cold surfaces.

"We've learned about these," Logan whispered. "In science class." He pointed. "It's a turbine room. We're inside of a nuclear reactor."

Hailey nodded. But there were a few differences between the nuclear reactors Logan learned about in school and the nuclear reactor before them now: this one didn't seem to be turned on. And this one was *filled* with Markless. Thousands of them milled about in the arena-sized space, huddling in clusters. "Logan," Hailey said. "He's brought us to the heart of Beacon's Markless community."

"The capital." Logan laughed. "We finally get to see the capital."

Logan and Hailey had never seen anything like it. They'd never even *heard* of anything like it.

"Someone down here *has* to know about Acheron," Hailey said excitedly. "They just have to!"

"I don't know," Logan said. "But we're certainly closer than we've ever been before."

Logan and Hailey walked wide-eyed around the space, through the rows marked carefully by tape sectioning off parts of the floor. This section for one huddle, that section for another . . .

And yet something about the community was amiss. All around them, Hailey and Logan heard murmurs and whispers. Markless children ran by, adults pushed past, breaking the boundaries of the space that they themselves had set. Everyone was headed toward a corner of the room, just out of sight.

What's going on? Logan wondered. And he followed the flow.

A crowd was gathered in a little alcove sectioned off by the tubes. As Logan neared it, he heard a voice ringing out across the space.

It was a voice Logan knew.

He pushed his way up toward the front of the crowd, just past the turbine, pulling Hailey by the hand through the assembly of Markless.

There, in the middle, speaking on behalf of the huddle of Dust that stood behind him, was Peck.

NINE

BEACON'S SHADOW

1

INALLY.

The Dust was together again.

"Leadership suits you," Logan told Peck as the rest of the Dust gathered around. "Seems wherever you go, people can't wait to follow."

"Let's hope so." Peck smiled. "Anyway, I've had a few days to get them riled up."

"Riled up?" Logan asked.

The crowd had broken up after Logan's and Hailey's entrance—had cheered and whooped and hollered at the Dust's reunion—but had tactfully respected their privacy after a few moments' celebration.

"They seemed to expect us," Hailey said uneasily. "Peck . . . what have you told them?"

Peck shrugged. "Everything. We knew you'd come. And even if you didn't, we knew we'd need their help if we're going to find Acheron. We can't do it on our own."

"Tell me about it," Logan replied. "Hailey and I have been

trying all week. We've looked into everything we could find on every major building in City Center—there's no sign at all of a prison."

Peck nodded. "So far, Markless here don't know anything about it either. But I've told them our mission. And they're willing to help."

"Peck wants a coordinated citywide search tomorrow," Blake said. "Spent most of the evening rallying the troops down here."

"They're on board," Peck said. "They're eager to help."

Logan was shocked. "That's amazing, Peck! We're really doing it!"

Peck smiled. "We really are, my friend. We really are." He put his hand on Logan's shoulder. "Come. Let's walk. This is your new home. And I'd like to show you around."

The Markless community inside that turbine room was everything Logan had come to appreciate about the underpass he'd found in New Chicago—except bigger, more organized, and more astounding. Peck led him around the space, explaining what he'd learned about it during his time there so far.

"During the States War, when Beacon was first constructed, after the rupturing of the dam, this fission reactor was built to power what General Lamson knew would become his capital. It would remain the source of the city's power for three years—right up until the war was won, when the United States became the American Union once and for all.

"At that point," Peck continued. "This reactor was shut down, its doors closed permanently."

"Why?" Logan asked. "Didn't they still need the power?"

"No," Peck said. "They needed *more*. And so, right next to us, Lamson built a second reactor—a *fusion* reactor, capable of putting out *far* more energy than the defunct fission reactor we're standing in now."

Logan and Peck walked to the old, abandoned fission control room, gazing through the pane of glass that separated them from the computer-automated clean room that ran the fusion reactor next door.

"So why the sudden rise in energy consumption? Had Beacon really grown that much with the formation of the A.U.?"

Peck shook his head. "No. That's the whole point. It hadn't."

"I don't understand," Logan said.

"No one does." But Peck smiled. "Except . . . I have a hunch."

Suddenly Logan's eyes went wide with understanding.

"Acheron," he said. "Lamson needed the extra power for Acheron!"

Peck nodded. "Bingo."

The two of them walked back from the control room into the main area filled with the Markless community.

"There are many huddles in this space, Logan. Many people, each with fascinating stories of where they came from and how they got here." Peck stopped and looked Logan in the eyes. "They all want to help you find your sister. We're in this together. And check this out"—Peck pointed toward an area across the room—"That quadrant you see there? That's a Markless school," Peck said.

"School?"

"You bet. They've started their own." Peck chuckled, looking down at his feet, hands resting behind his back. "I've insisted the Dust begin attending first thing. Rusty, Tyler, Eddie, Meg—they all begin tomorrow. Even Blake will be taking some classes here and there, part-time."

"I bet they were thrilled about that," Logan said, shaking his head and feeling rather sorry for whoever would become Tyler and Eddie's new teacher.

And now Peck grinned. "When this thing with Lily is over . . . if we make it out alive . . . I'd like you to join that school too."

Logan laughed. "Really?" he said.

"Really.

"It's a deal." Logan nodded. And they shook on it.

"I noticed the book you're carrying in your pocket," Peck said. "So I figure you'll be interested in that area over there too."

"What is it?" Logan asked.

"A church."

"A . . ."

"Church." Peck laughed. "Don't look so surprised. You do realize there was a time when every community had one, right?"

"I guess so . . . ," Logan said.

"I mean, not since the Inclusion, of course. 'No god above Cylis'—that's the whole point. But underground . . . underground is a different story."

"Isn't that still kinda dangerous, though?" Logan asked, fingering the tattered old cover and the whisper-thin pages of the book in his pocket. "I mean, it's one thing to have a Christian book lying around, but to actually get caught with a real, Christian church down here—"

Peck's laugher interrupted him. "A Christian book? Logan, that's not *a* Christian book you're holding. That's *the* Christian book. It's the *Bible*—"

"Well, I know it's the—"

"The entire religion is based on it! It's all in there—the whole history of God and His promises to His followers.

"There is a God, Logan—just one—and all of this is part of His plan. He loves us. He wants a lot better for us than this. And all of those promises are in the Bible. Promises you can depend on." Peck's face was growing animated now. "It seriously doesn't get more Christian than that."

Logan laughed. "You've thought a lot about this."

"Oh, please—my life's work is thinking about things DOME doesn't want me thinking about. I've been reading that book for years! I'll tell you all I know, and I bet there are Markless down here who know a lot more about it than me."

"So, what, then? Now that we're here, we're gonna start going to church? As if we're not taking enough risks these days already?"

Peck clapped Logan on the back. "Believe me, Logan. It'd be hard for you or me to be in more trouble with Lamson and Cylis than we already are. We might as well do what we want."

"I guess that's true," Logan said.

"Just look around. It may not seem like it, but this space you're seeing—it's *freedom*. Concrete walls and all." He nodded. "You can think, believe, and speak just as you choose."

"It's a growing thing, then, isn't it?" Logan said. "This Christian movement."

Peck frowned. "Look. Everyone has his own reason for going Markless. Plenty of people down here laugh at the Christians. But there's a good bit of us who take this stuff very seriously. Just like they used to, pre-Unity."

Logan nodded. He was a little nervous, even now, just hearing these words—religion, church, God . . . he couldn't remember a time when they weren't taboo. But it was nice to see Peck so excited. And it was nice, finally, to feel part of a community again.

"Then there's the library, of course, along that wall," Peck continued. "The barter market in the middle. Food, clothing— you name it, they got it.

"There's a jazz band, if you can believe it, over by the ventilation ducts." Peck pointed. "Over here is the exercise station. They have weights, courts for ball games, a lane for racing . . ."

And Logan couldn't help but laugh. "We're really gonna be set down here, aren't we?" he said. "Once Lily is with us. We'll really have everything we need."

Peck smiled, but something about it was a little sad. "Maybe," he said. And then he nodded. "Yeah. Maybe that's true."

2

It was a dreary day back in New Chicago. The underpass was cold and wet with a wintry rain. Two weeks had passed since Logan had been chased off by DOME, and the huddle as a whole was in high spirits. Nearly everyone had moved into the abandoned buildings along the sidewalk by the underpass, brushing off rubble from old beds, sweeping the floors clean of broken plaster and glass, making real homes for themselves.

And it was all thanks to Andrew. His deal with DOME had granted the entire huddle immunity, and as long as its members agreed to stay within the Ruined Sector, they could now do nearly anything they wanted.

No one but Andrew had known the terms of his deal with

DOME. Everyone had come to assume that Andrew was simply a masterful negotiator. And no one had questioned why he'd been given the largest, nicest brownstone still standing along the lakefront.

It was only Bridget who held out, who had remained in her old spot by a pillar of the overpass. She alone knew the full story of Andrew selling out a fellow Markless. And so she stayed put, reading the books in her library and listening to her shortwave radio alone.

"Sitting out here in the cold won't bring him back," Andrew said, walking up to her.

Bridget looked up, resting the book she had been reading on her lap.

"And it's certainly not proving anything to me. My conscience is free and clear."

"I'm glad," Bridget said. "You know, if you were anyone else, I might actually take this opportunity to suggest that maybe, *just maybe*, you should try *for once* to treat others the way you would have them treat you." She stared at him. "But honestly, right now, you're not worth the effort." And she looked back down at her book.

"Listen," Andrew said. "That guy was the worst kind of skinflint out there. I've seen the type. He thinks he's bigger than the system. He thinks the rules don't apply to him. He expects others to fall in line and pay the price for his actions.

"Now, maybe those cute little freckles of his were enough to sucker you into forgetting all that—but the tightwad got what was coming to him. He'd asked for it. And after everything he put us through? All this immunity is the least he could have done for us. We were *owed* it. And it doesn't do anyone any good for you to reject it like this."

Andrew paused, waiting for Bridget to respond. She didn't.

"Please, Bridget. It's raining. You're gonna catch pneumonia."

More silence.

"You done?" she asked.

Andrew sighed.

"Logan didn't get us into this mess, Andrew. DOME did. And Logan's the first person I've ever met—the *first* one—who's decided to stand up to them. Who's trying to do something about it. Sure, Peck's been goin' around for years, pullin' kids out and protecting flunkees. But even he never had the guts to stand his ground and fight.

"Logan is different. He's onto something bigger than you or me or any of this. If you can't see that, then there's nothing for us to talk about." Bridget turned her back to Andrew. He slinked away. And she went back to listening to the faint, comforting chatter of the shortwave radio beside her.

∃

The next day, Logan and Peck and the rest of the Dust were brainstorming next steps, and for the first time in weeks, they were actually looking forward to them.

"What do you think she'll be like now? Think she'll be the same?" Hailey asked.

"I don't know," Logan said. "She'll be eighteen. Last time I saw her was on her thirteenth birthday. A lot can happen in five years, I guess."

"Sure."

"But she used to be . . . well . . . she was always very quiet.

She was smart, much smarter than me, though she didn't brag about it. Never showed off. She has brown hair, or at least she did, and it's shoulder length, or at least it was . . . and she was athletic. Tall." Logan laughed. "I wonder if she's still taller than me."

"Think you'll recognize her?" Hailey asked hesitantly.

"Yeah." Logan smiled. "I do."

"Hey, you the kids they're callin' 'the Dust'?" some teenage boy asked, barging through the control room door.

"Yeah. That's us," Peck replied.

The boy nodded once. "You're the tightwads tryin' to break into Acheron, right?"

"That's right . . . ," Logan said. "But we're trying to find it first."

"Hey, yeah, right on," the boy said. "That's exactly what I thought. Exactly!"

Blake eyed the boy. "Why? What's it to you?"

"Well, I just might have someone for you kids . . . someone I think you might like to meet."

"Oh yeah? Why's that?"

The boy shrugged, smirking just a little now. "Because this someone—she might just know the way in."

The Dust eyed the boy suspiciously, but Logan lit up, trusting and eager to follow. "Where is she? Is she here?"

"Oh, she's here," the boy said.

And Logan leaped to his feet. "Then take us! Can you take us to her?"

The boy frowned now, nodding his head slowly. "I think that just might be possible," he said. "Just might." He winked. "For the right price."

It took Hailey's foxhole radio to seal the deal. The boy wouldn't settle for anything less. But they were on their way, the Dust marching straight toward the girl who'd take them to Acheron.

They made it all the way to the vents at the edge of the community before they saw her. The girl they'd been taken to see, waiting patiently, half in shadow, just inside the alcove of the steam vents in the corner.

"Took you long enough," Erin said. She saw Logan and smiled wide.

Ч

From there, things went not at all as Erin had planned.

She'd expected a hug, at least, from the friend she'd gone through so much to find.

She'd expected some small window of time, some grace period at least, to explain herself before the Dust all turned a cold shoulder.

In her heart, she'd expected Logan to be as happy to see her as she was to see him.

But Erin didn't get any of that.

Instead, the Dust pounced.

"*Who are you?*" Blake demanded, pushing the boy up against the wall. "*Who sent you? DOME? Huh? That it?*"

"DOME? No!" the boy cried, suddenly very much out of his

element. "Dude, I'm just the Tech Wiz! Shawn! I'm a Markless—
like you!"

"*Spill it*," Blake roared at Erin. "Who is this guy? If he won't
tell me, you will!"

Shawn was scared now, yelling at Erin, "*Dude, Erin, you said this
was cool!* You said these guys were your friends!"

"They are my friends," Erin grunted. It took Jo and Tyler and
Eddie together to pin her down. "They just don't know it yet."

But Peck was already stepping back. "Fellow Unmarked," he
called. "We have an emergency on our hands! It has come to our
attention that DOME—"

"Stop him—*stop him!*" Erin pleaded to Logan. "Or he'll botch
this whole thing!"

Logan stood, bewildered, between Peck and Erin, caught
right in the middle of his two friends.

But something about the look in Erin's eyes told him to give
her a chance. A small one, at least.

"Peck," he said, resting a hand on his shoulder. "Let's hold off.
Just for one minute, okay?"

So Peck cut short his announcement. He turned to Logan.
Then he looked to Erin, fuming. "You have one minute."

5

"Listen to me. *Listen* to me now." The Advocate towered over the
young Coordinator.

"I am listening, ma'am."

"Cheswick's call confirms it: DOME's security has been

compromised. We must assume the boy knows everything. He will make it this far. Now it is just a matter of time."

"But . . . Advocate . . . even with this security breach . . . is that really plausible? No one has *ever* made it this far. People have tried, but . . ."

The Advocate brushed a chin-length wisp of hair from her face, revealing briefly the Mark on her forehead. She closed her light-blue eyes. She sighed. "All the same. I believe this one will. And when he does—"

"But—"

"*Listen* to me. *When* he does . . . you must let him in. Do you understand?"

"No. No, ma'am. I'm sorry . . . I don't. Why? Why not simply capture him?"

"He is crafty, this boy. DOME has learned that much. We strike when the time is right, or we risk missing our opportunity altogether. Are you following me now?"

"But . . . Advocate . . . why not simply capture him on sight?"

"This boy's resolve is unique, Coordinator. It will take a specific approach to break him. But make no mistake. He can be broken. Do you understand?"

"Yes, Advocate."

"Good." The Advocate nodded. "Then be prepared."

ㄴ

One minute was not enough time for Erin to explain everything. Not by a long shot. So she had to go right for the bull's-eye.

"I know," Erin began. "I know about Acheron."

Peck rolled his eyes, unimpressed. "Congratulations," he said. "That makes DOME only one step behind us this time. Probably a record for you hotshots."

"I'm not *with* DOME," Erin said. "Can't you understand that? Don't you have *any* idea what I've sacrificed to help you beggars? What I've done to my family? My future?"

"You have strange definitions for *help* and *sacrifice*. Unless, of course, you're referring to how you *helped* DOME hunt us down and how you *sacrificed* the life of an innocent man," Peck growled.

"Please," Erin said. She looked at Logan now. "You can't. You *can't* go in there."

Logan laughed, feeling all the loneliness he'd experienced without Erin fall away under the weight of his anger. "Why?" he said. "You're gonna tell me it's too dangerous? Two weeks ago you're chasing me into a freezing river in the dead of night, leading the charge for my capture by the very people who *created* Acheron, shooting my guide and separating me from my friends . . . and now you wanna give me a speech on *safety*?"

"I've learned things, Logan. It's not what you think in there, in Acheron. You can't possibly succeed!"

Logan scoffed. "Six weeks ago you didn't even believe me when I swore to you Acheron was real. Now you're trying to share your expertise with me? *Me.* The guy who escaped a DOME Center. You think I can't break into a prison?"

"*First* of all, you escaped that Center because of *me*. *Second* of all, Logan—this place . . . no matter how dangerous you think it is . . . I swear to you, it's worse."

"Oh yeah? And why is that? Because you've already turned us in? Because DOME is on the way? As usual? Thanks to you?"

"No, you dimwit! Because Acheron is a *military base!*"

Peck stepped forward now. "What are you saying, Erin? Are you saying Acheron *isn't* a prison? That we've got this all wrong?"

"I'm not saying that," she said, still pinned against the wall by the rest of the Dust. "I'm saying it's both. The prison *is* a training base."

"A training base for what?"

"For IMPS."

"*Imps?* Little demons?" Eddie laughed.

"It's an acronym, you idiot. The International Moderators of Peace. Cylis is using Lamson to build an army."

Logan sneered. "What would Cylis need an army for? He's about to run the *Global* Union. Also known as *the whole world*. Why would the G.U. need an army when there's no one left to fight?"

"Because there *is* someone left to fight."

"Who?"

Erin grimaced against Jo's arm. "Us."

Peck was quickly losing patience. Her minute had elapsed. "Erin, how do you even know any of this?"

"'Cause of Logan," she said. "I studied his Pledge tape."

"You have *access* to that?" Shawn said enviously.

"Of course not. I hacked into DOME's system. Saw the Marker saying something that looked like 'Acheron,' so I followed the lead. And unlike for you beggars, when *I* follow a lead, it leads to actual information. So I kept digging, through DOME's deepest channels. Eventually found my way to a document. And what that document explained . . ." Erin trailed off, shaking her head.

"What?" Logan asked, egging her on.

Erin sighed. "Deep down," she said, "Cylis is a vicious, vindictive man. I can see that now. The idea of people anywhere, at any time, not pledging complete allegiance to him . . . it makes his blood boil. So he had Lamson build Acheron—and all the other places like it—to punish them.

"But I think Cylis soon realized that punishment wasn't going to be enough. *Punish* people . . . and they only resent you further." She shook her head again. "But if you can *break* them . . . if you can bring them over to your side . . ." Erin shrugged. "Cylis may be vicious . . . but he's also brilliant. So he made a brilliant decision. Who, in any country, is more loyal than a soldier? Throughout history, an army has been the very symbol of patriotic loyalty. To fight for your country, to die for your country . . . there is no greater commitment.

"If Cylis could take those who had committed themselves to him *least* and turn them into those who had committed themselves to him *most*—turn them into his own soldiers—then, truly, Cylis could rule the world. It does more than kill two birds with one stone—it proves a point. That there has *never*, in *history*, been anyone more powerful."

"Erin," Logan said. "Look. If your goal was to convince me now more than ever that we *have* to get my sister out of this place— you've succeeded. So tell me how to get into this place, already, and stop wasting my time."

Erin laughed bitterly. "Fine," she said. "You want to know so badly? Here goes: You're standing right on top of it."

Logan closed his eyes. He put his hand over his face. *Of course. Of course we are. We've searched City Center high and low; this whole time, it's been right under our noses.*

"Do you remember how General Lamson won the States War, Logan? He won by rupturing the dam that protected the old capital from rising waters. And then he had this hill constructed right above it, with the new capital built on top as a symbol of how peace had been won. Except City Center is *not* just a symbol, Logan. It's a decoy. It was put on this hill to hide the Markless prison underneath; to hide DOME's secret army. To hide it right here, in plain sight.

"Acheron isn't *on* the hill, Logan. Acheron *is* the hill. Your sister is right below us."

┐

"All right," Peck said. "We've heard what we needed to hear. Blake, Jo, tie these two up. Take anything they have on them. Erin and Shawn both. These next few hours are crucial. No risks. You got that?"

"Wait!" Erin yelled. "No! Logan, no! Hear me out! Lily *can't* be saved!"

"Different song," Peck said. "But the same old tune. Starting to sound awfully familiar, Erin."

"Peck, please—listen to reason!" But Jo had her gagged before she could say anything else.

"You okay with this, Logan? I need you on board."

Logan looked at Peck sadly. He wished he had a little more time to figure everything out.

Was Erin really here to help?

Or was she here for DOME, up to her usual tricks?

They'd come all this way. They'd risked so much.

And now they were *right there*.

Erin really could derail that. Just a pea-sized tracker, or a little strip of tape—or any number of the other spy gadgets Erin knew all too well how to use—and she could ruin this whole thing. She'd done it before. She'd done it at every opportunity, in fact.

"*You picked the wrong side of history,*" Erin had said back at the warehouse that night in November. "*You're alone now, Logan. I can't help you anymore.*"

So what made him think tonight was any different?

Logan looked Erin in the eyes when he spoke, summoning all the cold, hard resolve he could. "Take her to where she can't bother us, Dust. We have work to do."

▱

The Dust was stationed back in the control room, with Erin tucked very far away.

"Okay. We know it's under us," Logan said. He had intended to draw up a plan with chalk on an old slate that hadn't been used in years, but he realized now that this one fact was as much as he knew. So Logan drew a horizontal line across the board, and a dot underneath it. And then, sheepishly, he sat down.

"All right, go team!" Blake said sarcastically.

Logan buried his face in his hands.

"We know they freeze their prisoners," Tyler said, trying very hard to be helpful. "We learned that on the wagon, remember?"

"And snakes," Eddie said. "I heard they have snakes."

Logan shook his head. "Wait a minute. *I* heard they poke your eyes out, or they tar and feather you, or they put you in a fiery cell. I never heard anything about freezing or snakes."

"That's 'cause everything we heard was an urban legend!" Blake blurted out angrily. "Don't you guys get it? No one *knows* what's in Acheron—that's the whole point! Everything we've heard . . . it's all just stories. Stories that don't fit together at all. Because they're nonsense. They're made up!"

"Face it," Jo said to the group. "We know nothing."

"Not true." Logan pointed defiantly at the slate. "We know it's right under us. We *know* that."

"Yeah? And what good does that do us, exactly? Huh? We can't even *walk* in, let alone sneak in—we don't even know where the entrance is!"

"Actually," Eddie said, very slowly. "We might."

The Dust all leaned forward, eager but confused.

"Back at the mansion," he continued. "On the River. With Mr. and Mrs. Psycho and their kid, Psycho Jr."

"What about it?" Blake asked.

"Winston. While you all were stuck in the basement, he told me . . . he gave me details."

"Yeah, we know," Tyler said. "You told this story already. Like, fifteen times in the car."

"No. All I talked about was the hundred-foot-thick walls and the entrance—"

"—that might as well be a brick wall," Tyler interrupted. "We *know*."

"I know you know! But there was something else too! At the time, I thought it was a joke. But . . . when I pressed him on this . . . when I asked if that one entrance was *really* all there was, Winston said—and I'm quoting here—'That and the power source.'"

Peck narrowed his eyes. "Power source . . . like a fusion plant?"

Eddie shrugged, and he nodded a little.

"That's it . . . ," Logan said. "If we can find a way into the maintenance ducts on the other side of this reactor, we should be able to follow the power cables all the way into Acheron. Of *course*. Eddie—you're a genius!"

"Let me get this straight," Jo said. "We're about to launch our whole prison break plan on a story some random Marked told Eddie as a scare tactic while his parents were threatening to torture us?"

"You got anything better to go on?" Logan asked.

Suddenly, Jo smiled. "No," she said. "Actually—I kinda like this."

9

They spent the rest of the night planning, the Dust, all together, in the control room. It was time to break Lily out of Acheron.

Tyler's job was to keep watch over Erin. To make sure she didn't get away, and to head any suspicious behavior off at the pass. There would be no surprises; the Dust was determined. This evening *needed* to go according to plan.

The whole Unmarked community was on lockdown. Everyone was a part of the plan. To ensure there wouldn't be any intruders, it was decided that for the rest of the night, there would be no coming or going from the turbine room. The Markless were in this together.

Meg was good with numbers, always had been—astonishingly good, in fact—so it was Meg's job to keep watch over the community. She'd counted with ease the number of Markless underground to begin with—2,370—and if that number changed, even by a single head, Meg would be able to tell. She waited up on the cat-walk now, keeping watch.

Blake and Hailey rallied the Markless throughout the turbine room, mustering support and scrounging for help from whoever was willing. Already, their task had proved valuable; that evening the two of them had successfully found eight pairs of magnecuffs that had been hoarded among the crowd. "For disguise," she told Logan and the others. "You never know . . ."

"Thanks, Hailey," they said uncertainly.

But Peck smiled. "I'll make sure we use 'em."

Even Rusty had an important job, though the rest of the Dust dreaded the scenario in which he would have to make use of it.

If worse came to worst, Rusty was the decoy. He'd wait on the catwalk with Meg, and at the first sign of DOME interference, Rusty would run out into the upper hallways and exit into the alley outside. He would attract DOME's attention, keeping them on ground level for as long as he could while the Dust scrambled to close up shop below.

Every member of the Dust had a crucial role in the Great Prison Break of Acheron, though none more important than the prison breakers themselves. From the beginning, this job was Logan's and Peck's, and everyone knew it was theirs alone. During the planning that night, this particular division of labor came up for discussion not once.

Less expected, though, was Joanne, who partway into the planning volunteered to follow as backup.

"You don't even agree with what we're doing here," Peck said.

"Maybe not," Joanne told him. "But I believe in the fight."

Again Peck refused, but Joanne insisted, and in the end their argument prompted Eddie to volunteer as well.

Peck was very proud in that moment to have the friends that he had. After all the fighting and doubt had passed . . . after all the hopelessness and second-guessing had run its course, the Dust had stuck together.

It was time to save Lily.

10

Logan went first. Peck and the others followed close behind.

Once they'd made it past the maintenance rooms and into the power tunnels of the fusion reactor, they had to crawl, shimmying on their stomachs, pressed against a humming coil on one side and a concrete wall on the other.

They could not have turned around if they wanted to.

There was not enough room for that.

The tunnel into which Logan and the others had entered eventually branched off into an even narrower tube, with an even lower ceiling, so small that they had to keep their heads turned sideways just to fit. Logan tried hard to hold back the encroaching claustrophobia, but there were moments when he felt certain that he'd end up stuck in this tunnel forever, blocked in by the unimaginable weight of the skyscrapers above them.

He pushed on all the same. One inch at a time. One elbow in front of the next.

Eventually, the tube led out to an air duct that ended about six feet off the ground, in a corner of a large vestibule, which Logan could see through the duct's grated metal cover.

"How's it look?" Peck whispered. "What's in there?"

Logan hated being in the confined space of the air duct. But the thought of venturing out into the space he saw before him now . . . that was much worse.

"It's the holding room, all right," Logan said.

Peck took a deep breath. "Okay," he said. "Logan and I descend. Jo and Eddie, you know what to do in the holding room."

But Logan shook his head. "No. Change of plans. Only I descend."

"Logan, we talked about this. I need to be a part of—"

"A part of Lily's rescue—*I know*," Logan replied. "But, Peck, I think someone needs to stay in this vent—"

"Absolutely n—"

"*I think someone needs to stay in this vent*," Logan repeated, "because I'm looking at the number of guards in there. And I think there's a good chance we're going to need two tries at this."

Peck frowned, though Logan couldn't see it. "Two tries? Logan . . ."

"Peck. Listen to me. I'm not liking these odds."

11

Eventually Peck agreed to wait behind in the air duct while Jo and Eddie prepared their part and Logan made the first attempt to sneak into Acheron.

Logan removed the grate carefully, trying not to make any

noise or draw any attention to his entrance. His goal was to slip undetected into the newest batch of arriving flunkees and make sure that no one got any bright ideas about that air duct.

When Logan finally did jump down into the vestibule and clamp on his own sets of magnecuffs—one for his wrists, one for his ankles—he decided he liked the tunnels better, claustrophobia and all.

The holding room was as gray and filthy and neglected as one might expect a prison holding room to be. Flies swarmed around in the air and followed flunkees wherever they went, and as everyone's hands and feet were bound, there was nothing anyone could do to swat them away.

Worse than the flies, though, were the guards. The "Moderators." The IMPS. They were everywhere, dozens of them, all taking shifts herding the Markless from a set of metal sliding doors to the main sign-in desk, and beyond that, to the elevator at the room's end. Once there, it seemed certain there was no coming back.

That, of course, would be Jo and Eddie's job to fix.

Logan could see the mass of newest arrivals put into a line as they slowly approached the sign-in desk, where a different type of guard stood by, labeled not as a "Moderator," but as a "Coordinator." Logan figured this must be a higher-ranked individual. He stood counting heads as the new arrivals shuffled past the desk and into the elevator behind it.

There was something odd about that Coordinator, though, along with the Moderators who manned the room. Something Logan had never seen before.

The men were Marked. But not on their hands.

Each one of them was Marked on his face.

When Logan stepped toward the sign-in desk, one of the many Moderators stepped sharply in front of him.

"Don't recognize this one," he said to the Coordinator. "Didn't see him come in with the others."

Logan felt his heart speed up. He was sure he would faint.

Stay strong, Logan told himself. *This is for Lily.*

For a long, agonizing moment, the Coordinator leaned in and peered at Logan. He raised an eyebrow. He eyed the magnecuffs. Then he studied Logan's face again. "Must be some mistake," the Coordinator said. "This one goes to level one. Let him through."

It worked.

He couldn't believe it worked!

As Logan passed the sign-in desk, his magnecuffs automatically released. He walked freely to the elevator, where another team of Moderators packed him in so tight with the rest of the flunkees, he could have lifted his feet from the ground and not fallen over.

12

Luckily for Logan, his elevator ride was short. One floor down, and he was off. He was inside. Level one.

He'd made it into Acheron.

Except it was nothing like he'd imagined.

He'd heard of the fire. And ice. And snakes. He'd heard of the blindness. And tar. And desperation. He'd heard of no escape.

Instead . . . what Logan saw before him . . . was *nice*.

TEN

ACHERON

1

THE ACHERON LOGAN STEPPED INTO WAS LIKE a vast, interior courtyard, miles across and intimidating in its scope, but otherwise peaceful and calm. Scattered between the stone walkways were large patches of grass—real grass, none of that fake plasti-grass stuff—and flowers that perfumed the air. The space was covered by a high, vaulted ceiling, and even *that* seemed warm and inviting. The whole thing was a screen that projected a bright sky with puffy, white clouds slowly sweeping across the blue background and shifting into countless different shapes.

The sun peeked out from behind them, warm and yellow and shining with long rays that stretched out in all directions, kissing every surface with its golden glow.

Everywhere there was the silvery sheen of nanodust from fresh Marks, the long trails of which wisped about in a gentle, artificial breeze.

Water flowed from a large fountain in the middle of the courtyard, bubbling smoothly in troughs between the many rambling paths and garden patches.

Scattered about the space, people relaxed. All except the newest arrivals were wearing a uniform, military in look, consistent with Erin's warnings and the guards in the waiting room. But there was nothing militant about the way these people behaved.

People walked freely about, and from this distance, Logan could just barely hear the many snippets of casual conversation about this thing or that.

Could it be? Could every last story Logan had heard of Acheron be wrong?

2

The water trough Logan walked along eventually brought him to the large, spraying fountain in the courtyard's center. Around it were benches, tiled walkways, arches curtained with thick ivy, and small trees of all kinds. Like the Moderators in the vestibule, these people were Marked on their faces, but that seemed to be normal here, maybe something people didn't even really notice after a while.

It took some time for Logan to muster the courage to speak to anyone. He spent several minutes just watching, pacing around the fountain, listening and waiting for the right moment to make a move. What kind of prison was this? There weren't even cells or locks.

Finally, Logan approached a teenage boy on a bench.

"You're new here," the boy said. "Must have just arrived today." The boy pointed to Logan's forehead.

"Yeah," Logan said. "Just got in."

"I'm fairly new here myself. But they did make me a Counselor today. That's my rank," the boy explained kindly.

"You a flunkee?" Logan asked.

"I was," the Counselor said. "Everyone here was."

Logan nodded. "So why'd you flunk?"

But the Counselor looked at him, confused. "What do you mean?" he asked.

Logan frowned. "Well . . . they must have told you *why* you flunked . . . right? I mean—did you steal something? Talk back to your Marker? Stir up trouble as a kid? What'd you actually do?"

The Counselor nodded. "There are two kinds of people here in Acheron. Flunkees—and criminals. You can't be both."

"But . . . what if you, I dunno . . . let's just say you attacked your nurse and threatened your Marker during your Pledge, and *then* you flunked? Wouldn't you sort of be both, then—a criminal *and* a flunkee?"

"No. Not technically. Not once you got here. You'd be a criminal. Criminals are divvied up among the lower levels, each punishment fit to the crime." The Counselor looked around. "This here's the flunkee level." He smiled. "It's much nicer." He patted Logan on the back. "But stop worrying about it. Since you're here, you're obviously not a criminal."

Logan sat down on the bench, and he had to laugh. "So they really do get ya," he said. "One way or another. Everyone's Marked in the end."

"Oh yes," said the Counselor. "That's extremely important. For the safety of all of us, you understand."

Logan blinked. "How long have you been here?" he asked.

"Two years."

"And how long did it take you to believe that?"

The Counselor looked at him appraisingly. "Me? I was a Moderator within a couple of hours," he said proudly. "But some minds take much longer to see the truth. Days, sometimes. Weeks. Even years, in the most stubborn cases. You'll understand it soon enough."

"I've heard rumors," Logan said, "that this is actually an army."

The boy nodded. "With these Marks, we become the International Moderators of Peace. Every level funnels into the IMPS eventually. Though lower levels serve their time first."

"What is it you do?" Logan asked. "As an IMP, I mean?"

But the Counselor shook his head. "We do what we're asked. We don't ask what we do." He shifted his weight. "Anyway, things are expected to pick up with the signing of the G.U. treaty. That'll be any day now."

"So I've heard," Logan muttered. He noticed a few IMPS sitting on a nearby bench staring at him. Logan found himself looking down, rubbing his forehead self-consciously.

"Doesn't seem like they train you very hard here," Logan continued. "Do you usually just sit around in the grass all day?"

The Counselor looked at Logan as though he'd just said the dumbest thing possible. He didn't respond. And Logan felt his face go beet red. But after a moment, the Counselor patted him on the knee and laughed. "I like you," he said. "Stick with me. You're gonna do all right here."

"Um, thanks," Logan replied. And then he culled every ounce of courage he had.

It's now or never, he thought. *No turning back.*

"You know, actually . . . I'm sorta . . . wondering if someone might be here . . ."

The Counselor narrowed his eyes, not quite understanding. Logan could guess how weird that question must have sounded—to be looking for someone in a place you weren't supposed to know existed.

"Do you go by names here, ever?" Logan asked the Counselor. "Anything other than your rank?"

"It's not how we address one another," the Counselor said. "But we learn each other's names. Sure."

Logan cleared his throat. *Here goes.*

"I'm wondering if you know a girl by the name of Lily Langly. She would have come here about five years ago."

The Counselor's eyes lit up. "Lily! Of course! Everyone knows Lily Langly!" The Counselor stood up from the bench. "Advocate!" he called. "Advocate Langly!"

And as if on cue, Logan's sister emerged from behind a gauzy curtain hanging across an archway into the courtyard. She was older, hardened somewhat, with a wide Mark spanning her forehead. But in every way she was still his sister, right down to the chin-length brown hair, the blue tint of her eyes, the lightness of her step, and the way she seemed to float as she walked . . . it was all somehow exactly as Logan had remembered.

Logan had pictured this moment countless times, had rehearsed what he would say, had imagined how his sister would respond . . . for years, he'd had it all planned out. But as it happened, he forgot all that. Instead he sat, speechless.

So Lily spoke first.

"Get up," she said, a few feet from the bench. She didn't smile. She didn't reach out for him. "Now."

Logan looked up at her, instantly confused. All across the courtyard, IMPS were staring, whispering, pointing . . .

He did as he was told, though he found himself wiping his face quickly and clumsily with his hand as he did. He sniffled twice, took a deep breath, exhaled sharply. *Be strong*, Logan thought. *You've made it this far.*

Seeing all this, Lily turned and walked swiftly back toward the arch through which she'd entered. Logan took a few quick steps to follow, and soon he was walking beside her, stepping in double time to keep up with her long, cool strides.

When they'd reached one of the larger patches of grass and had some privacy from curious onlookers, Lily spun around and looked at Logan sternly.

"What are you doing here? And what are you thinking, asking for me by name?"

It was not exactly the reunion Logan had pictured. For months now, he'd pictured Lily waiting helplessly for him in some cell, hoping against hope that someday, freedom might come . . . knowing that it was impossible, that none would ever find her . . . that none could be so cunning, or selfless, or brave. He imagined the look of gratitude and relief on her face upon seeing him—her younger brother, the hero, coming to free her, to wake her from her nightmare.

Instead, Logan stood slouching, overwhelmed, embarrassed, feeling younger than he had in years, while his sister looked on, rolling her eyes.

"You flunked, didn't you? You flunked your Pledge. Logan, how could you be so stupid?"

For a moment, Logan stood with his mouth open, as if words were intended to come out. But none did.

Lily shook her head and began leading her brother in a wide lap around the courtyard.

"I would have," Logan finally said. "I would have flunked. But I escaped, Lily. So that I could rescue you. Lily—DOME didn't bring me here. DOME doesn't know I'm here at all. I've come to break you out."

"That was a mistake," Lily said simply.

"No. Lily—no, it's not! I know what you're thinking—but it's *not* impossible. The whole Markless community is on our side. Everyone in Beacon—we're all working together on this. To get you out of here!"

"You've brought *Markless* into this?"

Logan stuttered for a moment, trying to regain his thoughts. "I—of—Lily—of course I did. They want to help. Lily—they want to help you!"

Lily looked very frustrated now, not at all touched or relieved or anything else Logan could have predicted. Just *frustrated*. That was it.

"Did you ever *think*, Logan? Did you ever stop to *think* about the consequences of your actions here?"

"I—*what?*—of course I thought—"

"You come here, halfway across the country . . . you leave Mom and Dad, you drag innocent people into it . . ."

"Lily, listen to me, please. You have to trust me. This isn't some half-baked plan."

"Oh, it isn't? *Really?* Because you have *no idea* what you're up against, Logan! No idea what's really going on. Don't you have any sense of how fragile this situation is? You're a *traitor* now, Logan. Do you know what that means? It means you're headed *straight* down to level nine."

Logan was growing frightened now, very frightened, by his sister's anger. He racked his brain desperately for something—anything—that might knock some sense into her. That might get her to cooperate.

"Peck," he said, finally. "Your friend, Daniel Peck. He's here. He came with me. He and I—we're . . . we're in this together! For you!"

"Daniel's here? You brought *Daniel* too?"

"Yes. Yes! Let us help you, Lily. Please. Let us help you get out of here. We'll run away. We'll all run away together. Just come with me now, Lily. Come with me, and we'll never look back. Will you do that for me, Lily? Please?"

"It changes things, having Daniel here."

Lily stopped now, by a trough. She leaned down and let the water run over her hand, and for a full two minutes, she didn't say anything. She didn't look at Logan. Instead, she looked out toward the stone archway through which the stream flowed. Finally, she nodded. "Okay," she said. "Here's the plan."

∃

For Peck, it had been an excruciating couple of hours. He was lying on his stomach in the air duct, face pressed against the grate for any sign of Logan or Lily, and by this point, even just keeping his head up was a chore. His neck was cramped and sore, sending sharp pains down past his shoulder blades and all the way up into his skull. His head ached, his arms were numb, and his legs throbbed terribly.

Three hours, Peck told himself. *You promised yourself that. To succeed or fail, Logan needs time. You can't jump the gun on this. You're the last chance for the plan to succeed. There won't be another.*

The minutes passed, and new prisoners came and went. Each time it was the same for them: arrive through the sliding metal door, line up at the sign-in desk, cross to the elevator, and disappear into Acheron. How many had it been now? Peck had lost count long ago, and yet another batch arrived now, all shaking and crying and wide-eyed.

In each group, there were one or two stragglers. One or two that would thrash and scream and refuse to board the elevator. Invariably, these new prisoners were allowed to throw their fit. Never once did the Moderators intervene. The vestibule they'd been brought to was so depressing on its own—so filthy and stuffy and swarming with flies—that it never took long for the prisoners to break down, to convince themselves that anything beyond that elevator couldn't be much worse than where they were now. It happened every time.

Every time, that is, except with Eddie and Jo. The two of them managed to raise a stink with each successive group ever since Logan crossed the sign-in desk. Because it was the deal they had made: to stay right there, ready to spring to action at a moment's notice, the instant Logan and Lily reappeared, to clear the way among the dozens of guards, to create the diversion necessary for Lily to make her escape through the air duct.

Nothing about the plan was foolproof. But this was the end-game, after all. There was no going back.

Lily was the symbol. Free her, and make a statement. Free her, and pave the way for the rest.

The Markless were taking their stand.

It was hard for Peck to watch Joanne and Eddie suffer in the waiting room as long as they did. It was hard to watch them endure so much for a cause, Peck knew, they only believed in for him.

But in the end, it was worth it. Logan emerged. With Lily. Through the Moderator's entrance next to the elevator, just beyond the desk.

Eddie and Jo moved in to surround them, to clear a path through the crowd of guards.

It was happening. They were *right there*. Logan and Lily both. They stood at the far end of the room and waited eagerly for Eddie and Jo to bring them back to the ducts. To Peck. To freedom.

Peck unscrewed the grate in front of him, heart racing, blood pounding in his ears.

They were here.

They were really going to do it!

4

Lily's plan was simple. "There's only one way out of here," she said. "And that's the Moderators' exit, connected to the pathways we IMPS use to travel throughout the building. I'll just sneak you into it, and we'll be on our way."

"Wait a minute," Logan said. "You're telling me everyone here has *access* to a pathway leading out to the prison's main exit?"

"Yeah."

"Well, why in the world doesn't everyone just *leave*?"

Lily looked at him as though she hadn't understood the question. So instead of answering, she slipped silently into the Moderators' exit, and Logan followed nervously behind. Something about this—just to walk out through the holding room like that, right there, out in the open, nothing sneaky about it . . . somehow that plan felt awfully risky, even to Logan. Something about it was hard for him to trust.

And yet here they were in the middle of the room, just shy of the sign-in desk, everything going according to plan.

And that's when Lily stopped. She stopped right there at the desk. Right as Eddie and Jo were about to reach them.

Logan's body went rigid, stone-limbed with fear. He braced himself. For something . . . something coming . . .

What are you doing? Peck thought. *Come on—we're so close!*

Lily stepped swiftly to the Markscan at a podium by the sign-in desk. She looked into it as it scanned her face. Then she leaned down, even closer. She touched something on the screen. And she spoke.

Her voice rang out, amplified by some speaker system across the vestibule and, Peck could only assume, throughout all of Acheron.

"This is Advocate Langly," she said. "Reporting intruders, and attempted prison break, and treason. Repeat. Treason. I have apprehended the perpetrators. Requesting immediate backup for transport to level nine."

Peck shook his head in horror. The unthinkable had happened. The Lily he knew was gone. Replaced by . . . something else. An Advocate. An IMP. A puppet of Cylis. The struggle was quick. The guards descended on Logan and Eddie and Joanne as Lily watched. Logan swung a few times, ran a few feet, and was swiftly overpowered. Trapped alone out in the open, with the element of surprise taken away from them, Eddie and Jo never stood a chance.

Peck saw no emotion flash across Lily's face. No remorse. No fear. Nothing but the flat, black mark on her forehead as she stood by and betrayed her own brother.

Peck's heart sank. All the adrenaline left him, sucked right out of his belly into the cold metal duct. He had no energy left. But what could he do? What could he possibly do?

And so Peck fled, through the vent, hardly believing this turn of events. Back to tell the others. Back the way he came.

5

When Peck made it into to the control room alone, everything was chaos and confusion.

"What happened?"

"Was it really there?"

"Did you make it?"

"Did you find her?"

"Where's Lily?"

"Where's Eddie?"

"Where's Jo?"

"Where's Logan?"

"Logan—he found her—they were coming—captured—" Peck spoke in short bursts, still barely believing it himself. He slowed himself down, taking deep breaths so he could explain what had happened.

"Logan did find Lily. She's an IMP. She didn't want saving. She played along until the end. And then she turned us in. She turned her own brother in."

The news was met with blank, disbelieving stares across the control room. Distantly, the whirring of turbines from the fusion reactor droned a low, unnerving hum. No one spoke.

Finally, Peck turned, walking swiftly away from the Dust.

"Where are you going?" Blake called.

And Peck yelled back, stone-faced, still walking, not even turning to look. "To get someone," he said. "We're gonna need the help."

ᗡ

The first thing Erin did was spit at him. "Well, *of course* she did, you idiot! What did you *expect* would happen?" Erin was lying, hands still tied behind her back, beneath a tangle of pipes in the corner. Tyler stood over her, keeping watch for any sudden movements.

"How many ways do I have to tell you misers—Lily was labeled disloyal during her Pledge. So they've made her into a soldier. Just like they've done every other flunkee. Just like every other Markless they could get their hands on, through whatever excuse of 'law enforcement' they could come up with. Lily is an IMP! Highly trained and brainwashed. Why *wouldn't* she have turned Logan in?"

"Erin. Please." Peck approached her now. "We were wrong. And I know you have no reason to help us after what we've put you through. But if you care about Logan . . . tell us what you know. Do you have any ideas . . . any at all . . . that might give us a chance at rescuing Logan and Eddie and Joanne? Because however hard it was for us to get to Lily . . . this will be harder. They'll be labeled traitors, Erin. She sent them to level nine. And if the rest of what Eddie heard about Acheron is half as accurate as what we've confirmed so far, that means they'll be tortured, Erin. Tortured. Please help us. Before it's too late . . ."

Erin was silent for a long time. She breathed slowly and

deliberately, just staring into the distance, but inside she was frantic, desperate to come up with any sort of reasonable plan.

"I think . . . ," she said finally, "I think there might be a way."

┐

Back in the control room, Erin stood on top of the old panel, speaking quickly to an energized group, and it wasn't just the Dust surrounding her. There were a couple hundred Markless now crammed between the rows of rolling chairs and tablescreens and switchboards.

"Here it is," Erin said. "I'm layin' it all out, not pulling any punches: You can make your way across the holding room. You can make your way to Logan's level. You can make your way down past the winds, or the darkness, or the reptiles, or the tar pits, or the fires, or whatever it is that's actually down there . . . you can even make it all the way back. But as long as Acheron is filled with prisoners willing to fight for the idea of Acheron, that place really is guarded with an infinite security.

"This isn't some case of knocking out a few hourly-rate security guards, or hacking into some lame security feed, or sneaking our friends past some silly trap. *Everyone in there* is an obstacle in our way.

"Logan's fellow inmates *are* his prison guards. IMPS. Every last one of them. *Not a one* is on your side. So how in the world do you break anyone out of a prison like that?"

"You don't," Blake said. "We can't."

"That's right. *But.*" Erin smiled. "There might be a catch. Because this network of prison guards? This endless chain of security? It's *also* Cylis's army."

"Right," Tyler said impatiently. "We get that part."

"Well, what if I told you," Erin said, "that Cylis is willing to use it? *This* document—" She borrowed from Shawn the tablet she'd given him earlier, and she held it up to the group, displaying her picture of Michael Cheswick's top secret page. "This document proves it."

"Wait a second," Jo said. "You mean to say that Cylis has used IMPS on A.U. citizens . . . already?"

"That's right," Erin said. "A test run. One early sunny morning in August. This page here confirms it."

Erin frowned. "Now, I know it sounds crazy. But if we can force Cylis's hand—if we can coax him into using this IMP army of his in a big way—well, it would clean Acheron out. It would pull all those IMPS right out of their cage."

"And since the IMPS *are* Acheron's guards—" said Peck.

"No IMPS means—" continued Tyler.

"No security." Jo nodded.

"That's right," Erin said. "Leaving Acheron vulnerable . . . and giving us the opportunity we need to break our friends out."

"But what could we possibly do that would prompt Cylis to use that kind of force?" Jo asked. "Even if every last Markless in this community agreed to it . . . there's just no way to mobilize a movement of that size and importance . . ."

And now Hailey smiled, two rows over in the control room, swiveling smugly in an old rolling chair. "I think I have it," she said. "I think I know what we can do."

The group laughed when Hailey suggested it. But it was a nervous laughter. The kind that showed they knew she was right.

Blake sighed sharply when the room's jitters died down. "There's no coming back from this, you know. We're stirring up a hornet's nest here. This is a masterstroke, and we can't undo it once it's done."

"If it really is a masterstroke," Hailey replied, "then we won't ever need to."

ELEVEN

FOXHOLE

1

DANE HAROLD WATCHED THE SETTING SUN, and he smiled sadly.

For dinner that night, he'd caught a fish from the Potomac, and he had cooked it himself to share with Hans and Tabby. It was the first fish he'd ever caught. It was the first fish he'd ever cooked. And neither Hailey nor Logan was there to taste it.

He wondered about them as he walked along the valley ridge, preparing for his radio show, shivering just a little in the cool winter evening. They must have made it to Beacon by now. He wondered if they'd come any closer to finding Acheron. He wondered if they'd stayed out of DOME's grasp. He wondered if he'd ever see either of them again.

Things in the valley had been fine. Dane was the youngest resident by a large margin, but he'd been taken in kindly, he got along well with Hans and Tabby and the neighbors, and most important, he had his broadcast. Every night, he'd make the trek up to that little hut by the tower, carrying Tabby's guitar in one hand and his own griptone in the other. He'd sit at that hut's rickety wooden desk. And he would chat with Mrs. Phoenix and Sonya. Right there on the airwaves, though without names or specifics. He'd listen to their news, he'd give them his own, he'd answer their questions and they'd answer his . . .

And every night, once that was over and Mrs. Phoenix had officially signed off, Dane would play. He'd play everything he'd ever written for the Boxing Gloves, everything he'd ever learned or meant to learn growing up . . . he'd figure out tunes live on the air, make up chords, improvise melodies, try out lyrics . . .

Every night, he'd do this until the early morning hours, when Hailey and Logan were most likely to be listening, and then he'd repeat Mrs. Phoenix's news from the day. He'd add details of his own. He'd wish his friends good luck.

And in this way, Dane did bridge the gap between Hailey and her mom, between Logan and his grandmother, just as he'd promised he would do, despite the thousand miles in between.

Then, tonight, just minutes before he went on the air, something happened that was so unexpected, Dane knew right away that this new life of his was over for good.

"*Dane*," his griptone suddenly said in an electronic, auto-tuned middle C. "Dane. It's me—Erin. I've hacked your griptone. Hailey told me you said it would be possible. And you were right. Pretty cool, huh?"

Dane stared in disbelief at the instrument in his hand.

"Dane, listen. Lily betrayed us. Logan is captured. We need your help."

Dane couldn't answer—there was nothing he could do to reply through the griptone—but he leaned forward, holding the instrument reverently, listening carefully to its faint, auto-tuned words.

"If you're listening, Dane . . . here's the plan . . . and here's what you can do . . ."

Dane ran the rest of the way up the ridge. He sat in the plain wooden chair at the plain wooden table, and he spoke quickly into the transmitter.

"Markless. It's me. Dane-o-rino. No music tonight, though. Just listen. It's story time. And I know some of you might already know this one. But bear with me all the same." Dane took a deep breath.

"Just say what's on your mind," Erin had told him. *"And make your words count."*

"Two months ago a thirteen-year-old boy named Logan Langly discovered that his sister had been swiped by DOME. Swiped at her Pledge, five years ago, because in the eyes of her Marker, some part of her showed doubt.

"Doubt about Cylis, doubt about the Union, doubt about the Inclusion . . . who knows? All that matters is that, for one reason or another, Lily Langly vanished. Just as many of you have watched your own loved ones vanish.

"Now, I know that for some of you the name Logan Langly has come to mean something. Perhaps you blame him for the most recent raid on your home. Maybe you think he's brave. Or rash. Or heroic. Or crazy.

"Whatever you think—whatever you've heard—know this:

"On the evening of November 8, Logan Langly did something most of us have never dreamed possible.

"He stood up to DOME. He stood up to Cylis. Because he saw injustice. And because he decided that it could not stand, no matter the cost."

Dane took another deep breath. He leaned closer to the microphone.

"Perhaps you have also heard of a rebel group led by a teenager named Peck. Perhaps you have heard that they recruit kids. That they call themselves by that old slur against us: 'Dust.'

"Maybe you think they're misguided. Or stupid. Or selfish. Maybe you think they draw unwanted attention to us Markless.

"But here is the truth: the fight *is* happening. Whether we want it to or not. Whether we resist it or not. It's happening even as I speak to you now.

"They take away our rights, and we let them. They round us up, and we let them. They imprison us. We let them.

"We are the ones who slipped through the cracks," Dane said. "We are the ones who have been brushed aside. We are the ones they said could be forgotten.

"But Markless, hear this: if you allow it . . . Dust collects.

"Like it or not, Chancellor Cylis is forcing the G.U. treaty through Parliament. There won't be a public vote this spring—it's happening now.

"These raids, they're happening now.

"These loved ones. They are disappearing *now*.

"And so the time has come—now—to collect. To push back. To demand a *less* unified world. To demand freedom, whatever the cost.

"Because we are all Dust. Because we are not afraid."

∃

The broadcast spread like wildfire, through radio waves and razor blades, as far as Dane could send it, until his signal died out and others took over, each with its own brave broadcaster taking the message, running with it, making it her own, everyone's words and ideas and inspirations hopping from one huddle to the next, up, down, and sideways across the Dust of the American Union.

Back at the underpass in New Chicago, Logan's old friend Bridget was reading by candlelight when the message came on the radio beside her. She lowered her book, she looked straight ahead, and she listened.

"Markless everywhere," Mrs. Phoenix began. "Dust. The news has come. It is time."

4

When Andrew emerged from his comfortable brownstone, he stepped into an energized huddle and a mobilized underpass. "What is this?" Andrew asked of a Markless running by.

"A protest," the kid said. "We're fighting back!"

"Who's fighting back? Fighting back against what?"

The kid looked confused. "Against DOME, of course." He swept his arms in a grand gesture. "The Markless, all of us— we're fighting back!"

"Why now?" Andrew demanded. "What started it?"

"Some escaped flunkee. DOME went nuts trying to find him, and last night they finally did. So we're fighting for freedom."

"*Langly?*"

"That's the one."

"*His* freedom?"

The kid shook his head. "Our freedom."

"Listen to me," Andrew said. "You're not seeing this clearly.

If DOME really has gone nuts over this kid, what makes you think they won't just arrest all of us, the whole lot of us, all across the country, the second we make our stand?"

The kid smiled. "Then the Marked will finally be forced to see how DOME treats us. Then it'll finally all be out in the open. Out for everyone to judge." The boy shrugged. "That'd be okay."

Andrew didn't wait to hear any more. Immediately, he darted over to a pillar and climbed up onto its base, holding on to the side with one arm, and waving the other for the huddle's attention.

"Markless! Huddle! Listen to reason! We have immunity! DOME granted us immunity! For actions I took! Don't you get it? We don't need to fight!"

But all around him, the huddle continued scurrying back and forth, gathering supplies, preparing to climb, preparing to march along that old abandoned overpass, all the way to New Chicago. Where they would be seen. Where they could not be missed. Not a single member stopped to listen to Andrew's speech.

"Andrew." Bridget walked up to him, shaking her head. She spoke quietly, only to him. "You've never understood and you never will. This isn't about immunity. If we'd wanted comfort, we would have Pledged a long time ago."

Andrew jumped down beside her. "You did this, didn't you?" he said. "You mobilized this while I was asleep."

"In your little brownstone? That's right," Bridget said. "And you know what I *didn't* tell everyone? That Logan was here. And that you were the one who ratted him out in the first place. You know why? Because I believe in turning the other cheek, and I believe in forgiveness and grace. So you're welcome. For saving your sorry skin from this mob."

Andrew stood, silent as he watched his former huddle pack up and leave.

5

Michael Cheswick had not had a good month.

He was sitting at his office in the tip of the Umbrella when the call came in.

The desk rang six times before Cheswick finally answered it.

Cheswick tapped an icon on his desk, and the connection went live, a holographic face appearing in front of him.

"Sir," Cheswick said nervously. "Thank you for returning my call."

The head in the hologram nodded slowly.

"As I am . . . sure you are, by now, aware . . . the protests have been . . . growing. They are . . . coordinated, it seems. Across the country. Not just the cities, but everywhere.

"As for New Chicago . . . Markless here have made it . . . too difficult, I'm afraid, for my agents alone. We have only a hundred agents here. The numbers we're looking at on these streets . . ." Cheswick sighed, calculating a quick estimation in his head. "By now? I'd guess we're looking at . . . *thousands*." He paused, and then he said it again. "Many thousands, sir."

The hologram before him nodded.

"Therefore . . . General . . ." Michael Cheswick could not believe he was asking for this. He knew how weak it made him look. "I am requesting the assistance of the International Moderators of Peace."

The head nodded again, more slowly this time.

"I do realize, sir, that we've yet to use Cylis's army in such a . . . high-profile capacity. Nevertheless . . ." Cheswick cleared his throat. "Things are escalating quickly, sir. The sooner our response . . . the more forceful our response . . . the better."

General Lamson was still for a full minute. His gaze, even across the hologram connection, was penetrating and laser focused.

"Is that . . . may I take this as confirmation, sir?"

The gaze continued, unrelenting.

And Michael Cheswick cleared his throat. ". . . Sir?"

┗

The scene in City Center was pure chaos. The Markless—Dust, as they all now called themselves—were out on the streets, shouting slogans, blocking traffic, engaging the Marked Beaconers around them in friendly debate.

DOME's forces were not enough. Agents set up barricades that were easily trampled by the mob of the Dust. Police stood with shields that did nothing to stop the protesters.

The Dust marched on. Toward the Capitol Building. Where they would camp on the steps. Where they would dare DOME to retaliate, for all the Marked world to see.

┐

There was only a handful of Dust left down in the control room deep under Beacon; Peck, Blake, Tyler, Meg, Rusty, Hailey, Shawn, and Erin stood huddled around the old security feed of the fission reactor, monitoring any sign of movement from below. Erin and Shawn had hacked it together, turning it on for the first time in years.

"So far, so good," Blake said.

"Yeah," Erin agreed.

"And you really think this'll do the trick?" Peck asked. "You really think they'll release the IMPS?"

"Your guess is as good as mine," Erin said. "But we're certainly asking for it."

"I still don't understand," Shawn said. "How did you know that this might even be possible? What was it you saw on that page you found? What did it take to bring the IMPS out of their shell the first time around?"

Erin looked uncomfortable. "Oh. It doesn't matter," she said. "We can worry about that once this is over."

"Well, now you have to tell us!" Tyler demanded.

Erin waved him off.

"Come on! Settle it by bet? I have a game we can play . . ."

Erin rolled her eyes. "Biological warfare, if you must know. Don't worry about it, all right?"

But Peck narrowed his eyes. "What do you mean, biological warfare?"

"It's just this . . . this *thing* DOME's had planned from the beginning."

The whole group stared, now, at Erin, very eager for her to continue.

Finally, Erin did. And once the floodgates were open, the words came out fast. "They give us shots when we Pledge," she said. "I always figured it was a numbing shot. But . . . turns out it isn't. It's a vaccine. DOME's been inoculating its Marked citizens since the very first Pledge."

"Inoculating you for *what*, exactly?"

"For . . . well . . . for a situation like this, actually. For a time when they might feel the need to just . . . wipe all you Markless out."

For a moment, no one among the Dust dared even to breathe.

"Project Trumpet. It's . . . a plague, basically. Deadly. They've been keeping it in their back pocket, just in case the Markless ever got out of hand." Erin looked uneasily from one member of the Dust to the next. She clearly didn't want to be thinking about this, much less talking about it.

"So now what?" asked Blake. "You're saying they've unleashed it on us?"

Erin shook her head. "On the contrary." She laughed a hollow little laugh. "DOME screwed up. Turns out these inoculations . . . they aren't protecting us Marked from the plague. They're making us sick."

Peck crossed his arms. "I don't understand."

"You see, this plague . . . it was actually unleashed a long time ago. It's been in the air—all around us—for a long time. Since the beginning of DOME."

"Okay . . ."

"It's a nanovirus. DOME took this crazy flu strain, and they used nanotech on it. Makes the virus totally dormant . . . until DOME turns it on. Until they sound the trumpets, so to speak."

"Project Trumpet."

"Exactly." Erin laughed halfheartedly again. "Anyway. With the G.U. treaty about to go through, and with you Dust raising a real stink back over the summer . . . well . . . Cylis must have decided it was time. Time to turn on this virus . . . time to take care of you Markless once and for all."

Erin smiled now. "It was the perfect plan, really. As long as DOME kept its secret, the whole thing would just look to us Marked like those unhealthy skinflints were getting sick and dying on their own. Cylis would be blameless. No PR hassle, no needing to explain himself . . . as messy as biological warfare is . . . politically, it was his cleanest option.

"*But . . .*" Erin sighed deeply. "Instead, DOME flipped the switch and turned the nanovirus on and discovered that this nanovirus isn't actually *catching* if you just breathe the stuff, or if you ingest it. Turns out the virus doesn't spread like a cold or flu *at all*. Because of a mistake in the nanotech modification process, this virus now only spreads by blood. So all you Markless are safe. In fact, the *only* way for the virus to infect a person is if it's actually injected into you—into your bloodstream—like with a needle."

A slow look of understanding washed over Peck's face.

"What? What? Guys, I don't get it," Tyler said.

"You see, Tyler," Erin explained, "the way vaccines work . . . it's not like other medicine. It's not something that treats the illness, the way antibiotics kill bacteria, for example. Vaccines work by actually *giving* you a weakened version of the virus. That way, your body's immune system can learn to fight it in its weakened state, and if your body is ever infected for real, it already knows how to handle it. It knows how to kill it, right away, so that the real virus can't hurt you."

"Okay . . . ," Tyler said.

"Well, so, here's the joke of it," Erin continued. "That vaccine nanovirus that DOME's been injecting into the Marked? It's been dormant too, this whole time, right in the bloodstream. And now that it finally *isn't* dormant, DOME is learning that—'Oops, sorry, everyone!'—even the weakened state of the nanovirus, once it's turned on, is more than powerful enough to make a person deathly sick.

"DOME's vaccine didn't inoculate anyone. All it did was infect us. And now that it's 'live,' we Marked"—she pointed at herself now—"are the ones starting to drop."

Tyler's eyes went wide.

Peck nodded slowly. "So that's why Cylis is so intent on pushing the G.U. treaty through Parliament—he knows it'll never pass once this news leaks."

"That's right," Erin said.

"But . . . when will it all happen?" Blake asked.

"No one knows yet. It could be slow in coming or it could be fast. There've only been a few cases of it so far. They've contained the outbreaks by assassinating the sick, covering up their tracks with stealth missions by the IMPS . . . but according to reports, it's probably just a matter of time before every last Marked is . . . well . . ."

"Wait a second," Blake interrupted. "Erin . . . wait . . . then . . . but . . . *you're* Marked . . . so that means that you . . ."

Erin shrugged. "Look, let's not get all weepy about it, all right? One thing at a time. Right now we're all on the clock." And she turned back to the tablescreen. "Come on," she said. "Focus. Let's run through this plan again."

By the end of the day, the IMPS were mobilized and moving out. The Dust could see them as little blinking dots on the fission reactor's hacked security feed.

"I guess it's time," Peck said.

Erin nodded. "I guess it is."

"Everyone clear on this?" Peck asked. "Rusty, you hold the fort up here. Everyone else, we descend. Meg goes first. When we get in there, Meg, you run straight for any guards left in the vestibule. There shouldn't be many now, the way they've been leaking out these last few hours.

"When the coast is clear, Erin, we use your Mark at the sign-in desk to call the elevator. Then, Erin, you stay behind and hack computer security."

"Just give me five good minutes with it," Erin said, "and I'll have Acheron's security feed as useless as the tycoons who designed it."

Peck smiled. "Spoken like true Dust, Erin." And Erin didn't even flinch when he said it.

"Shawn, you stay right with Erin," Peck continued, "and do whatever you have to do to erase all those Markscan traces she'll be leaving behind. You'll cover our tracks all along the way—can you do that?"

"Dude. Please. I'm the Tech Wiz!"

"Fine." Peck rolled his eyes. "Everyone else, we cross the holding room, board the elevator . . . and we hope against hope that it accesses every floor. We need to take that thing all the way to level nine to get Logan and Jo and Eddie. No matter how awful it gets. We take them. And somehow . . . we make it back up." Peck looked around. "Anyone not crystal clear on this?" he asked.

The Dust all glanced around at one another. Everyone knew it was hardly a plan at all. Everyone knew the odds of success were slim. But no one spoke up. It was time to move in.

TWELVE

MARKED

1

THE HOLDING ROOM SHOWED THE FIRST fingerprints of the Dust's plan in full effect. Where before there had been dozens of IMP guards, now there was only one, the coordinator at the sign-in desk.

"He's alone," Erin whispered, peering over Meg's head and through the grate.

"Is that surprising?" Blake whispered.

Peck nodded. "Last time there were more."

"Good," Erin said. "So it's working. Security's depleted."

"Meg. Will you do the honors?" Blake asked.

And Meg nodded gleefully. She unscrewed the grate of the air duct in front of her, sliding out on her stomach and falling to the ground below. Erin gave her a little tap on the foot as she did, for good luck.

The guard never saw it coming. Meg had him clobbered before he even knew what hit him. By the time Erin and the Dust made it out of the air duct, he was sprawled unconscious across the floor.

"Go, go!" Peck whispered, and Erin ran to the Markscan to call the elevator.

Except.

The Markscan flashed red.

"Call it, already!" Blake whispered, waiting eagerly at the entrance. "We're here—call it up!"

"I can't. *I can't!* It's not working." Erin was growing frantic. "Why isn't it working?"

"You're Marked, aren't you?" Tyler demanded. "Make it *happen!*"

And then Erin looked at the IMP splayed out on the floor. And she saw the Mark tattooed across his face.

"Of course," Erin said. "How brilliant . . ."

"Erin, we're naked out here! Make this happen before someone sees us!"

"A Marked hand can be stolen," Erin said. "With extreme measures, but still . . . it's possible that someone could cut someone else's hand off."

"Like that Rathbone guy the Dust met?" Hailey asked.

"Yeah, just like that," Erin answered, shuddering a little. How gross. She picked up the IMP now, by his armpits. His head rolled lifelessly to the side. "A Marked *face*, on the other hand . . . no chance. It's DOME's way of keeping IMPS IMPS, and making sure no one else can infiltrate the army." She held the man's head up against the scanner. It blinked green and called the elevator their way.

"Good," Hailey said. "Now, hurry up to computer security before we make it to the surveillanced floors."

Erin looked up at the mainframe room perched over the vestibule with a narrow metal staircase spiraling up toward it. Then she looked, irritated, at the IMP in her hands. "Shawn," she called. "Help me drag this lug up there, will you?" And as Shawn did, the rest of the Dust boarded the elevator and disappeared into the depths below.

2

Logan was freezing to death.

Around him was a vast cavern, smaller than the other floors of Acheron, but dimly lit, so that, from where Logan sat, he could just barely see the ragged stone walls around him, just barely make out the stalactites hanging from the high ceiling above.

The entire floor was a frozen lake. Down as low as he was, all the water from Acheron flowed to here, pooling on the ground, slowly washing over the space, slowly cooling, slowly turning to layer after layer of milky-white ice. At first, Logan stepped lightly, wading around on the frozen surface in the ankle-deep ice water sloshing atop it. But it was too cold to keep that up for long. After half a day of it, Logan sat, exhausted, numb, slow, right down on the ice, letting the cool water wash over his legs and waist.

So Logan rested, now, stuck up to his belt in the frozen surface of the lake, and it was torture. Pure, vile torture. Logan thought back to his time in the snowbank beside the stream when he'd nearly died from hypothermia, and he remembered it as mild and pleasant by comparison.

He knew, because he was told, that the way out was within his grasp. He needed only to commit to Cylis. He needed only to commit to the Mark. That one simple thing, and Logan would be free of pain. But he had to mean it. Deep down, he had to mean it.

Please, *God*, Logan prayed, remembering everything he had read in his tattered book. *Give me strength now. I am tempted. I want to give in. I am so tempted.*

Do not let me.

Do not let me give in.

I am ready to die.

I would rather die.

Please.

Give me the strength to die.

Ǝ

On the upper levels of Acheron, Erin and Shawn were frightened and desperate.

Erin had the IMP's face pressed more or less permanently against the Markscan, and still she couldn't manage to hack the security feed. Not to her satisfaction, at least.

"I could get it to turn off," Erin said. "But something so obvious is bound to sound an alarm."

"No, no. Much better to have the loop," Shawn said. "Some old, boring history feed on repeat—that's what we need."

"Don't you think I know that?" Erin snapped. "I'm *trying*, Mr. Wiz."

But Shawn only looked at her, confused. "What do you mean?" he asked. And he pointed to the tablescreen in front of him, to the security feed of the first few floors. They were totally clean. No sign of the Dust anywhere. "Didn't you hack this already? Isn't this your work? We'd surely be seeing them by now."

Erin looked at the feed, shocked. "No," she said finally. "I had nothing to do with that."

Someone had beaten them to it—someone had already hacked what Erin was trying to hack, had already done what Erin was trying to do. Someone else was helping the Dust. And whoever it was, that person was way ahead of them.

4

The ninth level was empty of Moderator guards. Peck, Tyler, Meg, Hailey, and Blake exited safely from their elevator, straight into the dark heart of Acheron.

The five of them were speechless.

All of the rumors were true.

But none of the rumors were true.

Finally, Peck and Tyler and Meg and Hailey and Blake understood what had been described to them all this time.

After the uniqueness of the courtyard for flunkees on level one, each of the eight levels below it had, in fact, been exactly the same. Each was nothing more (and nothing less) than an enormous, sterile white floor filled with a seemingly endless array of desks. And at each desk was a criminal, serving his time.

The desks were simple—just a little white surface with space enough for a little black computer.

The computer attached with cables to a helmet. The helmet was placed on the head, covering everything down to the neck.

Peck walked to one of them now, lifting it from its empty desk. "Of course," he said. "It's genius. The helmet attaches to the person through a brain-computer interface—it can read the criminal's mind, and the criminal's mind can read it." Peck shook the helmet, frustrated by how obvious it should have been. "This helmet, through a simple BCI, can make its subjects feel *anything*. It can convince its subject that he's endlessly on fire. It can convince him he's being eaten alive by snakes. It can convince him he is freezing, or boiling alive in tar, or going blind, or anything else at all.

"All of the rumors are true.

"And none of the rumors are true."

"But I don't get it," Tyler asked. "What is it that's keeping the helmet on? Why doesn't whoever's wearing the thing just take it off?"

Blake examined the helmet himself, and he pointed carefully to the inside. "That's why," he said. "This simple mechanism, right here. Take the helmet off, and it triggers this switch; the wearer's forehead will be instantly Marked."

"So then," Hailey said, "you *choose* the length of your punishment."

Peck nodded slowly. "Everyone holds out for as long as they possibly can. Everyone makes the decision feeling certain that they did the best job they could of avoiding it."

"And everyone believes," Hailey said, "whatever point they were at, that Cylis and his Mark saved them from torture and pain and certain death. No one ever regrets it."

Blake shook his head, "But in the end, no one escapes. Everyone is Marked."

"Well, we're here to make an exception to that rule," Peck said. "Let's just make sure to break Logan and Joanne and Eddie's computers before we touch any of their helmets. See if we can't disable the Marking mechanism first." And the five of them set out in search of Logan and Joanne and Eddie—to find them in a sea of bodies and desks, to find them with their faces completely hidden under the heavy helmets of their punishment.

"Hey, no sweat, right?" Tyler said. "Meg—I'll race you—best two out of three."

5

Logan was delirious when the Dust finally found him.

In the darkness, Logan recognized the voices, could hear them all the way across the lake, could hear his own best friends walking out on the ice, sliding fast across the slushy water and frozen surface below it. He was sure they were in his head, but he called out all the same, rasping dryly, tearing his throat raw. "Hey! I'm here! I'm over here!" He never expected an answer. It was not the first time he'd called out that day.

"Found him. I found him!" Hailey yelled, recognizing the muffled cries from several rows over. "Logan!" She ran to him, immediately wrapping her arms around his body, and Peck followed close behind, kicking over the desk and shattering the computer on the ground.

"Help me get this helmet off him! Quickly! *Now!*"

"But what if it Marks him?" Hailey asked.

Peck gestured to the sparks flying from the hard drive. "I think it's sufficiently broken, don't you?"

In the distance, Tyler and Meg sprinted down another aisle, destroying every computer they could get their hands on. "Best— game—*ever!*" Tyler yelled.

"You really think that's all it takes?" Hailey asked.

"I don't know," Peck said honestly. But he held his breath, and he said a prayer, and, very carefully, he and Hailey removed the helmet from Logan's head.

It took him several minutes to know whether or not any of them were real.

Where is the lake? Logan thought briefly. *Wasn't I freezing just a moment ago?*

But as soon as those thoughts had come, they had gone. Logan lay on the ground, delirious . . . but Markless.

"So what was the punishment?" Tyler asked, running over to him and trembling from the excitement of leaving so much destruction in his wake. "Was it cool?"

Logan frowned, lost in his memories of it. "It was . . . agony . . . but Cylis . . . Cylis would have saved me . . ."

"No, Logan. *No.* Cylis would *not* have saved you." Logan could feel Peck's hands gently patting his face, but it was as if through a bubble, as if they were very distant and as though Peck himself were speaking from across a wide canyon. "You're Dust, Logan— you're Dust; do you hear me?" The words were muffled at first, barely audible, barely registering. But as Peck repeated them, again and again, their meaning began to take shape. Logan could feel that canyon closing up, could feel the bubble as it broke. Slowly, he pulled himself up from out of his BCI-induced delirium.

He *had* been saved. But not by Cylis.

"Found Jo!" Blake called from just out of sight in the dim, sterile space.

"That's good!" Peck yelled. "Keep an eye out for Eddie."

"Uh . . . guys," Hailey said. She pointed toward the edge of the darkness at the opposite end of the vast room. A Moderator had appeared.

"Intruders!" the Moderator yelled. "Traitors!" He ran straight for them, stumbling a bit, arms out.

And yet, in the moment, the Dust could not bring themselves to flee. Meg watched with her hands to her face. Tyler fell to his knees. Blake stood stoic and numb.

"Ed . . . ," Peck mumbled as the group fled, finally, toward the elevator. "Forgive us."

The Moderator was Eddie.

ᑕ

"Shawn! Shawn," Erin said. "Look—they're coming back out." Erin pointed to the Moderator's exit at the side of the vestibule. Peck, Hailey, Blake, Meg, and Tyler led Logan and Joanne out by the arms. "Let's get outta there!" Erin said to Shawn. "Logan's safe. I can see him, Shawn! Logan's safe! Jo too!"

"Can't move yet," Shawn said. "Whoever set this security loop in motion, I've gotta find their Markscan trail. I've gotta delete it."

"Why? Who cares if some tycoon Moderator gets in trouble over this?"

"My job is to cover our tracks," Shawn said. "Completely. I'm not about to cut loose just because of a surprise along the way. I don't *work* like that."

And Erin looked at him admiringly. From one hacker to another.

"Besides," Shawn said. "I don't like free rides if I don't know who's driving. You wanna know who's helping us, don't you? Don't you think it's just the tiniest bit suspicious?"

"You're right. Just go—go, already," Erin said. And she waved him along impatiently.

Shawn was digging deeper now, much deeper, into Acheron's immune system database. Surely, there must be some clue, some-where, as to who this mystery hacker was. Acheron's systems were as secure as systems got. There was a heavily firewalled Intranet within its walls, but no Internet, to be sure. No way to hack into the prison from the outside. For anyone to loop the security feeds, that person would need to sit at this very desk, hacking this very tablescreen. But who besides Erin could have done that?

"Seriously, can't you go any faster?" Erin asked after just another thirty seconds. The Dust had made their way across the vestibule. "Checking scan logs—that's, like, your area of expertise, isn't it, Mr. Tech Wiz? So make it happen already."

"Hey," Shawn said slyly. "As I recall, you couldn't hack this thing *period*."

And sure enough, after several more seconds of searching, Shawn found it. The lone node in the database, stamped with precisely the same time as the footage pulled for the security loop. The condemning evidence. The person who'd compromised Acheron's computer security before Erin ever even had the chance. The person who'd enabled the Dust's escape.

Except the cell was wiped clean. Whoever was responsible, they'd already covered their tracks.

And yet, in what must have been the haste of the hack, one detail did remain.

Shawn could hardly believe it.

The hacker was an IMP.

⌐

"Where's Eddie?" Erin asked when she and Shawn joined the Dust down below.

Peck was unscrewing the air duct grate in the corner, working fast, concentrating hard.

"Hey—guys. *Where's Eddie?* He coming or what?"

Hailey was the only one willing to respond. She looked over at Erin. She frowned. And slowly, silently, she shook her head.

目

Once Logan and Joanne stabilized, the Dust moved above ground, out of that empty turbine room, out from under Beacon's shadow. And it didn't take long for them to find the Beacon protests.

The protests were everywhere.

The Dust—the larger Dust, thousands and thousands of them, co-opting that name—were entirely above ground now, visible, deliberately lining the streets at every level, blocking traffic, making noise, camping out at the DOME headquarters, on the Capitol steps . . .

But while the protests were peaceful, the scene in Beacon was not. Erin looked on, horrified by the violence she'd stirred. All around them, IMPS marched through the streets, revealing themselves, pushing back against the protesters with all means of force, magnecuffing everyone they could grab, dragging them away, not caring about the Marked onlookers or the disturbed faces they made.

Slowly, Logan approached Erin. He put his hand on her shoulder. She turned to face him. "I'm told this was you," Logan said. "You started this."

"I . . . I guess I did," Erin said, sounding shell-shocked and empty. "But Logan." She looked at him. "They did this for you."

The new year came. The G.U. treaty was signed. And across what could now only be called the Global Union, the Markless protests continued. The IMPS remained a constant presence.

By radio, the Dust heard nightly reports from Dane about the situation out west. Like a giant game of telephone, he relayed, without fail, everything he'd heard, passed on straight from the mouths of Mrs. Phoenix and Grandma, out from the little, unassuming town called Spokie, suburb of New Chicago.

The story was the same everywhere. Markless rising. IMPS crashing down on them.

A new era had begun.

It was another week before Logan or Erin or Peck or any of them could tell up from down. They mourned Eddie. They mourned what they had done. They wondered, hopelessly, what was next.

Slowly, Logan warmed back up to Erin, and Erin to him.

She hadn't gone back home after that night she left. She imagined her parents were beside themselves with worry. But she feared that if she left Logan's side, she would never find him again.

It wasn't safe enough to set a meeting place and simply hope for the best. Not anymore. The IMPS had made sure of that.

10

It was clear, with protests continuing all around them, that it wasn't safe for all of the Dust, the original Dust, in Beacon any longer. Not for Logan. Not for Peck. Not for Erin or Hailey.

The rest of them were determined to stay, to be a part of the community they'd found in the city. To be a presence there. To help with the movement blossoming all around them.

And Peck agreed that this was for the best. But for him, for Logan, for Erin and Hailey, everyone knew it was time to move on.

They'd been planning to leave, to head for the countryside, when Erin came down with the first signs of a fever.

"You can't deny it any longer," Peck said to her. "You have to come to terms with this thing. There must be something we can do."

"What thing?" Logan asked. "Peck, what are you talking about?"

"I'm sick," Erin said simply. "All the Marked are. Or will be, anyway. I think."

"How? *What?* Why?"

Erin took a deep breath, and she asked Logan to sit down.

Over the course of that night, Erin told Logan everything she'd found out. About Project Trumpet, about how it had led her to Acheron, to her plan with the IMPS . . . and she told, too, of the truth she had learned. About what was coming. For every last Marked in the G.U. It didn't always kill quickly, she said. But it did kill.

She told of the vaccination. She told of the shot at the Pledge.

And throughout that whole story, Logan looked at his own empty wrist. He remembered his own Pledge.

He remembered the shot he'd received.

But he didn't speak up.

Because it couldn't be, could it? Logan *wasn't* Marked.

Was he?

11

Another week, and Logan, Erin, Peck, and Hailey were ready to part ways.

"Do you think you'll find the cure?" Jo asked. "You think there's any cure at all?"

"We don't know," Logan said. "But we have to try. Or else the Global Union's about to get a whole lot messier."

It took until that night, their last night all together, for them to talk about what had happened the day Logan tried to sneak Lily out of Acheron. Periodically, Erin would ask about it. The betrayal. About how he was doing. About what he was thinking. But each time, Logan would close his eyes, and he'd shake his head, as if brushing off some thought too big and painful to wear just yet.

And then, finally, with Logan and Erin and Peck's Dust all sitting atop the fifth-tier Beacon grid, in a moment of rare peace, looking out over the crackle of rebellion and the distant noise from half a mile below . . . with all of them listening to Dane strum his guitar on the nearly-busted speaker of Hailey's latest foxhole radio, Logan opened up.

"Here's the thing I can't get out of my head," he said, unprompted. To no one in particular. To himself, almost. "What if she didn't betray us? What if it was the only way?"

The Dust just stared.

"The only way for what?" Erin asked.

Logan smiled, bemused. "What if Lily didn't need saving? What if Lily has her own plans?"

The Dust all looked now, intently, respectfully, waiting eagerly for Logan's next words.

"Lily. She's ascending the ranks of Cylis's army. A faithful servant." He shook his head. "She's close, now, to Lamson. To Cylis. Closer than any of us ever dreamed we could get."

"Yeah, because they broke her," Joanne said gently. "Because she's been brainwashed. Like Eddie. Like everyone else in that awful place."

Logan frowned. "Maybe. Or maybe she's been five years ahead of us all along. Maybe the reason she was so angry to see me was because I'd gotten in the way. Because she figured *she* was going to have to save *me*. Maybe she worried that doing so would blow her cover."

"Cover?" Peck said. "Logan, I'm sorry, but you're grasping at straws here . . ."

"She was surprised that you were there, Peck. She said that it changed things. It was as if . . . it was as if she revised her plan once she learned that I had backup."

"Revised it so that it included *betraying* you?" Hailey said incredulously.

"Well . . . yes. As if suddenly it seemed worth the risk to turn me in. Because with all of you on my side, I still stood a chance of escape, even without her help."

"So you think Lily turned you in on the *chance* that you might escape, because somehow that was preferable to the idea of ruining her big plan?"

"That's right," Logan said. "Maybe the stakes here are higher than any of us had ever imagined. Maybe we almost ruined the whole miserly thing."

"What *thing*?" Peck coaxed. "Logan . . . even if you were right about any of this . . . what could Lily's plan possibly be?"

Logan looked at him, distantly. "I agree, Peck. It seems like we've lost her. She turned me in. She gave us up. She left us for dead. It seems like we've lost the Lily we knew. But *what if* . . .

"*What if* we haven't? What if somehow, someway, Lily's still on our side . . . ?

"Because then . . . well . . . of all of us, she's positioned herself, now, right where she needs to be."

"Positioned herself . . . for what?"

"For the fight. Dust, don't you see? It's only just begun."

ABOUT THE AUTHOR

EVAN ANGLER has escaped. Hopped the first train out of Beacon, made his way across the country. . . . If he's lucky, he can buy himself some time in Sierra, lie low for a while . . . but he isn't counting on it. His first book, *Swipe*, gave him trouble enough already. His second book, *Sneak*, is only making matters worse.

Sometimes Evan wishes he'd never met Logan or Erin or Peck or any of them. But the Global Union needs to know what they did. It needs to remember. Before it's too late . . .

If you've finished this book—good. Hide it. Burn it. Give it to your own worst enemy and tell the authorities he has it.

That's my advice to you. For what it's worth.

Evan Angler